GREEK WEEK

A MORG MAHONEY MYSTERY

BY R. L. CHERRY

Books by R.L. Cherry

Historical Fiction
Three Legs of the Cauldron

Suspense
Foul Shot

Morg Mahoney Mysteries
Christmas Cracker
It's Bad Business
Greek Week

Father Bruce Mysteries
St. Nicholas Murders
St. Christopher Murders

ACKNOWLEDGEMENTS

While real life experiences do inspire fictional ones, this is purely a work of fiction. The only person in this book who existed in the real world was the beloved late Father Tim MacCarthy. If you think you know who any of the other people in the book really are, you are wrong. They are only figments of my rather fertile imagination. That being said, real people helped me make this book a reality. First, the fiction writing group of Sierra Writers of Nevada City, CA, and, after I moved, the mystery writers of the High Sierra Writers of Reno, NV, have listened to me read it and offered many wise criticisms. My fine editors, Dave Hershberger, my sister Donna (Big Sis), and my daughter Noëlle laboriously went through the manuscript, finding many more errors than I wish to admit. Last and definitely not least, my wife and muse, Kelly, not only edited this work, but has supported and encouraged my writing efforts for many, many years. Here's looking at you, kid.

TUESDAY MORNING

Chapter 1

Death by drowning is death by drowning, no matter what the longitude, latitude, water temperature or year.

As I stood on the deck of the cruise ship Scandinavian Superstar with a tarped lifeboat looming above, my best friend, Heather Pierce, was tightly hugging her college sorority sister, Mindy Maudlin, to her side while I looked over the scene where Mindy's husband, Bix, had disappeared into the depths of Davy Jones' Locker.

Heather reached out and gently touched my arm as she softly spoke. "Morg, did he fall overboard?"

While my dad had cursed me with the name Morgana, I hated it and went by Morg. It had a nice, deadly ring to it. And was great for a P.I.

"It's possible." I crouched down for a closer look. Personally, I didn't much care what had happened to the letch, but Heather wanted me to help for Mindy's sake. "He also could have jumped or been pushed. I'll let you know what I think after I've had a chance to process what I see here."

"Well, waste too much time on stuff that's not important." She frowned as she hugged Mindy more tightly. "This is really hard for Mindy and I want to get her to our suite to calm her down."

I glanced over at them. Both Heather and Mindy looked like they'd walked off an ad for Neiman Marcus: classy work-out clothes, perfect make up and beautifully styled hair. When Heather had shaken me awake about an hour ago, she'd said I had to go with her A.S.A.P. I'd managed to pull my thick, curly locks into a pony tail and eschewed any makeup before throwing on jeans and a lightweight cotton shirt.   As for this being tough on Mindy, she looked as upset as if she'd run over a squirrel with her Mercedes. Maybe less. With a disgusted shake of my head, I turned back to my work.

There was no crime tape, no police presence, and no investigators dusting for prints at the scene of Bix's disappearance. The crew politely kept passengers from entering the deck in that area, but people hung over the rail above, trying to see what was happening. It's like when there's an accident on any of the freeways; traffic slows to a crawl as gawkers hope for a quick view of bloody carnage. Maybe that sounds a bit jaded, but I've seen it too often.

I studied the scene. The railing was too high for anyone to accidently stumble over it and fall into the sea. Bix's sport coat had been found lying on the deck by the railing, wallet in a pocket. Since a rain had dampened everything and the crew had pawed over the evidence, the gloves I had procured through the Purser were superfluous. I had his watch in my hand, found by the crewman who had found his coat and didn't consider that picking it up and stuffing the watch in his pocket might hinder an investigation. The crystal was broken and one of the leather band's pins was missing. It read 3:17, the hands evidently frozen at the time when Bix had gone over the railing, which was how the rescue boats knew where to search. There was a gouge in the white paint on the railing and some white paint on the watch. And a little blood. The Captain had said Bix must have fallen against the rail, drunk, and knocked off his watch as he fell overboard, cutting his hand, and dropped his coat as he tumbled over the railing. No one had seen him fall. That scenario sounded as likely as me winning the lottery. And I never bought any tickets.

I pulled off my gloves and turned to Heather and Mindy. "Mindy, where were you at 3:17 this morning?"

Heather glared at me. "Mindy's in shock over this. What are you suggesting, anyway?"

Mindy didn't look like she was in shock to me. While she was dabbing at her eyes with a kleenex, I couldn't see any tears. Heather had described Bix and her as Ken and Barbie. While I doubted that her measurements were so out of proportion as the doll's, she was tall and trim, with high cheekbones and long, blond hair. And she showed as much real emotion as the doll. She looked at me and then down at the deck. "I was asleep in my cabin."

"I don't suppose anyone can corroborate that."

"If you mean was I sleeping with anyone, no." She sniffed, bringing up her kleenex. "If I'd known I was going to need an alibi, I could have hooked up with one of the deckhands."

Heather stamped her foot. "Morg, stop this now. Mindy is in shock."

I shrugged. "If you think my questions are harsh, just wait until the cops have at her. I'm not sure who has jurisdiction here, FBI, Coast Guard, *Federales*. Better hope it's not the last one."

She waved a dismissive hand. "I'll get my lawyer out here on a helicopter, if it comes to that. Right now, I'm taking her to our suite."

As Heather pulled Mindy away, I gritted my teeth. I was only on this cruise because Heather said she didn't want to be alone with her Sigma Iota Nu sorority sisters from her Stanford college days after almost no contact with any of them for over fifteen years. But she had quickly renewed friendships and I was like a fifth wheel, forgotten in the trunk until needed.

Heather expected me to find what had happened to Bix and I was cooperating, as was the captain. Staying in the Grand Escape Suite, one of the two best on the ship, did give her a little clout, as well as being friends with one of the vice presidents of the cruise line. Heather had used both to have me involved, no doubt touting my detecting skills.

So far I was at sea in more ways than one, somewhere in the Pacific Ocean. It was day three of our seven-day cruise along the so-called Mexican Riviera and we would reach Cabo San Lucas tomorrow. Now one of the 2,824 passengers, according to the Purser, was feeding the fish. The Purser had been there with the Captain and Staff Captain when I arrived, but now only the Chief of Security remained with me. The others had quickly gone about their duties, which included notifying whatever authorities needed to be notified and launching tenders to look for Bix where the ship had been when he went overboard, about two hours ago. As if there was any chance of finding Bix still treading water.

I studied the scene again. Broken watches with the hands conveniently stopped, a coat with a wallet inside left at the scene and a fresh scratch on the railing with paint from it on the watch were a little too convenient. So what could explain them? A suicide would work if the person committing it wanted the authorities to know where and when he'd jumped. The crew kept the ship freshly painted, even as we sailed. I'd seen them touching up paint several times before. It would be obvious that the railing was freshly scratched to even a casual observer, especially since there was no rust in the scratch. Of course, it could be that the watch crystal was broken during a fight with his killer and was a real clue.

I looked down at the watch. It was gold with a gold face with "Rolex Oyster Perpetua" lettering below a crown. I was no expert on Rolexes, but it felt too light. I looked closer at where the watch had scraped the railing, flicking off some white paint. The gold was scratched off, revealing base metal. It was a fake. When I got back to the suite I shared with Heather, I'd give the coat and wallet a closer inspection. Something was rotten in the state of Baja. Or at least the waters off its coast.

I glanced at my watch. It was 7:16 in the morning, an ungodly hour to be up. The sun wasn't even really up, so I shouldn't have been either. I regretted my wardrobe choice. I hadn't expected the Pacific Ocean off Mexico to be this cold. A spring storm had returned, sending cooler weather, winds and even a little rain our way the night before. I felt it as I shivered. The waters were choppy, so it was fortunate I didn't get seasick. But I did get cold.

The Chief of Security suddenly laid his white coat across my shoulders. Now I regretted skipping any makeup. He was maybe in his mid-twenties, tall, blond and handsome. A modern Viking many women would gladly let ravage them. At least in romance novels. He smiled winningly. "I saw you shake with cold. Is this coat okay, Miss . . .?"

"Mahoney. But just call me Morg." I glanced at his name badge. Olav Larsen. I smiled. "Thanks, Olav. It's a little cooler than I expected."

"Yah, Morg Mahoney." He looked around. "It is 12 or 13 now. We had a rain early in the morning."

"I noticed." I nudged Bix's coat, still wet. "Okay if I take this?"

Normally, I would leave everything alone for a forensic team to evaluate. But too many people had already handled the evidence. Besides, with the dampness, fingerprinting anything here would be a waste of time. I had no idea who would have authority over any investigation, other than the ship's Chief of Security, and I was reasonably sure that Olav had no crime-scene investigation training, so I wanted to see what I could find.

He shrugged. "Not a problem. Your friend says you are very good at your job. You are, what, a woman Sherlock Holmes?"

I chuckled. "I wish. I'm just a humble private investigator from Long Beach. But I loved reading the Sherlock Holmes stories and books as a kid. Maybe that's why I got into it."

He patted his chest. "Me, too. I like the movies too. Robert Downey is very good."

I grimaced. "He's flashy, but Jeremy Brett was the best in the television series he did for ITV."

"I have not seen that." He nodded thoughtfully. "So I will look for it."

"Did you take a sample of the blood on the watchband to check against Bix's?"

He cocked his head, puzzled. "Who else's could it be?"

I raised my eyebrows. "Maybe a killer's?" I sighed. Any chain of custody for evidence was long gone. "Well, I'd better get back to my room. I'll get a swab of the blood and give it to you to run DNA after the cruise is over. And see if there's anything I can learn from this." I lifted Bix's coat, a navy blue blazer. There was a dry spot under it.

"I would be most happy to assist you." He smiled. "I will go with you to study the coat."

I was tempted, but it felt little like cheating on someone else. Although Father Robert, the studly Episcopal priest from Buggy Springs, and I had dated, even spent a weekend together, we were not an item. Since nothing salacious had happened, I could say there was no commitment. Separate bedrooms and all that. But I did feel that there was something between us and I doubted that Olav was looking for anything long term. He was a hunk, but I'm not the type to hop into bed with guys for a short-term satisfaction. "Thanks, but I can handle it. Just send someone by in a half hour to get the blood swab."

He looked a little disappointed, maybe expecting more for his kindness, so I started to take off his coat. "No, no." He held up his hand. "You keep the coat and stay warm until later. You call me from your room and I will come for it. Okay?"

"Thanks."

I turned to go, but remembered something from last night.

"Did you find a gym bag around here?"

He cocked his head. "Jim bag? Was not his name Bix?"

I chuckled. "A gym bag is what people carry to take their work-out clothes to the gym. It's like a small overnight bag. Bix had one with him late last night."

He shook his head. "We found only the coat and watch."

The gym bag was missing. Was that significant or had it fallen overboard with Bix? I wondered about it as I headed back to the suite I was sharing with Heather, at her expense. I started for the elevator, one warm coat on my shoulders and another wet one in hand. Maybe I was taking Olav's gallant action a little too suspiciously. I paused and turned. "Olav, when did it rain this morning?"

"I am not sure. Would you like me to check for you?"

"Yes. Thanks."

He grinned. "I am glad to help, Morg Mahoney."

I wasn't sure how much it mattered, but I was curious about the rain. Small details sometimes were very important. I thought about the RMS Titanic, since it was the morning of April 15th, a fateful day in cruising history, even if this ship wasn't sinking. I'd read up on what happened when I realized our cruise was going to be at sea on that day. True, the pride of the White Star Line had sunk over a century ago after it struck an iceberg while sailing in the frigid Atlantic Ocean. Also true, I was sailing on the much-warmer Pacific Ocean with nary even an ice cube in sight outside of the many bars on the Scandinavian Cruise Line ship, the Scandinavian Superstar. However, if the key to the binoculars' storage case hadn't been left behind, maybe the iceberg would have been spotted by the crew in time to avert disaster. If the passenger potholes hadn't been left open when the evacuation began, the ship might have not sunk so quickly. Yes, details were important.

Chapter 2

After I went back to the suite I shared with Heather, I wanted nothing more than to grab a nap. To say that I'm not a morning person would be like saying the Pope is not an atheist. Heather was already there with Mindy, but I slipped into my room without saying anything. They seemed to be in earnest conversation over a couple of glasses of early-morning champagne in the living room and didn't look my way. Was it a wake, or maybe a celebration?

Once in my room, I used a Q-Tip to take some blood off the watchband and put it in a plastic bag I found in a drawer. It wouldn't stand up in a court of law, but the ship didn't exactly have a homicide department. Then I inspected Bix's coat. The seam where the sleeve met the right shoulder was ripped apart. Sign of a struggle? I looked inside it. The label said Brunello Cucinelli, however, close inspection revealed that it was hand-stitched in by an amateur. I wasn't familiar with the name, but I'd bet the coat was like Bix's watch: a cheap fraud. Except for a leather wallet, there was nothing in the pockets. After checking Bix's driver's license from the wallet in his coat, I found that his real name was Harold Bixby Maudlin, Jr. No wonder he went by Bix. Maybe the old song was wild about Harry, but it's not a popular name unless you're in the British Royal family. I booted up my tablet and googled him. Most of what I found was about ten years old, when Bix had been under investigation for irregularities in his mortgage company, HBM Investment Fund.

The early 2000's was the time of the real estate bubble when buyers were getting loans they couldn't afford on over-valued properties and homeowners were refinancing their homes to get cash to buy more property or just spend. Subprime lenders were making big profits on fees and interest and borrowers were making big profits on rising prices. At least on paper. Greed reigned supreme. And then the bubble burst.

Lenders who made unwise loans to unwise borrowers found themselves with a slew of foreclosures as buyers were forced out of houses no longer worth even close to their mortgages. Too many lenders played games with their accounting, making themselves look healthier than they were. And some mortgage brokers played a modified Ponzi scheme, getting more investors who helped fund paying interest to other investors when defaults started piling up. That was HBM Investment Fund's *modus operandi*. But when no more suckers could be found to invest, the well dried up.

If you were "too big to fail," the government propped you up. If you were not, you went bankrupt and the principals might end up in jail. Size matters. While HBM execs, including Bix, had been lucky enough to somehow escape criminal charges, the company had received no government aid and HBM went belly up. Now Bix had a new company named H-III Investments. I did more checking into its financial health as well as Bix's with a couple of programs that are not quite kosher, but good for digging dirt. Since I had Bix's basic information, I unearthed a lot of mud.

While Bix escaped criminal charges, civil suits had pretty much wiped him out. He'd gambled that his company would survive when the Feds hadn't filed charges and lost. Even though his company going bankrupt didn't affect his personal assets, most of his wealth had been in the company. It hadn't been that he wanted to help the investors or even his company, but it had been his hubris that he would always come out on top. "You've heard of the Teflon President?" he'd once bragged in an interview in the *Los Angeles Times*. "Well, I'm the Teflon businessman." However, what settlements didn't take, court costs and his own lawyers did.

I leaned back in my chair. Although it was possible that Bix had finally realized he'd never climb out of the hole he'd dug and hopped over the side, it was just as probable one of his suckers had either stalked him on board or just happened to be on the same ship and offed him. Trying to compare the huge passenger list with the also large number of people he'd bilked would take a lot of time and resources. Then again, there was always Mindy. Her grief at his apparent demise was about as much as mine for a cockroach I'd accidently stepped on at the pier before we'd boarded. Maybe that was because both victims were so similar. But I hadn't been married to the cockroach.

I needed more information and it wasn't going to be easy with Heather protecting Mindy like a mama bear guarding her cub. Did Bix have a life insurance policy? If so, how much? How were they getting along? From what I'd seen since we got onboard, not well. Were things bad enough to kill for? I would have to tread cautiously and that was not something I did well.

My eyelids were growing heavy. I'd stayed up late the night before. Make that this morning. It started with enjoying some jazz in one of the ship's bars. I took a power nap to clear my head. Well, since a power nap should be ten or twenty minutes, I took several power naps without waking. It was almost noon when I woke. I did feel better. I pulled out my notebook and made a list. I needed to find out who saw Bix last, what he was doing and if he was with anyone. I needed to find out when Mindy left the patio party at the suite early this morning, if anyone saw her after she left the suite and her activities until Bix's "accident" was noted. I doubted that she would be very cooperative with me. After all, I was just the hired help to her.

After a refreshing shower, I did my usual minimalistic makeup, pulled on a pair of jeans and knit top, and opened my door. Our butler, Alasdair, was in the bar, noting supplies on a pad. Yes, the suite came with a butler. No, I had no idea what it cost.

Alasdair smiled at me. "Good afternoon, madam. Are you well today? Miss Pierce asked me to restock the bar."

Wearing a white shirt, black trousers and vest, and a striped tie, he had an almost military bearing. He stood a little less than six feet, a little stocky, but not fat. His salt and pepper hair was neatly cut and his smile was warm, but not too familiar.

We'd established a rapport early on when I found that he was from the north of England, near where Heather and I had visited over a decade ago. I liked him, but I had a problem having a butler hovering about.

"Fine, Alasdair. And you?"

"Very well, thank you. Would you like something to drink? Coffee? A Jameson perhaps?"

He already knew me well. "It's a little late for one and early for the other." I considered what lunch in the dining room with the Greek crowd would be like. "I'd like lunch here, though. How about fish and chips?"

"Very good." He gave a short nod. "I'll have them sent right up. Anything else?"

"No, thanks. Well, except for how the hunt for Bix is going."

"You're referring to Mr. Maudlin, the, ah . . . unfortunate gentleman who fell overboard." He slowly shook his head. "So sad. We sent three of our tenders to search where he likely . . . ."

"Hit the drink. So, are we circling back, too?"

He nodded. "A United States Coast Guard plane is searching already, but they didn't have any vessels close enough to respond, so our tenders are working with it. We're headed back now. As I understand that if no trace of Mr. Maudlin is found in a couple of hours, our tenders will return to the ship and we will be resuming our sailing for Cabo San Lucas."

"That's it? Will the Coast Guard come on board to investigate?"

"They have no authority to do so. Besides, the poor chap probably fell overboard, intoxicated."

"I see." Evidently, the strange items he left behind and the gouge in the railing's paint were not important, best forgotten. But not by me. "Is Heather here?"

"Miss Heather and the other lady are out. They went for breakfast and are meeting some of their friends at the gym afterwards. Is there anything else I can do for you?"

Since "other lady" was the wife of the missing Bix, Mindy seemed to have recovered nicely if she were heading for lunch and a workout so soon after the loss of her hubby. I remembered watching *Downton Abbey*. The servants knew far more than anyone else. "Do you know when the 'other lady' left the party here early this morning and where she went?"

He shifted uneasily. "She left here about half past two this morning. I, ah, helped her to her suite."

Helped her? She was drunk, no doubt. "Any information you could find about her and her husband, Bix, would be most helpful." I paused. "I'm supposed to find out what happened when he went overboard."

"I will ask around."

"Thanks, Alasdair." I smiled. "You are a gem. And I asked you to call me Morg, remember?"

"Thank you, Mada—." A smile tugged at the corners of his mouth. "Morg."

Sunday Afternoon Before

Chapter 3

There's something exciting about standing on the deck of a cruise ship as it sails, especially when it's your first time. It brings to mind images of a time when air travel was unknown and couples regally strolled along the deck in tuxes and evening gowns after dinner, sipping champagne and laughing. First class on the Titanic without the berg. Even though I'd had a number of misconceptions, my first cruise was a thrill. At least, at first.

Heather and I stood on the verandah deck of the Scandinavian Superstar, crowded with people in T-shirts, shorts and sandals taking videos with brandished cell phones, and looked out at houses and restaurants as we left San Pedro Harbor. Since I'd bought a knee-length, navy blue, fit and flare dress and red wedge sandals for this occasion, I felt very overdressed. The white silk scarf knotted around my neck for the full nautical effect and Forties-style curled hairdo I'd overpaid my hairdresser to do up felt ludicrous in the present company. Even Heather wore some wide-legged linen pants, crop top and sandals instead of a dress. I was like Shirley Temple at a rap concert. I say that because some weird blend of a mariachi band with rappers blared over the loudspeakers. What was it called? Oh, yes. Reggaeton.

I had expected to have throngs of well-wishers along the dock that we would throw streamers at, like I'd seen in old movies. But I guess cruises have become too common and people too blasé for such theatrics any more. Just like the captain didn't personally greet each cruiser with charm and a witty comment. So much for the "Love Boat" reruns I'd watched as a kid. Still, it did have a rowdy, party atmosphere on the deck as we sailed off into the evening and I sipped the too-sweet rum concoction called "Mariachi Madness" an army of waiters were pushing that cost way more than it was worth. At least it came with a souvenir glass that I'd never use again. Actually, it cost Heather way more than it was worth, since Heather had paid for the best suite on the ship and all drinks were included.

Like any other sin, when you've taken charity once, it's easier the next time. Now I still remember enough of my catechism at St. Joseph's in Crestline to know that it's neither a venial nor mortal one. In fact, the Church says it's not a sin at all. Maybe it's more of an infraction, like speeding. Or more like that piece of death-by-chocolate cake. Once you break the diet and have one, you say, "What the hell, put a couple of scoops of cookies-and-cream ice cream on there. And cover it with hot fudge." Now my dad always considered taking charity one of the worst possible sins. Worse than when he blew away an unarmed kid who bungled a robbery. But then, he never took charity. Even after his "retirement" from the force, he'd never let anyone buy a round without him buying one as well. That's why he was often broke. And drunk. Anyway, I learned from him that you never accept charity. When I let Heather pay for our trip to England over nearly two decades ago, that was a first for me. Not that I'm complaining. It was a great trip and this not-so-little orphan was sort of adopted by a wonderful couple there. I'm just explaining why I so readily accepted the cruise from Heather.

While Heather was my best friend, we were worlds apart in many ways. I grew up with a cold, distant father and no mother to serve as a role model, struggling to make ends meet on my dad's retirement income from the San Bernardino County Sheriff's while living in the Valley of Enchantment, a speck on the map of the San Bernardino Mountains. Heather grew up with a cold, distant father and no mother, struggling to make ends meet on a seven-figure income from her wealthy banking family while living in Palos Verdes Estates on the Southern California coast. So, except for three zeroes on our yearly income and that one of us had rusting VW vans up on blocks in neighbors' front yards while the other had new Ferraris parked in the neighbors' garages, maybe we had very similar childhoods. Riiight.

If Heather weren't my best friend, I'd probably hate her. She's one of those people who are just too perfect. A Stanford grad from a filthy rich family with a drop-dead bod and a face to match, she's got enough beauty and class to supply a small city. Or maybe a mid-size one. And then, there's her personality. Perky and generous. She's the kind that guys fall all over themselves to impress. I know. I've seen them do it often enough. She's been such a good friend, though, that I overlook all those faults. And when she came into my office with the tickets and said we were going on a cruise to Mexico, I didn't even put up much of a fight. To be honest, I planned on paying my way, since I was working on a case that looked to pay well. I'm not impoverished, but I've never learned to budget my money. If I score big, I spend big. If work is slow, I make use of my charge cards and scrimp. The case went sour, but I still went on the cruise. The plans were already in motion and tickets had been purchased.

I'd just finished a disappointing case for Bennie. That's Bennie Rothstein of Rothstein and Meyer, a lawyer who is in the same building in Long Beach as I am and throws a lot of work my way. He hired me to help his client who was being sued by a previous employer, a large computer peripherals manufacturer, who claimed the guy had stolen proprietary information from them when he'd split and opened his own company. The guy told Bennie it was a phony, trumped-up charge and that he had proof. He not only wanted to fight the suit, but counter-sue for big bucks for defamation of character. He'd convinced Bennie of his innocence, so much so that Bennie had taken the case with most of his fees on a contingency basis. A hefty contingency, but still a contingency. So Bennie hired me to prove his case.

In my investigation, I found that his "proof" was the phony part of the case and he was as guilty as Harvey Weinstein. If I could figure it out, the snoops from the guy's ex-employer would too. Bennie dropped the guy for lying to him, the guy went bankrupt and then found some slime-ball shyster to go after Bennie. Bennie would beat the case, but the whole mess was going to be an expense without much income. When it came to paying me, Bennie did cover my out-of-pocket expenses, but nit-picked over my time so much that I ended up with far less than I'd hoped. I wasn't happy, but Bennie had been too good of a client for too long for me to say anything stupid. With my quick temper, though, I was glad Heather had given me a way to get away from Bennie for a while, at least until I cooled off.

As I stood on the deck of the ship, sipping my sickly-sweet drink and watching California slip away from us, the tension I'd been storing after Bennie's meager payment had barely covered my outstanding bills finally eased. It was a cruise, even if not exactly what I had expected. I was determined to relax and enjoy it.

As usual, there was something more to it than Heather just wanting the two of us to get away as a couple of friends escaping from the everyday routine. This time it was a reunion. It wasn't some formal high school reunion like I had gone to not that long ago, where you dieted madly for a couple of months to wear a dress that you pretended you'd had hanging in the closet, all to impress a bunch of people you'd never liked and wouldn't see again for another five or ten years. This was a seven-day cruise with a group of her sorority sisters from Sigma Iota Nu, of which she'd been a loyal part in her days at Stanford and most of whom she'd not seen since graduating. A different type of Greek week, so to speak.

From correspondence since she'd heard of the reunion, Heather told me that all of the ones she'd been close to were married now. All except her. Hence I was invited as a back-up companion in case it didn't go well with her sisters. That may sound jaded, but I prefer to be a realist. From the fact that none of her "sisters" had searched us out before the sailing, it seemed Heather had been wise to have me tag along as basically a paid companion. But then I'd been a bodyguard once to an aging rock star who liked having women around to watch him strut his stuff in the nude around his hotel, so at least this time I wasn't having to watch some nude, middle-aged guy and pretend I wasn't disgusted. All life is made of compromises, and some are worse than others. Plus the view of the disappearing coastline was pleasing to see.

My reverie was broken when two slime-balls started putting the make on Heather and me. I should say, one put the make on Heather and I got the leftovers. I had my drink, but Heather had opted not to brave the rum concoction making the rounds on the waiters' trays.

Suddenly a drink was pressed into her hand from behind us and a contrived-baritone voice unctuously whispered to her "A killer cocktail for a killer lady."

I say whispered, but that only means that he didn't yell, since the noise level was so high that anything below rock-band level was a whisper. We both turned to see who was the source of the unwanted liquor and this ludicrous line. He was decent looking, with thick black hair, high cheekbones, and a strong chin. Standing about six feet, he had an athletic build, more of the swimmer's than the body-builder's, but fit-looking. His clothes were California casual: Hawaiian-print shirt, baggy khaki shorts and Van's without socks. If not for the bad come-on and the heavy gold chain and medallion, Heather might have gone for him. And for the obvious leer in his eye and cocky awareness of his own good looks. Heather had fallen for some creeps before, but this guy was just too creepy.

Before she could respond, I felt someone else close at my side, offering me a drink as well, and heard him say, "Yeah, and here's some dynamite for a dynamite chick."

I turned to my suitor to see the Ghost of Disco Past looking me eye-to-eye. I know Seventies retro was popular in some places a while ago, but this was too much. Baby-blue bell-bottoms and a wide-collared, polyester paisley shirt that he probably got from Goodwill was open enough to show several gold chains were way over the top. His longish almost-blond hair was combed straight back and flipped up off his neck. He was about my height, five foot nine or so, but had a big edge on me in weight. A smaller chest than mine, but a much bigger waistline. He flashed me a bedroom smile to match his eyes. My first impulse was to upchuck. My second was to throw my drink in his face. But I restrained myself. It was too early in the cruise to make enemies. Quickly, Heather spoke before our conquests had a chance to add any more witty lines. She would know there are limits to my restraint, but it would have been better if she had let me explode and be rid of them for the rest of the cruise.

Looping her arm through mine, she said, "Thanks for the drink, but no thanks. My friend here takes care of all my needs." Then, if that weren't enough she emphatically added, "All of them."

It did set the two bozos back on their heels. With some varying and recurring combinations of "Um . . . Er . . . Yeah, I see . . . . Sorry, 'bout that," they awkwardly backed away and disappeared into the crowd.

"Great." I grimaced. "Now all those two overly-macho, brain-dead guys, the type who think lesbians are just needing a real man to turn them straight, will be hitting on us for the entire cruise. We'll be a challenge to them, you know. Couldn't you have figured a less dramatic way to have gotten rid of them, one that wouldn't have told any desirable guys on this cruise that we are off limits?"

"Maybe, but I wanted to get them out of our hair as quickly as possible." She gave me a wry smile. "And, if you look around, I haven't seen that many guys that are worth a second look, so I haven't really soured our chances with any hot candidates for a shipboard romance."

She was right about the visible selection of adult male passengers. I'd seen better choices in a police line-up. I wasn't really in the market for a relationship anyway since I had Robert back in California. And Heather was only here to see her old friends. Looking around at those wildly working at having a good time, Heather gave a resigned shake of her head and said, "Let's go to our suite."

"Don't you want to find your sorority sisters first?"

She shrugged. "I'll see them later tonight. We have a room reserved for cocktails and hors d'oeuvres at six." She paused. "That'll be soon enough."

"If you don't want to see them, why did you come?"

She looked off at nothing. "I don't know. I loved college. I felt like everyone loved me. I thought this group of my sisters would always be my close friends, that my life would stay the same. But life changes and so do people. I feel like I'm trying to step into the same stream again."

"River."

She came out of her reverie and stared at me. "Huh?"

"Heraclitus said you can't step into the same river twice."

She shrugged. "I don't know what Hercules has to do with what I was saying, but I'm going to our suite. You coming?"

I was more than ready to change to comfy jeans and a light, cotton blouse. I set my unfinished rum drink on the tray of a passing waiter. "Of course. We've got a bottle of Jameson there."

Chapter 4

Our suite was located midship on the top deck overlooking the pool, one up from where we were. As Heather and I walked to the stairs, the elevator stopped and the door opened, revealing an old man in a wheelchair with a young woman behind it. The man had a black shawl over his shoulders, clutched a fancy cane across his lap and a drooping, wide-brimmed black hat obscured his face. But the dark glasses that hid his eyes and black gloves that covered his hands gave him a sinister look. He might have been dead or a mannequin if not for when he raised his head slightly to look at us, but didn't smile or acknowledge our presence. Then he lowered his chin so that it rested on his chest. He said nothing, but a cold chill ran down my spine.

The woman took care of the talking. She was maybe in her late twenties, petite in all ways except her bustline. Neither that nor her blond hair looked God-given. Her white nurse-like pantsuit fit her a bit too tightly, making her look like some adolescent male's fantasy version of a medical professional. While her face was overly made up to be sexy, her brown eyes were cold and so was her voice.

"This elevator is going up to the Grand Escape Suite. Take another."

The doors closed as Heather and I stood in stunned silence. Then Heather spoke.

"Looks like we know who has the other Grand Escape Suite."

"Yeah. Dr. Strangelove and his hooker nurse."

Heather cocked her head. "Who?"

"You know, the evil scientist Peter Sellers played, the guy in a wheelchair with dark glasses and a black glove."

Heather looked confused. "Who's Peter Sellers?"

This wasn't going well. "Inspector Clouseau in *The Pink Panther*?"

"The Saturday morning cartoons I watched as a kid? They made a movie from it?" She paused. "Oh, wait, they did. I never saw it, but Steve Martin was in it, wasn't he?"

I chuckled. "The cartoon came from the movie, not the other way around. The Steve Martin one was a remake of the original with Peter Sellers. He was a great actor. *Dr. Strangelove* and *The Pink Panther* were movies he was in."

"I never saw them. When were they out?"

"The 1960's."

Heather rolled her eyes. "I wasn't even born then. Who watches movies that old? Well, besides you. You need to update your résumé."

I breathed out slowly before I said something appropriately insulting about the fact that I wasn't born yet either, but I have enough intelligence to know that everything worthwhile didn't start when I was born. I also didn't understand what loving old movies had to do with my résumé, but decided to let it go, too. "Well, I'm going to call our neighbor Dr. Stangelove anyway. With his faithful sidekick, Nurse Bimbo. I guess we won't be playing shipboard shuffleboard together."

Heather laughed. "Nobody plays shuffleboard any more, anyway. Let's go up the stairs."

Our suite was decorated mainly in chrome and bright colors rather than the rich mahogany and brass I had seen on the Queen Mary, permanently anchored in Long Beach. More brash and less class. Still, it had three large bedrooms that adjoined a larger sitting room-cum-kitchenette. Each bedroom had a king-sized bed and private bathroom. The living room with kitchenette was bigger than my whole apartment. I could get used to that.

Before we had boarded, Heather had ordered champagne so we could stand on the private deck above our suite and toast the sailing in style. As she pulled the bottle out of the ice bucket to open it, she grimaced. I could see that it was some sort of house brand. Not what she had requested. Heather had explained to whomever she had spoken before we sailed that she would like each day: bottled water and fresh fruit and flowers each morning with champagne on ice each evening. Tattinger champagne. There were flowers and fruit, plus champagne, but not Tattinger. Heather rang room service. Instantly, there was a knock at the door and I answered it.

A tall, trim man who looked like he should be the captain by his presence smiled at me. "I'm Alasdair, your butler. How may I be of assistance?"

Heather pointed at the champagne. "I ordered a bottle of Tattinger to be iced and ready when we sail. Instead I got this . . . ."

"Swill," Alasdair finished. "My apologies. All I was told was to make sure there was a bottle of champagne with no preference stated and was given that one to put on ice for you. It's the standard bottle given to any guest who requests champagne. I'm afraid there might be an extra charge for the Tattinger, however."

Heather snorted. "Do I look like I can't afford an extra charge?"

"Of course not." He bowed his head slightly for a brief moment. "I will take care of the matter immediately."

With that, he was out the door.

Heather looked at me with a raised eyebrow. "We'll see if he can deliver."

In the meantime, we decided to explore our accommodations. After our brief encounter with Disco Ghost on the verandah deck, the champagne sounded good. Heather opened it and we tasted it. Good wasn't exactly the right word. Pathetic was a better one. If I could tell, it had to be bad. Still, it was cold, bubbly and alcoholic, so we sipped it and walked out onto the patio and up the stairs to our private top deck to watch the shore slip away. There was something classy about standing on a private deck, sipping champagne as we sailed off into the sunset.

My reverie was broken as Alasdair appeared on the stairs, holding two filled champagne flutes. He handed one to each of us and took the ones we had. "Again, my apologies. I was able to get a bottle of Tattinger complimentary, since your original order was ignored. I have also brought caviar with toast points as a gesture of my good will. Shall I bring it up?"

Heather smiled, mollified. "That would be wonderful, Alasdair."

He went down the stairs and soon returned with a small table and a tray with the caviar, toast and a couple of plates. He set it between Heather and me and stepped back. "If you need anything else, please let me know."

Although a bit awestruck at the whole experience, I finally recovered enough to say, "Thank you, Alasdair."

After giving a quick nod, he was down the stairs again. The caviar was in a small, flat jar on ice with a ceramic spoon in it. Heather took a wedge of toast and put a dollop of the small, black eggs on it. She took a bite and closed her eyes. "Mmm. Not beluga, but not lumpfish either."

I followed suit. I took a bite, my first ever taste of caviar. It was somewhat salty and slightly fishy. It reminded me of a cross between salmon and oysters, but I'd rather have had either of those. I finished mine and Heather was still nibbling at hers. She sighed.

"Isn't that yummy?"

"Uh, . . . nice." I withheld my real opinion.

"Nice?" She rolled her eyes. "A candy bar is nice. This is heavenly."

Maybe it would taste better with harps playing in the background, I mused. "Maybe it would be better with vodka. That's what the Russians say."

Heather grimaced. "Vodka? What do they know?"

"Beluga caviar is from Russia, isn't it?"

She shrugged. "So? That doesn't mean they're experts on what to drink with it."

This was going nowhere, so I changed the subject. "So, are you looking forward to seeing your sorority sisters? Are these the same ones that I met when Nicole's fiancé disappeared just before their wedding Incline Village a few years ago?"

She shrugged. "No. They weren't there. These sisters weren't close to Nicole. We called ourselves the Southern Belles. I was closer to this group for a while, but there are a couple of them that I had a few . . . issues with a long time ago, back when we were in college. I haven't seen them since."

"Southern Belles?" I laughed. "You're from California, not the South."

"We were all from the southern part of America, even if not from the Deep South." She sniffed. "After all, I'm from *Southern* California, as you well know."

"But you haven't spoken to them for years. Sound like sisterhood ain't all that it's cracked up to be."

She shrugged again. "It's hard to explain. Once you join, it's forever, whether you get along or not."

"Like joining a religious cult?"

She rolled her eyes. "Not at all. If you've never been in a sorority, you can't understand."

I ignored the insult and sipped my champagne. "Guess I'll have to live with that."

Chapter 5

I was ready to go to the sorority cocktail party fifteen minutes before the six o'clock start. Heather was not. She was still in her room. I took a quick check in the mirror to make sure that I had not forgotten to take off any tags from the clothes I'd bought at Nordstrom's just for this cruise. I'm not a fashion clothes horse, but had splurged on three outfits, one of which I'd worn for our departure. Now I was already into my second one on the first day. I'd kept to my nautical theme. I wore an off-the-shoulder, long sleeved, silky navy blue top and a pair of wide-legged, white beach pants. I'd kept on my wedge sandals and moved my white scarf up to tie around my hair. I was pleased. One thing nice about a full bust line is it made the off-the-shoulder top look filled out. Eat your heart out, Heather.

At six, I tapped on Heather's bedroom door.

"What?"

"Uh, shouldn't we be going soon?" I hesitated. "We're going to be late, you know."

"Have a Jameson and relax," she called through the door. "No one shows up on time. It's gauche."

I followed her advice. The in-suite bar was a nice feature. I was almost finished with my drink before Heather came out of her room. She hadn't changed, which made me wonder what she'd been doing the whole time I'd been waiting. She poured herself the last of the champagne and finished it in one gulp.

She looked at me with a wry smile. "Well, once more into the fire."

I almost corrected her and said, "You mean, 'Once more into the breach,' from *Henry V*." But when I saw her face, I restrained myself. Her fear and reluctance was obvious. I realized that she'd been delaying not because of being fashionably late, but because she was afraid to meet her sorority sisters again after all these years. I'd known Heather for nearing twenty years and knew she hid a lot of insecurity with false bravado. Now was such a time. She didn't need some smart remark from me.

I took her arm in mine, saying, "Dawling, you look mahvelous." as we headed to the door. She gave me a little smile.

Although Heather had left messages on Facebook where she'd seen the information about the reunion cruise for the organizer, she'd had no response. When Heather made arrangements on her own for the cruise and posted it on the Facebook page, the only response had been a message about the cocktail party. The party was in the Oslo Room, a place set aside for private affairs two decks below ours. As we walked in the door, a woman about Heather's age was there to greet us. Or maybe she was a featherweight bouncer, to keep out the riff-raff.

The woman was tall, fit-looking and blond. The man standing beside her was a little taller, broad shouldered, longish brown hair and had a Ryan Gosling look, handsome and knew it. They looked like the typically country club type: both of them with their hair perfectly styled, and clothes that probably had designer labels. Ken and Barbie go on a cruise. But I noticed that he was getting a pot and his hair was a comb-over. A professionally styled comb-over, but still a comb-over. His glory was fading, while she still looked good.

Both of them smiled, he warmly and she coolly. Interesting, I thought. Her tone of voice matched her smile, not quite icy but close. "Why Heather, you're here."

Heather seemed surprised by this odd opening. "I couldn't miss a reunion of the Southern Belles. I left messages on Facebook that I was coming. Since I didn't hear from you, I made the reservations myself."

"Facebook is a pain to use. I guess I wasn't sure. You've always had a way of doing things your own way, anyway. But I made your name tag, just in case."

I was wondering what was going on. This was not the tearful reunion of sorority sisters I'd expected. Her companion looked uneasy and nervously spoke to us.

"It's nice to see you, Heather. It's been years since the last time we've seen you."

"Yes, it has. It must be eighteen years now. Since the wedding, I mean."

The woman broke in. "Since you're so late, you'd better get your name tag over there and mingle if you want to see any of our sisters." She gestured at the table behind her.

"Who else made it? Did Jennifer?"

"Jennifer and Dave are already here." The woman shrugged. "Somehow I thought she would've already told you she was coming, if she wanted you to know. After that wedding thing and all, I mean. Hasn't she called you lately?"

"I haven't even talked to Jennifer since the wedding. By the way, Morg, meet Bix and Mindy Maudlin, friends from college. Bix and Mindy, meet Morg Mahoney, my best friend."

We nodded to each other and Bix shook my hand. Evidently Ice Lady hadn't thawed enough to offer hers. And I didn't want frostbite, so I didn't offer mine to her. As soon as these amenities were finished, Heather continued. "Maybe we could all sit at the same table for dinner tonight."

"I made reservations at Restaurante Milano for everyone. Sorry, but they're full. I didn't know if you'd make it when I made the reservations. Besides, after what you did, I thought you might feel a little uncomfortable being with all of the Belles anyway," she said with a wry smile. "You can't undo what's been done, you know."

This woman is one catty bitch, I thought, mixing my metaphors. But I refrained from wading in. I was the outsider at the party.

"Well, it's great to see you both again," Heather said, obviously lying through her teeth. "If you'll excuse me, I'll get my name tag and, as you say, mingle."

Heather found her laminated name tag with a college photo and I used a felt-tip pen to put "Morg" on a paper one. Then we headed for the drinks table where a server poured Heather a glass of chardonnay and me a Jameson. At least they had my favorite. As we waited for our drinks, out of earshot of Mindy, I asked Heather what Mindy's problem was.

"We had a little . . . misunderstanding in our senior year. I thought she'd forget it after all this time."

"So Mindy's still holding a grudge from college days?"

"I guess so. Anyway, that's the story." Heather sadly shook her head. "Some reunion this is turning out to be."

I started to ask about the "misunderstanding," but I didn't. Looking at Heather's face, I could see that it wasn't the whole story, but that it was all I was going to get. Heather had always been open with me, but she was holding something back this time and I felt I should respect her wishes. Besides, she'd tell me when she was ready. I didn't even mention that it was odd that Mindy claimed not to know Heather was going to be aboard, yet a name tag with her name was ready.

Chapter 6

As we started to circulate among the other people in the room, I could see this was not my scene. I was never in a sorority. Working my way through Cal State Long Beach, I didn't have the time, money or inclination to join one. Maybe I'm like Groucho Marx and wouldn't want to join any club that would have me as a member. Judging from that crowd, I hadn't missed much. Most of the men and women seemed to know Heather. The men would smile while the women would hug Heather. But it's my business to read people and there was one thing I knew: some of these women really did not like Heather. Some were just too melodramatic, too clichéishly effusive. Phony squeals of delight didn't cover their true feelings. It was all, "You look wonderful" and "You haven't changed a bit," but no "I'm sure we can fit two more for dinner" or "We can find a way to squeeze you two in tonight." With some of them, it might have been jealousy.

As I've said, Heather had enough money to buy whatever she wanted. Add to that a face and body that swimsuit models would kill to have and a fashion sense that made her elegantly sexy, you have the stuff green monsters are made of. A couple of the women were what would be termed "attractive" but none of them had the raw material to compete on Heather's level. And for some hips and bellies were growing, faces were sagging or looking like a lift or two had been done. The way Heather's clothes draped on her body had natural class, while some women's attire looked too forced. They appeared to have trotted out their best duds and baubles for a simple cocktail party.

Four of the women had come over to embrace Heather, each the same and different. There was that feel, that "sorority-ness" so to speak, about them, but they seemed sincere in their welcomes. Each one also left a particular impression with me. Linda, was a tall, leggy blond in a silvery jumpsuit and diamond choker that reeked money, but she was too thin and her nose was a little too big, making that the most memorable part of her face. She had a hairdo that was a bit like celebrity chef Anne Burrell's gone wild, more a scarecrow-like clump of straw. Sheri was a petite woman with short-cropped brown hair that accentuated her elfin face, but had a fireplug body that her expensive-looking short, lacey white dress only magnified. Kathy was as tall as Linda, but with curly, black hair, shoulders like a football player and a full bust. She was wearing a mid-calf length black dress with large pink flowers. It was loose from the bust down, which almost hid her stomach and hips. Jan, a bleached blond was average in height, weight and had decent looks. She wore a simple, black cocktail dress and was the least unique, except for her Southern drawl. Texas was my guess, but accents are not my forte. I mentally tagged them as Scarecrow, Fireplug, Fullback and Texas. When they found that Heather was not dining with the group, they insisted they all meet for a drink afterwards.

One woman came up and just smiled at Heather as she stood there.

"Jennie," was all Heather said.

As far as outward appearances go, they came from the same mold. Both of them were stunners, with great bods and perfectly coiffed hair framing their flawless faces. If I weren't such a mature person, I might have felt envious of two women winning the genetic lottery for great looks while I hadn't. Well, maybe I did feel a little envy, but Heather's been such a good friend, a rare commodity for a smart-mouth like me, to allow it to greatly affect me.

With long, mahogany-colored hair and green eyes, in contrast to Heather's blond, blue-eyed beach-babe look, Jennie was the darker side of the All-American beauty queen. Although she was a little bustier than Heather, that didn't take much and her trim physique made her look really built. Except for her height of almost six feet, Jennie reminded me of Rita Hayworth. Probably none of the others there would even have known who

Rita was, but I was a classic movie nut and *Gilda* was a favorite of mine.

The woman was wearing a black sheath cocktail dress with a high neckline and three-quarter length sleeves that didn't hide her figure while not flaunting it. There was a noticeable difference in Heather's and Jennie's eyes. I've always thought of Heather as Bambi-eyed, although a deer has black eyes and Bambi was a male. It's in the sense of the innocence and harmlessness of the cartoon fawn of Disney fame. She seems to trust everyone and I've never seen Heather willfully hurt anyone. What I saw in Jennie's eyes was a cat: watchful and wary. She spoke with a husky voice.

"You made it, Heather."

"Jennie," Heather said, making a move as if to hug the other woman. "It's been so long. You're looking wonderful, just like you did in college." With no reciprocal move from Jennifer, Heather stopped after a couple of hesitant steps. Jennie smiled oddly as she spun the stem of her wineglass between her thumb and index finger, taking her time before responding.

"Jennifer. I prefer Jennifer now, Heather. And thanks, it's nice to hear that I haven't changed. I doubt that I haven't changed, but I could honestly say that of you. You're the same sweet thing you always were. And yes, it's been a while since . . . the wedding."

Although I sensed something was unresolved between them, I still almost expected the two of them to run to each other. Perhaps they would have, but Ryan Gosling intervened. No, it wasn't the real one, but the guy standing next to Jennifer reminded me of him. With his long shock of blond hair and a five-day mustache and beard, I'm sure he was aware of the similarities. His face was not Ryan's, though. He had brown, deep-set eyes, with thick, dark, eyebrows and thin lips. He was wearing an expensive-looking grey suit with an open-collared lighter grey dress shirt with the initials "DW" embroidered on the collar. He casually draped his arm across Jennifer's shoulders. His grin looked a bit forced and his voice sounded carefully controlled as he said, "We're both glad to see you, Heather. Maybe we can get together after dinner for a drink and talk about old times."   But the meaning I got was a more polite way of saying, "Get lost."

"Yes," Jennifer said, seeming to close up, "that's a good idea."   As if just noticing the glass she was holding, she said, "Well, I'm going to get another glass of wine. We'll talk later."

Heather stood for an uncomfortable moment before she fled out the door. I glared around the room before I followed. What was going on? Why were two of Heather's sorority pals so cold to her? Peer pressure from Mindy and Jennifer for something to do with a wedding years ago? I didn't really give a damn. They had been rude to my friend.

I found Heather was waiting for an elevator. She was staring at the closed chromed doors, blinking back tears. I started to say something, ask her about this "wedding" stuff, but held my tongue. Something I wasn't used to doing. Finally, I asked, "Shall we eat at the Ocean Restaurant?" It was one of the two huge main dining rooms on the ship, for those who did not make reservations at an extra-cost specialty one like the Restaurante Milano. She nodded.

Chapter 7

We were ushered to an open table in the dining room with only two empty chairs remaining. Heather had somehow regained her composure and was smiling as we introduced ourselves to those who were already seated.

There was a man about our age in a tight, black polo shirt that showed his biceps, chest and expanding waistline. Facially, he was sporting a soul patch, a little beard that looked like a Hitler mustache that had slipped below the lips, and short-cropped brown hair. Next to him was a small man of about the same age with a similar shirt, but not so filled out. He also had a similar haircut, but no facial hair.

The bigger man grinned and stood, showing that he was wearing tight, black jeans, a belt with a big, silver buckle and rattlesnake-skin cowboy boots. "Hi, ya'll. I'm Rex Martin, CEO of RAM Security. We do our part to keep the whole damn world safe." He pointed at red, embroidered lettering on his shirt that said "RAM Security" with a rifle scope sight in yellow below. He laid a hand on his companion's shoulder. "And this is my Chief of Operations and good buddy, Billy Wilder." He chuckled. "But I'm one hell of a lot wilder than him." Billy stood, smiled and nodded. I wondered if he knew that he had the same moniker as a famous director and screenwriter of days past.

The only others at our table were two men who were more than a little strange. When introductions reached them, one of them rose from his chair and gave a short bow. He was tall and thickset. To use a dated word, he would best be described as portly. Dressed in a black, pin-striped suit with a striped tie on a casual night, he looked out of place. As he stood, smoothing his thinning black hair and touching his large, drooping mustache before he spoke, I expected him to sound like some stuffy East Coaster. Instead I heard a Californian, stilted in manner but without discernable accent. I mentally named him Wally Walrus, after Woody Woodpecker's cartoon nemesis I'd seen in reruns on Saturday morning TV in the late 80's.

"I am Baron Beaton, ambassador extraordinary and plenipotentiary to the United States for His Royal Highness, Prince David of Albany of the Royal House of Stewart, in exile, who is seated at my side." He gestured at the man next to him.

At that, his companion rose, gave a short bow, took Heather and my right hands in turn, and bowed as he kissed them. Then he solemnly sat down again without a word. Similarly dressed to Baron Beaton but with a purple sash diagonally across his chest, HRH Prince David was shorter than the Baron by a head and skinny, with long, black hair drawn back into a ponytail, and a goatee and mustache. His large, black-framed glasses dominated his thin face. The classic wimp.

On a trip to England some years ago, I had read a book that gave a short synopsis of all the kings and queens of England and Great Britain. I recognized Stewart, or Stuart, as being the name of the Scottish line that had reigned over both England and Scotland for about a century. As I remembered, James II had been kicked out and his daughters had reigned afterwards with the one who died in the early 1700's being the last Stewart monarch. Although a pompous nephew of hers named Charles Edward Stewart, popularly known as Bonnie Prince Charlie, had made a come-back attempt in 1745, he failed dismally in his military venture to regain the throne for the Stewarts. Ol' Charlie had died without a son and his only daughter had no legitimate children, so I wondered who this guy could be. "Prince David" must claim some link, but I was in the dark as to what it was. From the "in exile" bit, I assumed that Queen Elizabeth didn't exactly recognize his claim.

I had a hard time suppressing my curiosity, but the looming waiter wanted our orders. After a quick perusal of the menu, I chose a Caesar salad and lamb chops in a mint sauce. I was impressed with the choices on the menu. Heather ordered a garden salad and grilled salmon, then asked our waiter, who I guessed to be Southeast Asian, for the sommelier. He smiled, nodded and left.

A solemn-looking, burgundy-coated man with the required silver cup on a chain around his neck appeared with a wine list. No one else seemed to be interested in ordering, so Heather took the lead and ordered a bottle of zinfandel and one of Pouilly-Fuissé, charged to our room.

Me, I'm no wine connoisseur. I usually stick with Irish whiskey as my poison-of-choice and did that night. The RAM Security duo passed on wine, but our table royalty and nobility joined Heather in imbibing. When the sommelier served her, she swirled the wine in her glass, took a long sniff, and sipped a little before nodding her approval. As he poured for the other two, Wally mumbled a thanks before taking a healthy swig, followed by an embarrassing toast by the Prince.

HRH stood, raised his glass and spoke with what sounded like a French accent. "To the beautiful *Mademoiselle*. You are a rose among thorns." Then he clicked his heels like a Prussian officer and bowed.

I was not impressed, especially since I was apparently a thorn. Heather graciously managed a smile, but her flushed cheeks and panic-stricken eyes showed her true feelings. The baron applauded. Rex ineffectively stifled a guffaw and Billy chuckled, but they lifted their water glasses to salute Heather.

The Prince sat and Wally refilled his highness' wine glass as well as his own.

Heather and I had met real nobility when we'd been in England, some I'd liked and some I hadn't, but these two were poor imitations. While they hadn't offered to buy any wine or help pay for what Heather had ordered, Wally and the Prince seemed to be more than willing to do their part in emptying the bottles. So much for *noblesse oblige*.

The service by our waiter was attentive and the food up to the standards of a decent restaurant, but not great. The baron and the prince monopolized the conversation.

Wally stifled a burp, then took a gulp of his wine. "My estate is about seventy miles from Glasgow. I can't spend all my time there, since my dental practice is funding the restoration of my castle. As a knight of the realm, I have many duties here as well."

This yo-yo had been knighted by the Queen? "Don't you have to be a British citizen to be a knight? Have you renounced your American citizenship?"

He gave me a stern look. "I am still an American citizen. I have no use for titles from the usurping house of Windsor. I am a Knight of the Order of the Red Thistle, granted by His Royal Highness." He gestured at his companion with his fork and the Prince bent his head in a mini-bow.

I leaned back in my chair. "So you live in America. California?"

He waved his hand dismissively. "My California holding is in hills outside of Sage where I reside when I'm in the States and my practice is in Mission Viejo. But my real home is in Scotland. That's why I'm supporting Prince David and I am his Ambassador Extraordinary and Plenipotentiary for North America. I am also Grand Master of the Historic Knights Templar of the Prior of Sion. We want to restore Prince David to his rightful place on the Scottish throne."

I thought Rex was going to choke on his steak. He was coughing and laughing at the same time. Finally, he recovered enough to speak. "So you're going to kick out the Queen? Don't you think she and her army might object?"

The Prince spoke up. "When Scotland unites behind me, there will be no war. She will have no choice but to heed the will of my people. She is *faux*, what you call a fraud, yes? This is all explained in my book *A King in Exile: The True History of Scotland's Hidden Monarchy*. I have brought some autographed copies, if you would like to buy one."

Fortunately, the waiter was handing out the dessert menus and I took one, grateful to have something to read other than a book by a wacko. It was one comment made by the so-called

HRH David, though that gave me a nickname for him. He claimed the Queen was *faux*, but he was the fake. I mentally dubbed him *Faux Prince*, or FP.

Turning to more pressing issues, I ordered a "chocolate suicide" cake which was small, but rich and moist. Heather stuck to cheese with a glass of port. Wally tried three different desserts and FP had two. They also drained the last of Heather's wine. If I were doomed to sit with these two boors for every meal, I would have jumped overboard. Well, maybe I would just start dining in the suite. Whatever was necessary, I would avoid them for future meals.

At that point, Heather's cell phone rang. Or rather played the opening bars of Beethoven's Fifth. She pulled it out her purse, glanced down at who was calling and left the table. I didn't even know cell phones worked on cruise ships. Looked like there was no escaping the plague of the smartphone zombies.

Chapter 8

Rex gave me a bemused grin. "Looks like y'all are stuck with us, Hon."

I gave him the death stare. "It's Morg, not Hon. Got it, *Dude*?"

"Got it, Miss Morg." He laughed. "You're okay. I like a feisty woman."

I sighed. He wasn't worth the effort of another comeback about his trite phrase. Fortunately, he turned his attention to FP.

"So, Your Princeness, since y'all are a king, you must have a royal treasury. You should have the best security. That's RAM Security. No assassins'll get at you with me and Billy on the job. I'm a retired Navy Seal, ya know, and Billy's an ex-Marine." He pulled out his wallet and proffered a business card.

FP studied it through his thick lenses, but didn't take it. "I am in danger from the usurpers who have my throne and are worried that I will press my claim, but my funds are—"

"Tied up in long-term investments." Wally interrupted, as he wiped chocolate cake crumbs off his mouth. "I handle the royal accounts and there is no room in the budget for, uh, such matters at this time."

"So you're a baron, a knight, an ambassador, the royal treasurer and a dentist?" Rex grinned. "Y'all have more hats than the lineup at a Texas bar."

"Yes, I am a very busy man." Wally checked his wine glass, which was empty, then grimaced as he drank his water.

I was saved from enduring any more of this delightful dinner conversation by Heather's return. She was smiling, no, beaming.

"I'm sorry, but Morg and I have to leave. We're having guests come to our suite in a few minutes and have to get ready."

She grabbed my hand and half-dragged me away from the table. FP stood and solemnly bowed slightly as we left. Rex and

Billy called a good-bye, but Heather and I were already too far away for me to distinctly hear what they said.

As we left the dining room and stopped at the elevator, I pulled my hand away.

"What gives? Who are these guests that are so important you dragged me away from the table?"

She stood, looking at the closed elevator doors and impatiently tapping her foot. "Linda called. She, Sheri, Kathy and Jan wanted to meet up for a drink, so I invited them to the suite."

"Our suite? Why?" I paused. "And why drag me away? I don't think they'd care much if I were there or not."

"Because it's quiet and private. But if you'd rather not, feel free to go back to the table."

I considered our table company that night and turned toward the elevator doors. "This thing is sure slow tonight."

When we got to the suite, Heather called for Alasdair. "Would you order a plate of cheese and crackers. Not the cheap stuff, but good cheese, like brie and camembert. And no junk like Saltine or Ritz crackers. Maybe some mixed nuts. Not peanuts, though, a good quality mix." She paused, looking around the bar. "Some champagne, Dom Pérignon. Two, three, no make it five bottles. Oh, some strawberries to go with them. And a bottle of cognac. Martell XO, if you have it."

"Um, I will get the food, but there is a problem on the beverages." He tapped a pen nervously against a pad of paper he held. "The champagne included free with the suite is, well . . . ."

"Crap." Heather rolled her eyes. "I know that. Just get the best you have and put it on my tab."

"And I don't believe we have any Martell XO in stock."

"Just bring a bottle of the best have of that, too, and put that on my tab, too." She glanced around. "Please hurry. They'll be here soon."

After Alasdair quietly slipped out, I cleared my throat. "I think it might be a good idea for you to have some time alone with your sorority sisters. I've got some research on the Internet I want to do."

Heather turned to me and gave a weak smile. "Don't go. This is going to be fun. I'm sure my sorority sisters will love you as much as I do."

I managed a smile. "I'm sure. I'm so good with . . . ." Snobs? Rich bitches? "Strangers?"

Our discussion was, thankfully, cut short by Heather's cell before I was honest about my concerns. Heather answered it.

"Hello . . . What? Oh, I didn't think of that. I'll be right down."

She looked at me as soon as she disconnected. "My friends are stuck at the door to the stairs on deck 13. I forgot that they need our key card to get in. I'm going to let them in." She paused, looking around. "Would you open a few bottles of wine we have in the fridge and get out some glasses? It'll have to do until Alasdair gets back."

"Look, I'll let them in. You do the wine bit, okay?"

"Thanks." She started pulling wine glasses from the bar's glass-doored cabinet. "You're a pal."

I took the stairs down, first propping the door to the suite ajar. My key was in my purse in my bedroom and I didn't want to get it. When I opened the door at the bottom of the staircase, Scarecrow, Fireplug, Full back and Texas were there. I smiled. "Come in."

Fireplug looked behind me. "They're stairs. Can't we take the elevator?'

"Take's a room key and I left it upstairs. It's only one deck up."

Fireplug rolled her eyes. "Great. Just great."

They followed me up the stairs and into the suite. We took the long hallway to the living room. Scarecrow, Full back and Texas were right behind me, oohing and aahing over the room and the view. Fireplug was wheezing, not far behind. I should try to think of them by their names, I admonished myself, before I slipped up when I was talking to them.

"We had to take the stairs," Fireplug . . . oops! . . . Sheri gasped. "Your companion here forgot her key, so we couldn't take the elevator."

"Oh, I'm so sorry." Heather hugged her. "How many stairs did you take getting here?

Texas laughed. Was she Jan? "We only had to take the one flight. Sheri's just not into exercise."

Heather stepped back and looped her arm in mine. "I forgot to introduce all of you to my BFF, Morg Mahoney."

"Morgue?" Jan . . . yes, it was Jan, laughed. "What is she, a coroner?"

I forced a smile. I'd heard that joke too many times. "No, but I give them a lot of business. It's short for Morgana and I'm a P.I."

Scarecrow, or Linda, chimed in. "I don't remember you. Were you in our class?"

"Same year, different school. I went to Cal State Long Beach."

Linda looked down her nose at me, which was a long ways to look. "So you're not Greek."

"Mainly Irish." I fluffed my auburn curls. "Hence, the hair."

"No, I meant —"

"I know what you meant. I'm Phi Kappa Phi, if that means anything."

Sheri spoke up. "That's not a sorority, it's a fraternity. I went with a guy from Cal who was in it."

I shook my head. "It's also an honor society, like Phi Beta Kappa. Not that you'd care about anything —"

Before I could finish, the doorbell rang.

Heather looked relieved as she went to answer it, calling back, "That must be our nibbles and drinks."

When she returned, Mindy was with her, followed by Alasdair with a loaded cart. Stunned, would be how I would describe Heather's expression. Mindy glanced at the others, then turned to face Heather.

"I don't want us to continue this way. You hurt me, you know. But we're sisters and what we had was more important than Bix will ever be."

Tears ran down Heather's cheeks. "Oh, Mindy. I've tried to tell you how sorry I was. I thought you two were . . . . Anyway, we were both drunk that night. I don't even remember what—"

Mindy grabbed Heather's shoulders. "Stop. I forgive you. Knowing Bix, he probably spiked your drink. It's over and done now. I wanted to still be angry, but when I saw you again, I couldn't."

As Heather hugged Mindy, Alasdair quietly wheeled in the cart. I motioned for him to take it to the bar and helped him set up for the party that would be coming. It didn't take a detective, or a P.I., to figure out that Heather slept with Bix when she thought he was no longer with Mindy, possibly by date rape. Mindy waited twenty years to bury the hatchet and tonight was the night. Once Alasdair finished and slipped out, it was my cue to cut out, too. Pouring myself a splash of Jameson with ice and water, I exited to my room. I also grabbed a slice of cheese that looked like Irish cheddar and some crackers. What little I took would not be missed any more than I would be.

Chapter 9

As I sat at the glass-top desk in my room and turned on my tablet, I wondered if I was being petty, overreacting to the jibes from Linda, Sheri, Kathy and Jan. I sipped my whiskey. Maybe, but I'd worked my way through college with no help from anyone. I did not suffer fools or snobs well. While Heather, in spite of all her money, was not really a snob, she'd let peer pressure intimidate her to silence when I was being insulted. It was safer for all parties for me to vacate the party before I strangled someone.

After meeting our delightful dinner companions, I decided to do a little online research on them. I started with Prince David. While he called himself David Charles Robert Stewart, Duke of Albany, only he and his faithful followers did so. According to FP, his parents were both descended from Bonnie Prince Charlie, who married a French princess after the Vatican gave him a divorce. Only problems were that the Roman Catholic Church had stated there was no divorce and FP's Belgian birth certificate said he was born to a bar manager named Georges De Clercq and his barmaid, Marie. Only those who wanted to live a fairy tale believed otherwise.

Then there was the Baron. I do love Google. Wally did, indeed, have a Scottish barony. Technically, he was Walt Ferrier, Baron of Beaton, and had purchased the title. I could buy one, too, for a few thou. Yeah, I'm Lady Morg, you sorority snobs! I laughed at the thought. Not worth the money, though. Wally's "estate" did not come with the title and I wondered what it was like. A few acres of land with a ruined stone cottage? Considering what I found out about the aptly-named, desert-like community of Sage where he lived, no wonder he wanted to live a fantasy life.

I nibbled some of the cheese. Ah, it was Irish cheddar. Then I sipped some Jameson. I could hear laughter through my door, but was glad to be alone in my room. I feared it would be a long trip, with Heather back into her college friends and me on the outside. I sighed. Such was my life.

I had one more person to research: Rex Martin of RAM Security. The website for his company had many testimonies by satisfied clients, such as *Premier Claude J.*, *Sheik Abdul H.*, and *Lord Henry T.* There were also a few that gave full names, but they had no fancy titles. That gave me pause. There were claims of doing security for "multinational corporations" and "African and Asian governments," but no names were given "because of confidentiality agreements." This was sounding as real as FP being descended from Bonnie Prince Charlie. I went down to Rex's bio.

According to the site, Rex A. Martin had been a Navy Seal, in Team Five. He had once helped rescue five women scientists held by Al-Qaeda in an unnamed African country. After retiring as a Seal, he had been recruited by the CIA and had participated in Black Ops, including "eliminating numerous terrorist threats to our country." However, due to "national security," he could not give more details. Since then, he formed his own company and was lending his expertise to "those who have need of the services of a trained, professional security team of the highest caliber."

I shook my head. I was not a Seal expert and had never been in the military, but his résumé didn't sound real. All that was missing was his birthplace being Krypton or that he worked nights patrolling Gotham City. He was a perfect fit with Wally and FP. It wasn't like I was going to go on a crusade to expose all of them, but I didn't want to be around them. Hopefully, I would not have to sit through another meal with any of these phonies. Life was too short.

I Skyped Lois, the woman who was taking care of Sam while I was on the cruise. After a couple of rings, she answered. She seemed perplexed.

"Morg, is anything wrong?"

"No, I just called to see if Sam is okay."

"Of course she is. But isn't this your first night at sea? Shouldn't you be with your friend at a show or something?"

"I'm taking a break." I sipped my whiskey. "Too much excitement. Can I talk to Sam?"

"Sure. I'll put her on."

After a couple of minutes, Sam's happy face came on the screen.

"Hey, girl, you miss me?"

She barked a hello. Seeing her was a comfort. That little Border collie was always glad to see me. Lois came on the screen beside her.

"We've been having a great time. She's enjoying having a huge yard to play in with a couple of buds."

"Yeah, I bet she is." I felt guilt for keeping her in my apartment all day while I was at work. "Well, I just wanted to check in."

"You go have fun. We'll be fine."

"Okay. Talk at you later."

After we disconnected, I felt very alone. At home, Sam would sense if I felt that way and put her head on my leg, looking up with understanding eyes. She was my real Best Friend Forever. As I ate a little more cheese and crackers while I nursed my whiskey, the baby grand piano in the main room was being played. Well, considering how professional "Music of the Night" sounded, it was very likely due to the talent of the piano's inbuilt computer that could pound out quite a variety of tunes. Several voices were laughing and talking loudly. It was going to be a long night. Fortunately, I had earplugs and dug them out for when I went to bed. In the meantime, I pulled out the book I'd brought, *Crime and Punishment*. I'd started it when I was in college and never got around to finishing it. The Russians had a heaviness to their writing, an ominous undercurrent of depression, that made reading them a chore. Yet I felt I would never be truly literate if I had not read any Dostoevsky. Since I had been an English major in college, I felt it was incumbent on me to finish at least one tome by the Monk Photius. Since I had nothing better to do, it was a good night to work on that.

Monday

Chapter 10

I awoke to a faint clinking outside my door. Instinctively, I reached for the revolver on my nightstand. It wasn't there. Not only that, it wasn't my nightstand. Looking around, it wasn't my room. Then I remembered that I was on a ship and it must be Heather making the noise. I got up to check it out.

Since I am a sleep minimalist as far as clothing is concerned and I am staying with another woman, I almost opened the door while in the nude. At the last second, I threw on my jeans and a knit top, just in case. When I opened the door and went into the living room, Alasdair was collecting empty bottles and putting them on a cart. He glanced over at me and smiled.

"I trust you slept well?"

I breathed a sigh of relief that I had taken the time to dress. I checked the time. 8:39 in the morning. "Great. Have you seen Heather?"

"I believe she was meeting friends for breakfast. She rang me to clear the, ah, . . . refuse from last night while she was gone." He paused. "You must have had quite a night of it."

I looked over at the rows of empty bottles and dirty plates on his cart. "I guess you could say that." Even if I hadn't been a part of it.

"Will you be joining your friends for breakfast or would you like room service?"

"Just coffee. I'm not a breakfast person."

He went to the room phone. "I will order a pot of it for you."

"Thanks. Give me a half hour to . . . freshen up first." I headed for my room.

Once I had a quick shower, I put on a little makeup and donned fresh clothes. I did a quick check in the mirror to see if my new drawstring cargo shorts and loose-fitting white ruched T-shirt looked okay. Satisfied, I went back out. The living room and kitchenette were cleaned and a pot of coffee in a thermal carafe was on the glass-top table. Alasdair pulled out one of the chairs. As I sat in it, I reflected that I could get used to this. He poured steaming coffee in a cup that he had placed in front of me.

"Cream? Sugar?"

I shook my head. "Never mess with perfection." I sipped it and closed my eyes. "And this is perfection."

"If there is nothing more, I will leave now."

A thought hit me. "There are two suites on this deck, right?"

He nodded.

"So, who's in the other one, the guy who looks like Dr. Strangelove?"

"I'm not sure about who that doctor is, but the gentleman in the other suite is Jerry Steele. He and his wife."

"Wife? The blond chick? I thought that was his nurse. She looks young enough to be his granddaughter."

He cleared his throat. "I'm not sure about her age, but she is his wife."

"Jerry Steele, huh?" The name was vaguely familiar. "Wait, is that the sex magazine guy?"

Alasdair looked away. "Yes, I understand that Mr. Steele owned *Tomcat* magazine."

I chuckled. What neighbors, an old pornographer and his bimbo wife. "Thanks, Alasdair. I'm fine here, so feel free to take off."

He gave a short nod. "I'll collect the coffee pot before lunch." Then he left.

I mulled over this new information. There was something in the back of my mind that he was not a nice guy, not counting his publishing predilection. I grabbed my tablet from my room and set up on the dining table. A quick Google search had a ton of information.

Jerry Steele had just beat a pornography charge in Mississippi in 1986 and was walking out of the court house when someone stabbed him in the back with an ice pick. So many reporters, well-wishers and protestors were crowded around him that the perpetrator was never caught, although there had been three suspects. It left him paralyzed and, rumor had it, impotent. Some called it poetic justice, others karma, and a very few said it was unfair. His wife at the time, his third, had divorced him, claiming he was unable to perform his husbandly duties. Then came the really not nice part.

The three suspected pick wielders were a Baptist minister who had been a friend of the court in the pornography charges, a Neo-Nazi who had written letters to Steele about using photos of nude inter-racial couples and a feminist who had protested Steele's exploitation of women in his magazine. Within a year, they were all dead. The men had their genitals cut off and stuffed in their mouths. The woman had a sex toy stuffed in hers. Then his ex-wife was also found dead, drowned in her bathtub. She also had a sex toy in her, but not in her mouth. The connection was obvious, but no evidence of Steele's involvement was ever found.

After that, Steele had many young women become his companions, all of them "Sex Kittens," the centerfold feature of his magazine. One of them he'd married, then divorced. She wisely never commented on his sexual prowess and was still alive. Last year, he'd married Darla Darling, a former "Sex Kitten" and retired "adult film actress," according to Wikipedia. She was the one who had been pushing his wheelchair. Google images showed her in a nurse's outfit like what I'd seen her wearing yesterday. In his condition, looking was probably all he could handle.

Since then, he'd sold his smut empire for a mid-nine figures and even produced some "legitimate" movies, R-rated sexploitation ones, of course. They went directly to video, but reasonably successful for that genre. However, he had not made any for several years.

I turned off my tablet and sipped my coffee. It sounded like Dr. Strangelove was very ruthless and very wealthy. As Dorothy Parker once quipped, "If you want to know what God thinks of money, look at the people he gave it to." Obviously, God must have thought highly of me.

Chapter 11

Since I had no idea where Heather and her clan were, I decided to check out the ship. I had a small guide of the decks and used it to find my way around the floating city. Water features had little appeal, a thrill-invoking slide that looped out over the side of the ship or not. Hanging out, literally, in my bathing suit at one of the pools was not on my list. I'd only brought it to go snorkeling with Heather in Cabo. Later in the cruise I might try the gym or the running track, but not the first day. There were a slew of bars, but it was too early for drinking, even for me. Two activities were interesting. There was a go-cart track and a laser tag course. Right then, running someone off the track or shooting them sounded like fun. I started toward the laser tag course.

As I walked along the pool to get to the chance to shoot someone, I spotted FP and Wally. FP had on a white polo shirt, black Bermuda shorts with matching socks and sandals. Wally wore a bright Hawaiian shirt that tented over his belly, khaki cargo shorts and flip-flops. At least they weren't wearing suits this time. But what was interesting was the dapper-looking man in a subtle Aloha shirt, chinos and sandals that they had cornered against a bar. It was Bix.

I couldn't hear them, but Wally was shaking his index finger in Bix's face. FP was right behind him, hands on hips and chin jutting. Bix was holding up both his hands, a sign of surrender. As I approached, Bix looked at me and said something to Wally. He and FP turned toward me. Bix slipped away. When Wally looked back and saw Bix had escaped, he and FP headed the other way as well. Hmm, I mused. Looks like no one wanted to talk to me. What was that all about? How did Bix know those two clowns and why were they mad at him? I shrugged. It wasn't any of my business. I was only on this cruise as a "companion."

When I got to laser tag, there was a line, a long line. From those in it, laser tag was very popular with adolescent males. There were a few girls, but the maximum age of those in the queue looked to be in the late teens. That is, if you didn't count the few parents that were interspersed in the crowd and looked as out of place as I would. Somehow running around shooting kids was not what I had expected. With a sigh, I turned away. I meandered toward the go-cart racetrack, but didn't expect much better. It was, with more families and adults waiting to drive carts. But the line was still long and I was alone, so I canned that idea. It looked like a bar. It was still too early for a Jameson, but I could use more coffee.

On deck 10, I found a table in the Market Street Café, which had an interior balcony that overlooked a three-deck atrium. I ordered a latte. Not something I normally did, but I was getting bored and wanted something different. I was alone with four thousand people. Could it get any more fun? Then the Ghost of Disco Past, dressed in the ugliest purple, pink and orange Hawaiian shirt I'd ever seen and tight, white shorts, sat down at my table. He winked at me.

"Hey, cutie, where's your girlfriend?"

"Busy."

"My friend's busy, too. Perfect time for just the two of us to get better acquainted." He smiled and leaned closer. "Look, I know you're a lesbian, but I can give you a night that will turn you straight. A hard man is good to find, you know." Then suddenly, hidden by the table, his hand rested on my thigh, just above the knee.

I jerked in surprise. My latte had just arrived. I really needed the caffeine, but made the sacrifice. I knocked it over so it ran off the table onto his lap.

Disco Ghost jumped up and tried to wipe the brown stain off of his crotch, screaming, "You stupid bitch! I ought to—"

"Do what?" I stood, leaning across the table. "You touch me again and I'll twist your head off and spit in the hole."

His eyes went wide and his jaw dropped. He staggered back. "You're crazy. You're nothing but a crazy lez." Then he turned and fled.

Everyone in the café was staring at me, not saying a word. Although I didn't regret what I'd said, I wished I'd said it more softly. The waiter who'd brought my latte started mopping it up from the table and chair, avoiding my eyes. I was looking for the nearest exit when someone behind me started slowly clapping. A couple of other people clapped once or twice, probably thinking everyone else was going to join in, but stopped. I looked around to see who was applauding my brash actions. It was Rex.

He looked a little less like he was in a country bar, with no silver buckle or boots. His silky guayabera shirt hugged his ample gut, hanging over the top of his cargo shorts. Instead of cowboy boots, he was wearing sandals. All of them were black. I wondered if he had any other color in his wardrobe. He grinned at me as he continued his slow applause, the only one left doing so.

So embarrassed I could have crawled under the table, I hurried past him, out the door. He followed and called to me in a Texas drawl.

"Hell of a show back there, Hon. Remind me never to get on your bad side. I need my head."

I was tempted to tell him what I thought of him and his Hon, but refrained. I'd already made a big scene that people wouldn't forget and probably made an enemy for life. And it wasn't even noon yet. So I tried to be polite.

"I might have overreacted. I don't take kindly to being groped."

"Don't blame you. The guy was an over-egoed wuss. Maybe we could have a coffee sometime, as long as you promise to drink it instead of dumping it in my lap." He grinned and checked his watch. "I'd offer now, but I've got to meet my client. Got great assets." The way he said it, it sounded like "ass-sets."

"I'm busy now, too. I've got to meet some friends." I lied to save face. So sue me.

He turned and headed forward with a backward wave.

I stood for a moment, tempted to follow. What kind of client would he have onboard a cruise ship? What job could he have here? Then I gave in to temptation.

Following someone without them knowing can be difficult, especially for one person. However, I doubted he had any reason to think he was being tailed and I hung back in the crowds of people along the wide aisles. He went up a few stairs and entered double glass doors to the library.

I paused. Rex never struck me as a guy who would spend time in a library, especially on a cruise ship. I hung around outside the doors, trying to get a peek inside without being obvious. He was sitting at a table, reading a magazine. I ducked back before he saw me, found a chair nearby and waited. A few minutes later, a woman approached, another person who I didn't expect to see in a library. It was Nurse Bimbo.

As she entered the doors, she didn't notice me. Obviously, our chance encounter at the elevator had not made an impression. I gave her a minute, then chanced a look inside. She was seated at the table with Rex. He was talking, but I'm not a lip reader, so I had no idea about what.

I knew the identity of Rex's client, but not her business. However, I had no reason to pursue more information. Curiosity wasn't worth more effort. I headed back to the suite to see if Heather had returned.

I got back to our rooms to find them empty. No Heather, no note. Although she used her cell onboard, I did not want to get charged for some call about reducing my credit card interest, so I kept mine off. I dug it out of my room safe and turned it on. I had a text. "Lunch at Market Street Café at noon. Cocktail party in Oslo Room at five. Dinner in Rick's Steakhouse Américain at seven." I sighed. It looked like, other than meals and drinks, I was on my own.

I am not a social animal. I don't go to concerts, clubs or movies, unless it's a big-screen blockbuster. And not even always then. It was still an hour before lunch, so it looked like I had no excuse for not reading more of Raskolnikov's troubled life in St. Petersburg. At this rate, I would finish *Crime and Punishment* well before I finished the cruise. I grabbed the book and poured a cup of coffee as I headed for the patio.

Chapter 12

The Market Street Café has a buffet for breakfast, lunch and dinner. I really don't like buffets. It's the "more is better" philosophy of eating. I like eating, but know I need to keep it in check if I don't want to be waddling down the companionways before we returned to San Pedro. When I arrived for lunch, everyone else was already there, a plate of food and a glass of wine in front of each woman. They had shoved two tables together, giving seating for eight. Two were still open, both on the far end from Heather. She smiled and waved. I waved back and sat. I was at the end of the table with Fireplug beside me and the other empty chair across. She was in conversation with Texas, seated across from her. I should have eaten lunch in the suite.

The waiter served me water, but everything else was self-service. I headed for the buffet. There were a lot of items for salads, but I wanted something more substantial. The pizza looked like pre-made frozen from a grocery store. There was a good selection of Indian dishes, so I spooned up some chicken jalfrezi and lamb rogan josh over basmati rice. After grabbing a piece of naan bread, I went looking for something to drink. I didn't want a soft drink or coffee drink, so I went to the juice bar. It had beer and wine as well, but no whiskey. I settled for a glass of merlot.

Once I was seated again, I sipped my wine. I'm no expert, but it tasted cheap to me. And my food was barely warm. Fireplug was talking to Scarecrow, who was seated on her other side. Texas realized I was there and smiled. "Well, hi, y'all. Havin' a good time?"

I smiled back. "Fine and dandy."

"Meet anyone interesting?"

I thought about Disco Ghost and Rex. "A guy named Rodion Raskolnikov."

She frowned. "Sounds Russian. Now I'm not sayin' they all are, but some of them are mobsters, pretty dangerous guys. We've got some in Texas. You've got to be careful around them."

I thought about how Raskolnikov murdered a couple of old women with an axe in the book. "I suppose so."

Leaning forward, she rested her elbows on the table and cupped her chin in her hands. "So, is this Rod-iron guy hot?"

I thought about it. He was described as tall, handsome and in good condition, with dark, bedroom eyes. Not exactly that, but close. A lot like Father Robert, the closest thing I currently had to a boyfriend. "Yeah, he is."

"What's he do for a living?"

"He's a priest. I mean a law student." Oops! Mixing fact and fiction.

"Priest and a law student?" She leaned forward and rested her chin on her interlaced fingers. "Tell me more."

"Rodion is a law student. Well, former law student. He's in a book I'm reading. *Crime and Punishment.*"

"I remember that book. I had to do a report on it in my sophomore lit class. I gave up after the first few chapters and went to Cliff Notes." She cocked her head. "Super depressing, I think. Some guy kills a couple of old women, loan sharks or something, and ends up in jail. What was the priest's part in all that?"

"None. The priest is a guy I'm going with." Not something I wanted known at this table. "Sort of. I mean, we met and . . . ." I was giving way too much information.

Fireplug must have caught that last. She'd turned toward me. "You're doing a priest? You both Catholic? Would that be a cardinal sin if he gets promoted?" She smirked. "What's it like to do the horizontal mambo with a guy in a dog collar?"

"I'm a Roman Catholic, but he's not. And—"

"Buddhist?" Texas interrupted.

"Huh?" It took me a moment to get what she meant. "No, Episcopalian. And we haven't—"

"What's he look like?" Fireplug butted in. "Little, old bald guy with thick glasses?"

"As a matter of fact, he's thirty years old, over six feet, fit and damn good-looking."

Fireplug chuckled. "He's only thirty? You're a cougar. Is he a tiger in bed?"

I slammed my hand on the table. "Not that it's any of your business, but we haven't tangled under the sheets, okay?"

Everyone at the whole table had stopped talking and was staring at me. Except Fireplug. She was grinning like the Cheshire cat, taking delight in my outburst. I had to get out of there. The lunch was lousy and the company was worse. In another minute, I might just commit sororicide. Except I wasn't Fireplug's "sister," so it would be justifiable bitchicide.

I stood and glanced around the table. "If you will excuse me, I will take my leave."

Heather was staring at me, eyes wide. Without another word, I headed for the door. I was angry at Fireplug, but more at myself that I'd let her get under my skin. I considered shooting people, with a laser-tag gun, of course, to relieve some of my anger. I went up to its deck, but the line was still too long. Same with the one for the go-karts. So I went back to the suite to change. My last resort was exercise. If I couldn't fight a person, I'd fight flab.

The gym was well equipped, with modern treadmills, bikes, ellipticals and weight machines. Although each machine had a person or two waiting, the lines were far less than for laser tag and go-karts. With the requisite mirrors along two walls to make you feel guilty for hitting the buffets and a row of dumbbells in front of one of them, it was much like my normal gym. So was the attire. With my baggy sweatshirt and faded, loose-fitting shorts, I looked like a kid in high school gym class, but I was there for exercise, not preening. After a couple of hours, I was sweating and tired, ready for a shower and rest.

When I opened the door to the suite, Heather was there. As I entered, she handed me a drink, Jameson, no doubt, and smiled. "Have a nice workout?"

I took the drink, but set it on a table. I needed water, not alcohol. "Using 'nice' with a workout is oxymoronic."

She shrugged. "I enjoy the burn." Then she grew serious. "Can we talk?"

"After I get a shower. Otherwise this place will need fumigation."

"Okay. I'll wait for you."

I grabbed a glass of ice water and headed for my bathroom.

Once I finished showering and washing my hair, I threw on a pair of white, loose shorts and a navy blue top and went back to the living room. My hair was still damp, but I'd let it air dry. It makes my hair hyper curly, but so be it. Heather was sitting in a chair, gazing out the window as she sipped her glass of wine. I picked up the Jameson glass and sat across from her.

"So, what did you want to talk about?"

She seemed nervous, playing with her half-full wine glass. "I hope you don't mind, but I had keys made for the Belles. Well, except for Jennifer. It makes it a lot easier when they come up here, us not having to go down to let them in."

I shrugged. Not my call. I wasn't happy, but it I wasn't paying for the suite. "Anything else? Like how I was rude to your friends?"

She shook her head. "No, about how they were rude to you. Especially one of them."

"Fireplug." I thought a minute, searching through my mental data base. "I mean Sheri."

"Fireplug?" She stifled a grin. "Oh, Morg, you kill me sometimes. Yes, I mean Sheri. She does look a little like a fireplug. Jan told me about what she said. Sheri can be a bit . . . ."

"Bitchy?"

"I was going to say caustic. But, yes. Anyway, I'll make sure you sit with me at dinner and Sheri is at the other end of the table. I do appreciate that you came because I asked you to and I've been a little caught up with my old friends."

A little? "Look, I understand that it's like old times for you. No problem. But I don't fit in. The cow in the china shop, as it were. Why don't I eat here? I can order anything I want and Alasdair is good company."

She stood and walked over to me. "Morgana Mahoney, there is no way I'm going to let you spend this cruise alone in the room. You'll come to dinner and have fun with me. I'll make sure of it." She extended her free hand with only her little finger out of her fist. "Pinky promise."

I sighed. Heather must be the only woman who still did a pinky promise. "Fine, fine. I'll come to dinner and try to behave."

"And to the cocktail party."

I conceded defeat. "And to the cocktail party."

"Pinky promise." Her little finger was still sticking out at me.

I wrapped her little finger with mine. "Pinky promise."

"Good. Now let's go out and have some fun."

I held up my hand. "Not now. I'm beat from my workout. I'll meet you at the cocktail party."

She looked at me askance. "Promise?"

"I've sworn by my sacred pinky."

She laughed. We were good again.

After Heather left, I took my whiskey and book up to the suite's deck and settled in a comfortable chair. It was nice to be alone with such a beautiful view. Besides, I still was not fine with Heather's friends.

Chapter 13

The cocktail party was in the same room as the night before. But this time only Bix, Mindy, Jennifer and Dave were there. Bix and Mindy greeted us again, but Mindy was friendly this time, even to me.

Looking around, I was struck by the sparse attendance. "So, where did everyone from last night go?"

Mindy rolled her eyes. "Sheri and her friends will be here soon. I made the mistake of making it a public posting on Facebook about the cruise, even the welcome cocktail party, so everyone wasn't a Belle. Some Stanford alumni and even some people who weren't even Cardinals snuck in before I took up being the bouncer at the door to keep them out. I didn't make that mistake tonight." She hesitated, embarrassed. "No offense. I'm not referring to you. You're Heather's . . . companion?"

I gave her a phony smile. "None taken. I'm just a shirttail Belle."

She looked at me quizzically. I didn't explain that a shirttail relative can mean someone who is only an honorary relative, not really part of the family.

As we walked into the room, Heather grabbed a glass of champagne from a waiter, but I opted to wait until I could get my usual. Why change from a winner? When the Gang of Four showed, Heather made sure I was behind her and ran interference. I headed straight for the bar for my Jameson.

Jennifer was there, picking up a couple of glasses of wine. She smiled at me. Although she did look a lot like Heather, she did not exude my friend's confidence.

"You're here with Heather, aren't you?"

"Guilty as charged."

"Would you do me a favor?" She hesitated, glancing over at her husband, Dave, who was talking to another man. As she spoke, she kept her eyes on him. "Tell her I understand about the wedding." She hesitated again. "And tell her thanks for trying."

What was she talking about? "Why don't you tell her? She's right over there."

Before she could answer, Bix came up beside her. "Hey, Jennifer, how's it going? Long time, no see."

She stepped back. "Stay away from me." Then she turned and hurried over to her husband.

Bix turned to me and shrugged his shoulders. "You try to be friendly." Then he turned to the bartender. "Jack and Coke. Light on the Coke."

He looked at me, glancing down at my bustline. "You're Heather's friend, who's not a part of Sigma Iota Nu, are you."

"No, I'm not into that kind of sin."

He looked at me uncomprehendingly.

"The Greek letters sigma iota and nu spell sin in English."

The candle flickered to life. "Oh, I get it." He chuckled. "They lived up to that name at Stanford, too, especially the Belles. You're a real joker, aren't you?" He paused. "How would you like to hang out later, a couple of fifth wheels having fun?"

"I'll pass." What a letch.

He shrugged again. "Suit yourself. I can always find someone who appreciates *my* company."

After he left, I watched Jennifer and Dave. He put his arm across her shoulders and possessively pulled her closer while glaring at Bix. She didn't resist. I also noticed that she was wearing a long-sleeved, high-collared blouse. It didn't take a genius to figure out the dynamics of that couple.

I shook my head. It reminded me of how one of Heather's ex-boyfriends treated her. The first time I met her, he'd been choking her. I'd put my .38 to his head and told him to let her go. But I wouldn't be pulling out my revolver and sticking it in this brute's ear. Unfortunately, I'd had to leave my beloved handgun home.

As I looked around the room, I was reminded of a novel by Katherine Anne Porter, *Ship of Fools*. Regarding that story of people on a voyage from Mexico to Europe, she wrote, "I believe that human beings are capable of total evil, but no one has ever been totally good: and this gives the edge to evil." From what I'd seen, this ship had more than one fool and from what I'd sensed about Dave, as well as from our deckmate of porn fame, Jerry Steele, more than its share of evil.

Since I took a stroll along the deck after my encounter with Bix, I didn't see Heather or the Gang of Four until dinner at Rick's Steakhouse Américain, one of the ones where you pay extra to dine. When I walked in, I was in love. The place had a décor much like Rick's Café Américain from the movie *Casablanca*. It had slowly rotating ceiling fans, ferns and wait staff wearing black pants with red sashes, blousy white shirts, open black vests and red fezzes. Being as *Casablanca* was on my top ten list of movies, I was enthralled. I looked around for a roulette table and an upright piano with a Dooley Wilson look-alike playing "As Time Goes By," but they were missing. Maybe the maître de would be a Humphrey Bogart look-alike.

As I stood, admiring the décor, a man who I assumed was the maître de came up to me and asked if I had reservations. He was dressed similarly to the rest of the crew, but had a black sash and fez. He was tall, Middle-Eastern looking and had a mustache, nothing like Bogie. I sighed. So much for my fantasy.

"I'm with some other women. I think we have reservations for seven at seven," I told him.

He nodded and smiled. "If you will follow me."

When we arrived at the table, Heather and two of the four amigos, Texas and Scarecrow, were there. Heather motioned for me to sit next to her. I did so and she rested her hand on mine, concern in her eyes.

"What happened to you? I didn't see you after we went to the party."

I shrugged. "After getting hit on by your friend's husband, I decided it wasn't my kind of party."

Her eyes narrowed. "Bix hit on you?"

"That dirtwad would hit on any bitch in heat," Texas drawled, then grimaced. "Not that you're a bitch. What I meant was—"

"I'm in heat?" I laughed at her reddened face. Texas obviously had a little of my foot-in-mouth affliction. If it'd been Fireplug, I'd have known it had been intentional. "Don't worry. I got what you meant. He's always horny and has no discrimination. No offense taken."

At that moment, Fireplug and Fullback came to the table. Fireplug obviously had caught my last comment. "Who's offensive?"

"Why, you, of course." I smiled sweetly as though I didn't mean it.

Fullback laughed. She was an alto, a very low alto. She nudged Fireplug. "She's got you pegged, hasn't she?"

Fireplug scowled at me, but before she could reply, Mindy arrived and plopped down across from me. "Sorry I'm late. Bix was making noises like he wanted to come along. I had to make sure he knew he wasn't welcome here."

Before anyone spoke, the waiter appeared to take our drink orders and all the women entered into that with gusto. They ranged from a Stoli Vanilla Martini to a Spicy Mint Avocado Margarita to a Cherry Bomb to a Land of the Happy, whatever the last two were. Heather had a chardonnay and got kidded for being dull. After ordering my Jameson on rocks with water, I leaned back and listened to the chatter, thinking about this group.

It was interesting that Mindy didn't want her husband along, not that I could blame her. In fact, none of the others seemed to have any male along for the cruise from what I had seen so far, nor had I heard them speak of them. Men were not important in their lives. No doubt, that had changed since college.

My reverie was interrupted when I realized that Heather was talking to me. I turned to her.

"Sorry. I didn't catch that."

"I was asking you what you're so deep in thought about."

How vapid the group was? "I was admiring the décor. It reminds me of the movie."

Mindy looked puzzled. "Movie?

"*Casablanca.*"

A blank stare from Mindy.

Halfback caught some of our conversation and entered in. "Is that one of those indie films? Who was in it?"

"I sighed. "Bogart and Bergman. It's a classic." I looked to Heather. "I watched it with you a few years ago, remember?"

She furrowed her brow. "Yeah, I think so. It's in black and white, right?"

"A black and white movie?" Fireplug chimed in. "Who'd waste their time on that? They're almost prehistoric."

"Hey, did you see *Ocean's 8*?" Texas asked, hopping right in there. "It's really cool. Women doing a big heist. Sisterhood, ya'all. We could do that."

"I saw it," Mindy said, then rolled her eyes. "But Sandra Bullock's getting a little old to be cutesy."

"She wasn't cutesy," Texas came back. "She was competent. It's an empowering movie."

I thanked God that my Jameson had arrived so I could keep my mouth occupied before I said something Heather would regret. Comparing a garbage rehash of a less than mediocre plot like *Ocean's 8* with *Casablanca*? True, I'd never watched the former, but I had read the reviews. That was enough.

I made it through dinner without strangling anyone, which I counted as a victory. I focused on the food. Unfortunately, it was not up to the décor. The Caesar salad was no better than any chain restaurant. My filet was medium well instead of medium rare and a little tough. The Béarnaise sauce had a canned flavor. Considering that it cost extra, a lot extra, for dinner in the Steakhouse, it was a rip off.

Chapter 14

After dinner, the group decided to go to the featured event in the ship's showroom, a gala adaptation of the Broadway show, *Priscilla, Queen of the Desert*. It was about two drag queens on a bus tour of the Australian outback.

"Oh, those guys make better looking women than we do," Scarecrow gushed.

I smiled. That wouldn't be hard for her. "I think I'll pass. Not my type of play."

Mindy rolled her eyes. "Because they're drag queens? Lighten up. It's artistic."

Like *Ocean's 8*, no doubt. "Not for me. Remember, I'm the troglodyte who likes black and white movies." I stood. "I'm going to check out the live music onboard."

Heather grabbed my hand. "You might enjoy the play, if you gave it a chance."

I slipped from her grip. "Not tonight. I need some time alone, okay?"

She gave a noncommittal shrug. "Okay. Your call."

As I was walking out of the restaurant, I noticed a *Casablanca* movie poster almost hidden by some potted shrubs. While the movie may have been the inspiration for the décor, the restaurant didn't follow it much other than that. As I stood there, the maître de came up beside me.

"That is a great movie," he said, staring at the poster.

"You saw it?"

"Of course." He turned to me, took my hand, bowed and gently kissed the back of my hand. "I am Youssef Harrak. When I was told this would be the plan for this restaurant and I would be the maître de, I watched it many times. You see, at first I dressed like Rick. I shaved my mustache so I would look more like him. I even practiced sounding like Mr. Bogart."

Considering he had what sounded to me like an Arabic accent, I was surprised. "That must have been very cool. What happened?"

He slowly shook his head. "Almost no one got it. They thought it strange, did not understand. A couple of them thought I was drunk. So the company told me to wear these very incorrect clothes. I am from Morocco and I never saw anyone dressed like this." He gestured at his blousy shirt, sash and vest, then sighed. "Soon the company is going to change everything, make the restaurant something completely different."

"That's sad." I put out my hand. "Thanks for letting me know I'm not alone in loving this movie."

He shook my hand. A couple that had just walked in caught his eye. "I must go now." He started toward them, but paused, gave me a wry smile and said, "Here's looking at you, kid." He had Bogie's voice down pat.

I grinned. "We'll always have Rick's."

He flashed a grin, then spoke to the couple as I left.

I wandered the ship, checking out the bars with live music. Most had a disc jockey who played Electronic Dance Music of some sort. I'm no expert on that type of sound, but had read about it and knew enough to avoid it and the frenzied, loud crowds in those bars. In one of them, I saw Disco Ghost dancing with a chunky blond with a very short, tight red dress. Fortunately, he was too focused on her ample cleavage to notice me. I used a ship's guide to locate each bar and reject it until I headed for the last on the list, a small place named O'Malley's Pub. As I approached, Nurse Bimbo came out the door. She wasn't in her nurse's outfit, but in a simple black dress. Nothing too sexy, except for being a little tight. She didn't even glance at me as she headed down the corridor. As I watched her, Rex came out of a side corridor and followed her. Was he watching her back or tailing her?

Inside the pub, a little combo, DJ and the Dukes, was playing blues. While the décor was a parody of an Irish pub, lots of dark wood and a dart board with no darts, the tunes were New Orleans or Chicago. The place had lots of empty seats, but one that wasn't empty caught my eye. Bix was sitting there. When he saw me, he turned away, drained his drink, and started for the door, carrying a gym bag. Maybe he was embarrassed at how he'd come on to me earlier. As long as I didn't have to talk to him, I was happy.

As he was leaving, a nicely-dressed Latino was coming in. He was about Bix's age, but shorter and stockier. His thick, black hair was slicked back in a pompadour and he had a pencil-thin mustache. Bix bumped into him, then said something. The man looked puzzled. Then Bix leaned over and spoke to him again. The man glanced at me, turned and left, followed by Bix. I wondered what Bix had said, but didn't really care. He was a slimeball.

I sat at one of the tables and listened. The quartet performing consisted of a piano, drums, string bass and a tenor sax. Their sax player had the most sensuous sound I'd ever heard from a live band. When he massaged the keys in "Harlem Nocturne," I almost melted in my seat. When they took a break between sets, I offered to buy him a drink and he accepted.

He was black, maybe late sixties, with short-cropped grey hair and goatee. He had a warm and friendly grin that reminded me of the actor, Lou Gossett, Jr. Standing maybe five foot six, the saxophonist was trim and fit looking. A black beret and turtleneck knit shirt gave him a cool Fifties "Beat" look. Not that I knew from experience, but I'd seen enough photos and movies.

When the cocktail waitress came by, he ordered a Jack and Coke, then turned back to me and flashed a winning grin. "Not often do I get picked up by such a lovely lady, Darlin'." His voice was a mellow baritone with a slight Southern drawl.

"I, uh . . . ." I didn't want to be insulting, but he was old enough to be my father plus a few years. And I felt like an Amazon next to him.

He laughed and gently patted my hand. "Not to worry, Darlin'. I know you're just being nice to an old man. You're a sweet child and I shouldn't have had you on that way." Our drinks had arrived and he lifted his glass. "Cheers."

"You just caught me unawares." I clinked his glass with mine. "Cheers. You are a great sax player and not an old man."

He snorted. "Good player? Yes. Very good? Possibly. Great? No way. Charlie Parker, John Coltraine, Cannonball Adderley, they were great. Lot more I could mention. Since I'm more a cool jazz kind of guy, there's Stan Getz. He was white, but I try not to hold that against him." He grinned again.

"I'm with you on that. I can appreciate Bird, but I can't take his music very long. I'm into slow jazz. I loved your 'Harlem Nocturne.' My dad had a record of it done by The Viscounts."

"They were okay, I guess. But not good." He shrugged. "Listen to Illinois Jacquet if you want to hear how it should be done. He played with Cab Calloway's and Count Basie's bands. He's also the guy who played 'C-Jam Blues' with President Clinton."

"Was Monica playing with Bill, too?"

He laughed and shook his head. "Not even goin' to go there."

I sipped my whiskey. "I'm assuming you're DJ and those are your Dukes. What's DJ stand for? Obviously, it's not disc jockey."

"Duke Jackson. Mama taught music and English and loved Duke Ellington, so she named me after him. I couldn't call myself Duke as a beginning musician playing in New Orleans in the Sixties. Sounded too pretentious. So I called myself Jackson until that bubblegum quintet came along and stole my name. Maybe not literally, but I couldn't use it anymore without people asking if I were related to that Michael kid. Hence, DJ was born." He glanced at his watch. "Anyway, thanks for the drink. Got to get back on stage. They don't want me sitting with the guests too long." He winked. "'Fraid I might lead them astray or something."

People would wander in, stay for a song or two, then leave. Jazz did not hold their interest. I stayed through all his sets, enjoying the sounds. At the breaks, DJ would come to my table and we'd talk about jazz greats and the travails of growing up a pint-sized black man (his words) in Dixie back then. By the end of the session at midnight, I was the only audience, but DJ and I were friends. After saying goodbye to him about one in the morning, I went to the suite.

Since the suite is about three times the size of my Long Beach apartment and has three bedrooms with ensuite baths, I didn't know if Heather was already in bed or not. Considering it was Heather, she might not be alone if she were in bed. I was very quiet as I closed the door. I was still a bit keyed up from the evening and early morning, so I poured myself a Jameson, went out on the private patio, climbed the stairs to the top level and settled in a chair to look out over the sea from my aerie. I was almost dozing when, to paraphrase the words of Clement Moore, out on the deck there arose such a clatter, I sprang from my chair to see what was the matter.

When I looked over the railing to the patio below, there was no St. Nick and his tiny reindeer, but Heather with her sorority bitches. Some of them waved champagne bottles and took swigs from them. The private hot tub churned to life and the party started shedding clothes. Some kept on their lacy underthings, but others went down to bare skin. Not all of them had bodies worthy of displaying. Although two of the sisters had brought their mates on the cruise, this was a "girls' night" gathering. The music of their teens was blaring. I may not have been into that scene, but who in my generation wouldn't recognize "Wannabe" by the Spice Girls? Several of the women were loudly singing along, regressing to their days of "girl power." Thank goodness that the suite was completely isolated from the other suite on this level and all the other cabins below.

While I wasn't trying to hide, the group was focused on themselves and didn't look up to my vantage point. Except for one. Mindy. In her underwear, she looked like one of those

Mixed Martial Arts female fighters: not fat, but lots of muscle, a person you wouldn't want to tangle with. She looked up and saw me. Then she took a swig from her champagne bottle and turned back to the gang without a nod or a wave. As she hopped into the hot tub wearing a black bra and thong, I backed away and sat in my chair. I sipped my Jameson and wished I'd brought the bottle. It looked like the sister-hoods would be a while.

By a little after three in the morning, the party was finally over. I should have just gone down the stairs, walked past everyone and gone to bed long before, but it felt like I would have been crashing Heather's private party, one to which I didn't belong, so I waited. When I did go down, the music was off and only the detritus from the little Greek bacchanalia remained.

Tuesday Afternoon

Chapter 15

A lthough I often wing it in investigations, following clues rather than a plan, I have found it helpful to lay out what I know before tackling a case and keeping it updated as I go along. For this case, I knew that Bix was missing, presumed overboard. Since the crew was making sure he wasn't still onboard by searching each cabin and checking I.D's , I would look into how he went overboard. One possibility was suicide. His life was a mess. Taking the "easy way out" was a possibility. However, from what I had heard and had observed, he was a self-centered egoist. Egoism, the philosophy associated with such a person, has self-interest as the motivation for all actions. That being the case, Bix would more likely be a sociopath than suicidal. Since the likelihood of Bix offing himself was slim, who else might want to do it for him?

In murder cases, the police look closely at the spouse or significant other, and for good reason. I'd read that about three-quarters of murder victims know their killer and of those about a third are close relatives. Although uxoricide (killing one's wife) is more common than mariticide (killing one's husband), those numbers are getting closer over the years. So Mindy was on the list. Bix had blown a fortune and money was a common motive for murder. She was definitely fit enough to toss him over the railing, especially if he were a little into his cups, to use an old phrase. I needed to do more investigation of their relationship. If I could get past Heather.

The others who seemed to have problems with Bix did not have a known motive. I didn't even know how most of them knew him. Well, Dave Wilkinson knew him from college, but just being irritating is not a normal reason to be killed. FP and Wally

Walrus definitely had some issue with Bix. Then there was Rex the ex-Seal security guy, if he really was one. He had seemed to be following Nurse Bimbo, but she had come out of O'Malley's Pub, where I had last seen Bix. They hadn't talked, as far as I'd known, but was it just a coincidence or a meeting? If Rex had been working for Dr. Stangelove, then maybe the good doctor had put a hit on philanderer Bix for meeting his bimbo. Love, especially a twisted love, was a definite motive and, for Rex, it would be money.

Then there were any investors in Bix's failed HBM Investment Fund. They might be after getting some of their money back or simply a little revenge for him taking it. It would be coincidental for any of them to be on this cruise, but you never know. I needed a list of who he bilked and for how much with his Ponzi plan and a list of all passengers on the cruise. Easier said than done. Heather should be able to help me get a list of the passengers, but I had no idea if she could get one of the investors. Maybe Mindy could, but it was no sure thing. I sighed. If I did get the lists, there were literally thousands of names to compare. I had my work cut out for me.

Sitting alone in the suite was getting nothing accomplished, so I set out to find some of the usual suspects. The first thing I found was something I already knew: it was one big ship. Finding anyone in this floating city would be by luck and I was so unlucky that I never even bought a lottery ticket. There must be a better way. I doubted if I could page my suspects to meet me in the library with a lead pipe. Then it hit me. There must be a ton of security cameras on board. They could not only help me find people, but investigate what happened to Bix. I went to the purser's desk.

A pert, blond young woman looked up from her computer screen and smiled. "May I be of assistance, Madame?"

I was in a bitchy mood and wanted to tell her that I was not married, but knew she was just being polite. Besides, best not to antagonize the staff that I might need later.

I returned her smile. "I would like to speak with Olav Larsen from security?"

"Might I tell him who is asking?"

"Morg Mahoney." I paused. "The woman who borrowed his coat early this morning."

Her eyebrows raised as she picked up a walkie-talkie, turned a dial and spoke in a language that I didn't understand, probably Norwegian. I didn't understand the reply either.

She smiled at me again. "He will be here very soon. Would you like something while you wait? Water or coffee, perhaps?"

"I'm fine, thank you." Evidently he hadn't forgotten me.

As I waited, I looked around. I spied a small camera aimed at me from the ceiling behind the purser's desk. No doubt it had many brothers and sisters around the ship.

A few minutes later, Olav showed. He was wearing a white, short-sleeved uniform with navy blue epaulets. And a big smile. He extended his hand. "Morg Mahoney, it is so nice to see you again. You had a lie down, I hope?"

I took his hand. He had a firm grip and, from what I saw of his arms, worked out a lot. "I did. Now I'm rested and ready to go with my investigation. First, I'd like to see the recordings from the cameras of the area where Bix Maudlin went overboard this morning."

He slowly withdrew his hand and his smile faded. "I am so sorry, but I cannot."

I was surprised. I was to have full cooperation. "Why not?"

"Our cameras have become . . . unoperatic."

"Unoperatic?" Did he mean nonoperatic, not suitable for opera?

"That is not the right word? They do no work."

"Ah." He was trying so hard, no reason to embarrass him. "How long have they been . . . unoperatic."

"Sometime yesterday night. The cameras work, but our recording is not. Nothing is recorded."

"What caused them to stop working?"

He shook his head. "We do not know. We are still investing."

"Investigating?"

He nodded. "Yes, invest-i-gating."

I thought this over. It was quite a coincidence that the security system goes out right before Bix goes overboard. Too much of a coincidence for me. The recording had to be part of the ship's computer system. "Has anyone had access to the computer other than the staff?"

He shook his head.

"Have you checked them out?"

He looked pained, as though it was his failure as Chief of Security. "The company is checking everyone who could do it. These people are good people, working for this line for many years. I have another man working to find out how it happened. I will find who did this.

"Well, let me see what you have. I also need to find some people onboard to question and need your cameras to find them."

"I am afraid I cannot." He looked away. "The captain has told me it was an unfortunate accident and I am not to do anything more. And I cannot help you."

I got it. A fatal accident was bad. But a drunken passenger falling overboard was far worse than a murder. It was PR damage control. The captain was stonewalling me and I needed Heather to break through.

Olav looked so cowed by having to tell me this that I touched his arm and said, "I understand. Thanks for what you've done."

He glanced back at the woman at the purser's desk who seemed absorbed in some computer task, then turned back to me and dropped his voice. "We are watching some cameras, but there are too many to watch them all. Hundreds. We have to watch places with lots of people, like the casino." He paused. "I am former Forsvarets Spesialkommando. Like your Navy Seals. I am trained for combat, but not as a detective. I will give you information when I can. I try to let you look at the recordings we have, but they are hours before the man . . . was missing."

"Thanks. I know you could lose your job over this. I appreciate it."

He stood upright. "It does not matter if I can help catch a killer." He handed me a piece of paper and a pen. "Give me the names of the men you want to find and I will do it for you. I will keep watch on them, too. You have a mobile?

I nodded. Looked like I would be getting charged cell fees after all. I wrote down my cell number and the names of Rex Martin, Billy Wilder, Dave Wilkinson, Walt Ferrier and David Stewart. As I handed them to him, I said, "There's no way you can watch all of them, so don't try. I'll let you know if any of them are real suspects after I talk to them. Let me know on my cell where I can find them. Start with Ferrier and Stewart."

He nodded.

I had a thought. "I didn't see a cell phone in Bix's coat. Do you have it?"

He shook his head. "Maybe his wife does."

"Thanks, Olav. You're one of the good guys."

He grinned. "Like John McClane?"

It took me a second to realize he was referring to Bruce Willis in the *Die Hard* series. I chuckled. "You bet. Like John McClane." But hopefully not going through so much killing and destruction before this was over. I wasn't ready to walk on broken glass in my bare feet. Yippee-ki-yay.

Chapter 16

Since it was now about two in the afternoon, I figured that Heather might be back in the suite. I needed her to lean on the captain. As I meandered through the corridors to get back, I mulled over what Olav had said. This didn't seem like suicide. The messed up security system ruled it out for me. Why go to all the trouble to kill the cameras before killing yourself? Plus this was no rash action. Getting to the ship's computer took knowledge and planning. In light of the camera problems, I couldn't rule out an ally in the crew either. It was getting more complex instead of easier.

When I came in the door to our suite, I heard Heather and Mindy talking. They must not have heard the door open and, since it was out of their line of sight from the sitting room, were unaware of me. Since Mindy didn't want to open up to me, I quietly shut the door and listened to see if she would be more forthcoming with Heather. I was close enough to hear her clearly as she was talking.

". . . so I'd had it with Bix. The way he came on to every woman on the ship was the last straw. When he did it with you and then Jennifer back then, it should have clued me in, but he blamed the two of you and I believed him." She paused and there was the sound of a glass laid on the table. "He was a great salesman. Con man, actually. He could have been a real salesman, done it honestly, but he thrived on building a house of lies."

"Hey, Min, he fooled a lot of people, not just you." It was Heather. "Like you said, he was the ultimate con man."

"Yeah, he conned me out of eighteen years of life and a lot of my inheritance. If I hadn't gotten a legal separation, I'd be broke now."

"Try to put it out of your mind. Let's go out on the deck." Heather again. "It's nice outside and I like it out there."

"Sure."

I waited until they went out onto the private deck before I went into the living room. So Bix slept with Jennifer, too. No wonder jealous Dave showed his dislike for Bix. Was he jealous enough to have killed him? Had Bix tried to duplicate his conquest? The killing showed planning, premeditation, but Dave must have known Bix would be coming onboard with Mindy and well could have plotted revenge. A good motive for a guy like Dave, from what I had observed. I needed to talk privately to Heather more about Dave. Dave had moved up a couple of notches on the suspect list, but Mindy was still keeping her spot.

We were finally arriving at Cabo San Lucas in about a half hour, so most passengers would be getting off to see the sights. While I wanted to do a little wandering around for the few hours we would be there, shortened considerably due to Bix's disappearance over the rail, I took the opportunity to stand near the loading area on deck 7 for the tenders to Cabo so I could observe my usual suspects as they disembarked. The line was long and edged along slowly as the crowd impatiently tried to get ashore.

Dave and Jennifer passed by me without acknowledging I existed. He was wearing an expensive-looking guayabera shirt with linen trousers and sandals, his face hidden by a Panama hat and reflective-lens sunglasses, never looking my way. She wore a flowing, pale yellow, silken jumpsuit with long, bell sleeves with a matching, wide-brimmed straw hat. She glanced at me, but her eyes were hidden behind large, round sunglasses and she seemed to look right through me without even a smile. Her outfit didn't fit. I mean, size-wise, it looked great. Would that I could carry off such a form-fitting outfit, but a long-sleeved jumpsuit in ninety-degree heat with ninety-percent humidity? I would like to talk with her about spousal abuse, but not then and there.

A few minutes later, Heather, Mindy, Fireplug, Scarecrow, Texas and Fullback were all together as they came by.

Heather grabbed my arm and tried to pull me into the group. "Come with us, Morg. It's going to be a blast. We're going to try to find the best margarita in town!"

"Next time." I forced a smiled. I don't like sweet drinks, even if the rim is salty. But I really don't like them if the company is acerbic.

Fireplug pulled Heather away. "Leave her alone. This is a Belle outing. Besides, she's probably trying to pick up some sailor. It's her only chance to get some this trip."

I gave her a half smile. "Unfortunately, all the sea dogs I talked to said you were their bitch."

Fireplug started toward me and I set myself ready to take her down, but Heather stepped between us, looking from Fireplug to me. "Why do you two have to go at each other like this? We're supposed to be having fun." She sighed. "It's probably better that you two are separated. You girls go ahead. I'll go ashore with Morg."

I shook my head. Way to go, Morg. You made her choose between friends she hasn't seen for years and you. And she chose you. Happy?

"Heather, I'm probably not even going ashore here. You go with your Belles."

She tilted her head and narrowed her eyes. "Morg, don't play the martyr with me."

I raised my hands in mock surrender. "I'm not. Really. It's way too hot for a Long Beach girl here. I'm more comfortable with the A/C on. Go and have fun."

She gave me a dubious look. "You mean that?"

I raised my right hand with three fingers up. "Scout's honor."

She rolled her eyes. "You never were a Girl Scout."

"Yeah, but I bought a lot of their cookies." I gave her a shove. "Just go. I'm not leaving here."

"Well." She glanced at the rest of the group who were looking impatient at the delay. "If you aren't going, then I guess I will. See you for a drink when we get back, okay?"

"Sounds good. " I forced a smile. "Let me know when you get back,"

As Heather's group went down the gangway, Fireplug looked back with a smirk. I gave here the Girl Scout salute, but with two fewer fingers. She returned it.

Mindy and the others had kept out of the interchange.

The next persons of interest were FP and Wally Walrus. In their garish Hawaiian shirts, cargo shorts and black loafers, they hardly looked like Prince David and Baron Beaton. Their wide-brimmed straw hats were cheap-looking. FP had white sun protection smeared on his nose. He also had a black eye that his sunglasses didn't hide. I walked with them as the line inched along.

"So, gentlemen, have you taken many cruises? This is my first."

Wally looked down at me. "This is our first. However, once we get a royal yacht in Scotland, I expect that we will take many more."

"Why did you take this one?"

Wally glanced at FP before replying. "It was a nice outing, a chance to get away from royal duties."

"Anything to do with Bix Maudlin?"

Wally was momentarily quiet, eyes bulging. "Uh, who?"

"Bix. You know, the fellow you were shoving around." I paused dramatically. "The dead one."

Wally brushed back his hair with a shaking hand. His knuckles were bruised. "I don't know what you mean. I don't know any Bux."

"Bix." I raised my eyebrows. "So you were shoving around someone you didn't know yesterday?"

Wally turned to FP, ignoring my question. "We need to hurry if we are to make the tour."

I stayed next to them. "By the way, what happened to your hand? It looks painful."

He held his hand behind his back. "Nothing. I . . . uh, banged it against a door."

We had reached the security area for disembarking, so I stopped. "You should report those dangerous doors to someone."

Chapter 17

Next to catch my eye was Rex and his companion. Rex had on a black RAM Security tank top that showed off his big biceps. And his big belly. However, few would notice him because of his companion. At his side was Nurse Bimbo. She wore a white halter top that did not hide her dark nipples and a white sarong that tightly wrapped her hips in diaphanous cloth. Rex smiled when he saw me.

"Hiya, Hon. Going ashore?"

I returned his smile. "Not sure, Dude."

He stepped close. "Come along with me."

I stepped back. "You already have company."

He glanced over at Nurse Bimbo, then wrapped his arm around her back. "This here is Darla Darling, the actress. I work for her husband and I'm her bodyguard." He leaned toward me and winked. "Ya know, in case one of those banditos tries to get too friendly."

In my eyes, he was getting way too friendly to be a bodyguard and, from the look Nurse Bimbo gave him, in hers, too. I stepped farther back. "You two have fun. I'll stay here."

He shrugged. "Your loss."

As they walked down the gangplank, she pulled away from his arm. I wondered about how Dr. Strangelove would feel about his employee copping a feel of his wife. He did not strike me as the forgiving type. I also wondered if Rex had more ambitions on Nurse Bimbo's body than just guarding it.

With the tourists ashore, I went looking for Olav, the Security Officer. I needed access to the video recordings. I went to the purser's counter and asked the blond Viking goddess behind it if she would let Olav know I would like to speak with him. Even in her white uniform and with her hair pulled back, she would turn every heterosexual male head. Why didn't they hire short, dumpy women instead of Nordic models? To make me feel inferior?

She shook her head. "I am so sorry, but Olav is not on duty."

"Did he go ashore? I didn't see him get off."

"I am so sorry, but I cannot give you that information."

"Why? Is he on a mission for the CIA or something?" I leaned closer. "It's okay to tell me. I have top security clearance with the CIA, the FBI, the NSA, MI-6, Interpol and the FSB."

She looked confused, her flawless brow creased. "I do not know what you mean. I have heard of the CIA, but Olav does not work for them. He works for Scandinavian Cruise Lines. I cannot help you or your CIA or any of those . . . strange letters."

My patience was wearing thin, but I fought to keep my temper in check. I did not need her to shut me off. "Look, Frigg, just call Olav for me. Tell him the female Magnum PI would like to talk to him. He'll know who I am and I'm sure he'll want to talk to me." I wasn't that sure, but show no doubt or fear to a Viking or they'll lop off your head with a battle axe.

"My name is Freya." She scowled and pointed at her name tag.

I stifled a laugh. "Sorry, wrong goddess. Anyway, call him. I'm sure he'll thank you. And you'd like to be on his good side, wouldn't you?"

She hesitated, evidently considering if it would put her on the good side of the Norwegian hunk.

"He has a cell phone, doesn't he? Or do you call it a mobile?" I forced it out. "Please. I will commend you for your helpfulness when I review the cruise."

She sighed, then picked up a phone receiver from the counter and punched in some numbers. After a couple of seconds, she spoke in what I assumed was Norwegian. She nodded, then said to me, "He will be here soon."

After an uneasy ten minutes or so, with the Valkyrie eyeing me suspiciously, Olav showed. He was wearing a tight, black T-shirt and shorts. He had a white towel across his neck and his skin had a sheen of sweat, like I'd interrupted a workout. He looked damned sexy.

He grinned. "What can I do for you, Morg Mahoney?"

Let me watch you work out? I was thinking like Heather. I smiled and thought of Robert. "I need some help with my investigation. I know that you are limited by . . . your orders, but any help would be appreciated."

He glanced at Freya who had suddenly become absorbed in her computer screen, then turned back to me. "I will meet you in ten minutes. I need to change."

"Don't change on my account. You look great." I grimaced as soon as I said it. That was not how I meant it. At least I hoped it wasn't.

"I have to change. It is the ship policy."

"Okay. I'll meet you at a bar." I could use a drink. "Where's the nearest one?"

"Hemingway's is on deck eight, right above us."

I gave him a thumb's up. "See you in ten."

As he walked away, Freya glanced longingly after him, then over at me.

I winked. "Don't worry. I'm not after your Viking warrior."

She blushed, returning her attention to her computer. I headed to meet Olav.

Hemingway's was set like Cuba in the 1950's, with a woven palm-frond ceiling and slowly rotating fans hanging down. The tables and chairs were rattan. The waiters were wearing Cuban wedding shirts, although the staff looked more like they were from Asia than the Caribbean. It was fairly empty since most passengers had gone ashore.

Olav joined me at my table in less than ten minutes. He was dressed in his white uniform, muscles bulging in his short-sleeved shirt. "What can I do for you, Morg Mahoney?"

I was barely into my drink, sipping it slowly. "Tell me about the cameras on the ship."

He thought for a moment. "I should not tell you this, but we are both professionals. We have one hundred and three cameras. They are in all public rooms and most corridors." He paused. "But none are in the cabins. Not one. You have complete privacy."

I wasn't sure if I believed him, but I hoped that was truthful. I'm not a prude, but I didn't like the idea of someone spying on me while I was soaking in the tub.

"Okay, now tell me about how the cameras stopped recording. Did they suddenly stop?"

He pursed his lips. "It would seem they did. I looked to see if the ones that record had anything, but there are no recordings after 21:23 yesterday."

"Wait." I leaned on my elbows on the table. "You don't all record?"

He shook his head. "Too many to record all of them at once, too expensive. Mainly we record public areas and main corridors."

That was disappointing. "I was hoping there'd be more recordings from the night Bix went overboard. It's possible he had a confrontation with someone or someones who might have something to do with his demise." I sighed. "Oh, well. Could I check the recordings you do have?"

He looked down at his hands, folded on the table. "I cannot do that. I tried, but it is against the company policy. When I asked, ah . . . ."

"And the captain told you not to cooperate with me." I was fuming. I didn't want to get Olav in trouble, but I needed to know if Wally Walrus and FP got physical with Bix that night. "Look, will you look at them? I need to know if Wally . . . uh, Walt Ferrier and if . . ." What was FP's real name? "If that Prince guy, David Stewart, got into it with Bix. Or if anyone else had a problem with Bix. Would you do that for me?"

His chin set in resolve. "I will. You can count on Olav. I will also ask the monitor staff from that night if they saw anything on the other monitors."

"You have people watching the monitors that don't record?"

"They watch all the monitors and call me if there is a problem."

That gave me hope. "How many are on duty?'

"There are five on four-hour shifts, to keep them alert."

My heart sank. Five watchers for over a hundred monitors. No one could effectively keep an eye on twenty screens at one time. But it was better than nothing, I supposed.

I smiled. "Thanks, Olav. You have my cell number. Call me if you find anything."

He saluted me. "I will do that." He hesitated. "And I am sorry the captain will not let me do more."

I patted his hand. "I appreciate your help. Don't get yourself in trouble."

He stood, throwing his shoulders back. "Trouble is my surname."

I stifled a laugh as he marched out. Why tell him he meant middle name?

Chapter 18

I considered my next course of action. Most of my suspects were ashore. I remembered that I'd seen Nurse Bimbo walk out of O'Malley's Pub and being followed by Rex. Bix had been in the pub when I walked in, but had scurried out. Rex now seemed to have a close interest in Nurse Bimbo. In light of Bix's aggressive way with women, I wondered if Bix and Bimbo had had any contact in the pub. Perhaps DJ could enlighten me. Although he wouldn't be performing this early, especially with few onboard, perhaps he might be getting ready or something. I headed to the pub.

As I came to the door, I heard a lone alto sax playing "Baker Street." Perfect for a jazz and Sherlock Holmes fan. As he came to the end of the solo riff, DJ sang the lyrics. The man not only had a way with an alto horn, but had pipes, too. I heard no other instrument except what sounded like a drum machine. I stepped inside. DJ was on stage, alone. He was in a Hawaiian shirt with a print of mainly black flowers, black jeans, a black straw short-brimmed fedora and dark sunglasses. He nodded to me, but didn't stop. I was glad he didn't. While "Baker Street" was more of a mellow rock song of the seventies, Duke made it sound like pure jazz.

Once he finished the song, he placed his sax on a stand next to a tenor one, turned off a drum machine and came to me.

"Like my axe on that tune, Darlin'?"

I cocked my head. "Isn't an axe an electric guitar?"

He grinned. "An axe was a sax before anyone started pluggin' in guitars."

"Learn something new every day. But I'm here to pick your brain about last night.'

"Pick away, Darlin'. Not sure you'll find much."

"A blond woman, a rather, uh, buxom one, maybe thirty or so, was here. There was also a man, about forty, tall, slim except for a little pot, blond, too, but with a bald spot in back."

He laughed. "Sure, I remember the woman. Looked a lot like my second wife." He paused. "No, she was my third wife. I think. Anyway, built like a brick . . . outhouse. Looked cheap, but probably cost a fortune. My ex-wife sure did when she left me and she was the one doin' the cheatin'."

That sounded like Nurse Bimbo. "What about the guy? Did you see him?"

He stroked his goatee. "Yeah, I did. He was at the table next to the one the blond bombshell sat at."

"Did they talk?"

"I wasn't watching them the whole time, so I can't say they didn't talk, but not that I saw." He looked toward the ceiling and closed his eyes. "He came in first and she came in maybe twenty, thirty minutes later. She left first, too. Only stayed a few minutes. One thing I do remember is that she didn't seem to be really into my music. Didn't even applaud when I finished a tune." He opened his eyes and looked at me. "Didn't leave any tip in the jar, either. But he did. Nice one. A twenty. I don't get many of those, so that's why I remember him."

I winked. "Obviously, she has no taste in music."

"Indubitably, Darlin'. Just like my third wife." He scratched the side of his nose. "Or was she my second one?"

"Thanks, DJ." I rose. "By the way, how many times have you been married, anyway?"

He grinned. "Six. My Mamma raised me a good Baptist, so I never slept with a woman who wasn't my wife. I'm what you could call a serial monogamist."

I laughed. "No wonder you have trouble keeping them straight. I'll be back later to enjoy your tunes."

To say I had suspicions would be an understatement. Why go into a bar and stay for only a couple of songs? And two people, not together or talking to each other, doing the same thing? Not very likely. Had she and Bix, the Lothario of the Greeks, been setting up a tryst? I would like to ask Nurse Bimbo, but getting to her when she was hiding out with Dr. Stangelove would be difficult. However, she and security-guy Rex who had been tailing her had been together going ashore and maybe I could talk them both. Since the time ashore had been shortened considerably due to the delay looking for Bix, passengers were re-embarking already. I set off to see if I could catch both Rex and Nurse Bimbo as they came back on board.

All the elevators were packed with returnees, so I started down the stairs at close to a run, dodging people coming up. A couple of flights down, I collided with a man as I slipped between an overweight couple who took up most of a stair.

I grabbed his arm to keep him from falling back down the stairs. He was not quite my height, maybe in his sixties, with curly, grey-black hair and a receding hairline. He caught his black-framed glasses as they slipped from his face.

"I'm so sorry," I panted, winded from my dash. "I was trying to catch some people as they came on the ship."

He regained his balance and breathed a sigh of relief as he glanced back at the long stairway behind him. Then he turned to me and smiled. "Not to worry. I am fine. No harm done." He paused. "Though I tink a slower pace might be safer."

His accent was pure Irish and his skin was as pale as mine. Unlike other passengers, he wore grey trousers and a black, short-sleeved shirt. The only sign he'd been in Mexico was a wide-brimmed straw hat clutched in one hand.

Since the man was now in no danger of falling downstairs, I released his arm. "You're from Ireland?"

"Guilty as charged, although I've been in the States for well over thirty years now."

His "thirty" sounded like "tirty," reminding me of Maureen O'Hara's brogue. Charging to catch Rex and Nurse Bimbo suddenly seemed less important. Besides, they were probably back on board, anyway. "I'm Irish, too." I hesitated a moment. "Well, of Irish descent on my father's side. I'm Morgana Mahoney, but call me Morg."

"Tim McCarthy." He smiled again. "It was nice to bump into you."

"Tell you what, let me buy you a drink to show I'm sorry for almost sending you down a deck backwards."

"I can't drink alcohol, but I would enjoy a cup of tea."

As we walked up the stairs at a more leisurely pace, we chatted.

"What brought you to America, Tim?"

"An airplane." The corner of his mouth twitched up. "Sorry, I've been asked that often and can't resist the joke. I'm a priest and I volunteered to take a parish in the States. I liked it and I stayed."

"Ah. That explains why the non-touristy attire."

He chuckled. "Yes, I'm afraid I don't have any shorts and flowered shirts."

We had reached O'Malley's Pub and went in. I was a little disappointed DJ wasn't there. We sat at a table and a waiter came for our order.

"The good Father will have hot tea and I'll have, uh. . . ." He couldn't have alcohol meant Father Tim was probably a recovering alcoholic. I turned to him. "Be honest, does it bother you to be around someone who's drinking?"

He shook his head. "Not at all. I have alcohol intolerance. Even a sip of communion wine causes a rash. Since I have asthma, I have trouble breathing, too." He gave a short wave of his hand. "But feel free."

"Well, if you don't mind." I turned back to the waiter. "Jameson, rocks and water."

"So, dear child, what is your occupation? What brought you on this cruise?"

It was nice to be called "dear child," especially by Father Tim. "I'm a private investigator and I came along with a friend. She wanted company." I paused. "At least at first. Anyway, she's also here with college friends. One of them, a man, was lost overboard and I'm investigating."

"I heard about that." His brow creased in concern. "Was he a friend of yours too? Would you like me to say a Mass for him?"

"I barely knew him and have no idea if he were Catholic, very lapsed if he were, but I'm sure he could use a Mass. You conduct services on the ship?"

He nodded. "The cruise line gives me a free trip for doing them. It's really the only way I could afford something like this. If you want to attend Mass, I conduct them every morning at eight in the Starlight Theater." He chuckled. "It's a little large for the few of us who gather each morning, but at least it's comfortable."

Eight in the morning? Why not at night? Most likely there was no space available at night for anything as unpopular in this current day and age as a Mass, much less the Theater. But it had been too long since I'd been to Mass. I sighed. "I'll be there in the morning. Just don't expect me to be awake."

Chapter 19

I went to the elevator up to the suite and punched the button. After a bit of a wait, the doors opened. The only two occupants were Rex and Nurse Bimbo, just the people I wanted to see. Rex nodded a greeting, but Bimbo disdainfully stared at me like I was a bug on the wall.

"This elevator is for the special suites." Obviously, she did not remember me.

I smiled, flashed my door key card and stepped inside. "You two have a nice outing in Cabo?"

Bimbo raised an eyebrow, but said nothing. Rex gave a slight shrug. "It was okay, I guess. We didn't have much time and it was pretty hot and muggy."

Bimbo punched the "close door" button. Small talk was not going to break the ice since the frosty air was colder than a freezer's.

I looked down at Bimbo. "I saw you last night in O'Malley's, didn't I? Weren't you with that guy who went overboard, Bix something?"

There was a flicker in her eyes, perhaps fear, but it quickly disappeared. She shrugged nonchalantly, her face now a mask of indifference. "I was there, but I don't know this Bix person. You say he went overboard? Went for a swim?"

Rex snorted with a big grin. "Yeah, went for a swim with the sharks. Liked it so much he stayed."

I shook my head. While I was no Bix fan, that was too much for even me. "No one will ever accuse you of being overly sentimental."

He laughed. "Yeah, you'll never catch me watching one of them chickie flicks."

I turned back to Bimbo. "Odd that you would sit almost next to the guy and not notice him, especially when so few people were in there."

She didn't meet my gaze. "I was just there for the music."

"Funny that you would only be there for a couple of songs then. You must not like Dixieland that much." I purposely misstated the type of jazz D.J. played.

"I love it." The elevator arrived and the doors opened behind me and she edged past me. "But I was meeting someone at another place."

"With Rex?" I turned to him. "Is that why you were following her?"

His eyes went wide, looking shocked, then he recovered. "Get out of the way. You're asking too many questions. You're no cop, so back off."

"But why —"

Rex shoved me back against the elevator's side wall, knocking out my breath and holding me there with his forearm pressing hard against my neck. He leaned close enough for me to smell the beer on his breath. His eyes were narrow slits. "Leave it be. The guy's gone. It ain't healthy to poke around where you ain't wanted."

Then he released me and I staggered to the back of the elevator. He and Bimbo got off the elevator and walked to her suite. She swiped her card to open the door and glaringly glanced back at me as she and Rex went inside.

I massaged my neck. Rex hadn't been gentle. I was angry with myself that I had let him get away with shoving me around. Although I have a black belt in Taekwondo, it's not the best for close quarters. I'd taken some Muay Thai, too, but he was bigger and stronger, plus had me up close and personal before I could react. Whatever the movies show, a woman has a natural disadvantage in those circumstances. But this wasn't over, I swore to myself.

My hand was shaking from adrenaline as I went into my suite. Our suite. I was reminded of that by the music playing loudly as I went in. The place was filled with the sound of Whitney Houston singing "I Will Always Love You." I sighed. Back to the 90's. At least it was a song I didn't hate.

When I walked into the sitting area, Heather and Mindy were sipping white wine. I went to the bar and poured myself a Jameson. A stiff one. I dropped in some ice and willed my hand to stop shaking.

"Well, did you have fun moping around the ship when you could have gone ashore?" Heather asked, her words a little slurred.

I spun around. "Yeah, a blast. I've been trying to do what you asked, investigate what happened to Bix. I get almost no cooperation from the ship's company now since some bigwig decided to let things die with Bix. But ol' dumb Morg keeps at it and gets slammed around in the elevator for asking questions. So because of that I missed out on the fun trip ashore with the girls who all hate me."

Chapter 20

For a moment, Heather and Mindy sat staring at me in stunned silence. Then Heather sprang up and ran to me as fast as her tottering legs would carry her. She wrapped her arms around me and pulled me close. Too close. I'm not a "touchy, feely" kind of person.

"Are you okay? I'm so sorry I got you into this, Morg. Who assaulted you? I'll call security."

I awkwardly patted her back. "I'm fine. Just a little rattled. Right now, I don't want to call attention to what I'm doing since the captain wants it all to go away."

"I'm so sorry about that. My friend with the Scandinavian Cruise Line texted me that the higher-ups wanted this all to go away and wouldn't be helping me. You. Us. Anyway, just forget I asked and let it drop."

I grabbed her shoulders and pushed her back. "No. No way he fell overboard or jumped willingly. There's something going on and I want to find out what. When you threaten me, it gets my dander up." I looked over at Mindy. "Do you want me to drop this?"

She looked down at her wine glass for a moment, then up at me, her chin raised. "No. You think he was killed. I don't want to be always suspected of killing Bix. I want to know who did it, even if only to shake his hand. Or her hand. But I want to know."

I looked at Heather. "Let's do this. But I need help, not obstacles. Will you do that?"

She wiped a tear away. "Let's do it. Whatever I can do to help, I will."

I glanced over at Mindy. "Same for you?"

She raised her empty wine glass. "To finding the killer."

I raised my glass. "The game is afoot."

Mindy look confused.

109

Heather waved her hand. "It's her Sherlock Holmes thing. Just go with it."

I always like to tie up loose ends. One of those was the bag I saw Bix with at O'Malley's that was not there where he went overboard. "Do you know anything about Bix's gym bag, what he might have had in it on Monday night?"

"I didn't even know he had a gym bag. Whatever he had in it, it definitely wasn't work-out gear." She snorted. "He never went to any gym as long as I knew him. That's why he was in lousy shape. He golfed and skied, or used to ski, but never was into exercising."

Dead end there. Time to move along. When someone kills someone, unless they are a psychopath, sociopath or some other path, there is normally a motive. Love, money revenge or whatever, most people have a reason to kill another person. Bix gave off motives like manure gives off stink. His financial misdoings were the most obvious ones. I needed to know who had been hurt by them. I pulled out my tablet and put it on the table.

"Mindy, do you have Bix's cell?" It was a place to start.
She shook her head. "He always carried it with him."
Great. So the fishies could now make calls on it.
"What do you know about access to Bix's company?"
She grimaced. "I hate to say it, but I never got involved with his personal finances. After he drained our joint account, I cut him off from all my money. Then I found out that he was even forging my name on some documents to steal more of my money. He did it so well I thought they were my own signatures at first and that I forgot I signed them. But eventually I figured it out." She hesitated. "He took a lot of my money and hopped into bed with any slut who would have him. That's why, even though we live in the same house, we're legally separated now. *Were* legally separated. " She shrugged. "I guess now we're permanently separated."

I sipped my whiskey. "Why not just divorce him? Wouldn't that have ended all the pain?"

She walked over to one of the large windows and looked out over the pool, sipping her wine. "Some of my ancestors came over on the Mayflower." She paused. "Did you know most of those on the Mayflower were not coming for religious reasons? The religious ones were called 'Saints' and the rest were called 'Strangers.' My ancestors were 'Saints.'"

"And this matters because?"

She gave a mirthless chuckle. "My grandfather was really big on the 'Saint' bit. He wanted the family to be 'Saints,' like it or not. He set up a trust fund for my mother that came to me. But if I got a divorce, the fund goes to The Mayflower Society. We're talking about over a hundred million here to a group of people who think their ancestry is the most important thing in life."

"But if Bix dies?"

She turned to me and sipped her wine. "Then I get it all. Not all at once, but I keep getting the big payments."

"You said that if you got a divorce, you'd lose the trust. What if Bix divorced you?"

"You're smart." She shook her head. "Then I got to keep the trust. So I offered Bix a payoff to divorce me, but he made a big demand. He was such an ass. He wanted me to pay him half of the trust as long as he lived."

"And now he's dead, so you pay nothing." I paused, thinking. "Why are you telling me this?"

"Because his lawyer has all the paperwork of our negotiations. I'm sure it will all come out in time." She looked back out the big window. "I'm not sad that he's dead. But I didn't kill him."

I mulled over what she had said as I sipped my Jameson. She definitely had a good reason for wanting Bix dead. Was she being honest or just playing me?

Chapter 21

Heather interrupted my mull. "Morg, I believe Mindy." She paused. "So, if you're so sure someone did, who else do you suspect?"

Heather had a point. I shouldn't lose sight of the fact that I had no proof Mindy did the dirty deed, so who else might have? I knew that Faux Prince and Wally Walrus had an unfriendly meeting with Bix the day before he disappeared. Why? Obviously, they must have known him. Then it hit me. What if Wally had invested with him and lost everything? He seemed very impoverished now for being a successful dentist. It was quite a coincidence that Bix just happened to be on the same cruise with him if that were the case, but it needed investigation. Plus, if Wally had lost with Bix, were there any other disappointed investors? While I doubted it, it was worth investigating.

"Mindy, do you know the main investors who lost money with Bix?"

She shook her head. "I stayed far away from his business, especially when I got the idea that he was not exactly ethical with his clients."

I sighed. "Too bad. I wish I had a way to find out who they were."

"Well, . . ." She pursed her lips. "I have Bix's computer and I know how to get into it, but I have no idea what's there and probably wouldn't understand what I found anyway. I never mess with financial stuff. That's why my trust's investments are handled by experts."

Heather leaned forward. "That's where maybe I can help. I know my way around spreadsheets, that's for sure. Just get me that computer, log me in and I'll look around."

Mindy finished her wine and set the glass on the table with a clunk. She stood and saluted Heather. "I'll be right back, *mon capitaine*."

As she bumped a chair on her way out I wondered how much wine she and Heather had already consumed.

Heather emptied a wine bottle into her glass. "So, you think it was someone Bix bilked?" She giggled, but ended it with a snort. "That sorta rhymes."

She proved she hadn't been a lit major. "It's a long shot. One of them just happening to be on the ship isn't very likely."

"Hmmm." She sipped her wine. "Any other ideas?"

"Maybe. His two big sins seem to have been cheating people and cheating on his wife. He might have done that, or at least tried, on this cruise and it came back to bite him. He may have made a pass at Nurse Bimbo."

She cocked her head. "Nurse Bimbo?"

"Dr. Stranglelove's wife. I mean, Jerry Steele's wife." I thought a few seconds. "Darla . . . Darla Darling."

"Okay." She leaned back. "You've really lost me."

"The people staying in the suite across from this one. He's got a reputation as a bad person to cross and Bix might have had something going with her. What about Jennifer and Dave? Bix hit on her at the last cocktail party."

"Dave saw it?"

"I think so. He sure reacted like he had."

Heather gnawed her lower lip. "You've heard about the wedding?"

"Heard of it, yes. Heard what it means, no."

She took a large swig of wine. "I went with Dave before he hooked up with Jennifer. You remember Jonathan, my abusive boyfriend?"

"How could I forget him?"

"Well, Dave was worse. He broke my arm once and dislocated my shoulder another time because he thought I came on to guys. I had warned Jennifer, but she didn't listen. That's why I did what I did at their wedding. It was my last chance."

She took a deep breath. "I was the only one of the Southern Belles who wasn't a bridesmaid or had any part in the wedding. Dave must have figured I would warn Jennifer about him. So when the minister asked if anyone can show just cause why they shouldn't be married, I stood up and shouted out what Dave had done to me. Nobody backed me up and the wedding continued. I ducked out before the reception and I haven't seen or spoken with any of the Belles until now."

I was stunned. That had taken real guts. Considering the marriage had gone ahead, it hadn't worked, but it must have made Dave livid. It explained why Jennifer had told me to tell Heather that she understood why Heather had done what she did at the wedding. It also proved why Jennifer wore long sleeves and a high neckline.

"So, do you think Dave could have knocked Bix overboard?"

"Without a doubt." She finished her wine. "And then went back to his cabin to finish taking out his rage on Jennifer."

Our conversation was cut short as Mindy returned. She set a laptop on the table and opened it. After it booted up, she entered the password and turned it around to face Heather with a smile. "He changed his password every year. It's capital B-o-o-b-s-2-0-2-0. Guess what it was last year?"

I raised an eyebrow. "Same, except it was 2019?"

Mindy shook her index finger at me. "Bingo! That's why you're a detective." Her sarcasm was dripping. She looked around. "Where's the wine?"

"Open another bottle," Heather said, with a wave of her hand. She was already punching keys. "So he used Zoho. Pretty simple. That makes this easy."

Mindy opened a bottle and poured herself a glass while Heather worked. I made conversation with Mindy while we waited. Maybe I'd get a better understanding of Bix.

"So, what was he like? Bix, I mean. I know he was into women. Figuratively and literally from what you say. Any other interests?"

She sipped her wine. "We used to go on fancy ski trips. Aspen, Alta, Vail, even Val d'Isère and Tignes. But Bix was way out of his league on the good slopes. Kept getting 'hurt,' the first time out or at least that's what he'd say. Then he'd spend time in the lodge hitting on ski bunnies. About eight years ago, he really did screw up his knee in Squaw Valley. On an easy run, no less. It wasn't bad enough to need an operation, but he had months of physical therapy. I knew his knee wasn't the only thing his PT had been massaging when I got home early from a trip and she was in my kitchen wearing only her panties. Anyway, that ended any pretense of a happy marriage and our going on ski trips together." She gave me a little smile. "But not for me. I'm good."

"Other than that, he spent a lot of time on his computer. Probably watching porn after I cut him off." She smirked. "He was also into movies, especially ones about successful cons. He loved *American Hustle* and *Catch Me If You Can* and even old ones like *Dirty Rotten Scoundrels*, *Trading Places*, and *A Fish Called Wanda*. He got his money's worth out of his Netflix account." She paused. "I should have been warned by them. I guess he followed their examples in how he ran his companies."

As she tapped the keyboard, Heather furrowed her brow. "This is not good. He was far worse than broke and still spending his clients' money. He never learned from the past, did he?"

Mindy chuckled harshly. "Never."

"I've got the client list now and I'm getting his old one from the cloud." She was silent for a few minutes, studying the screen. Then she leaned back, eyes wide. "Wow. Old home week."

Chapter 22

I walked around to see the screen to see what Heather found so interesting. There were four women's names on the screen that were familiar, at least their first names.

"Heather, what are the last names of uh, . . . Sheri, Jan, Kathy and Linda?"

She took a swig of her wine. "Well, Sheri's last name is Winston, or is now. She's been married a couple of times before, but now she's married to Bob Winston. She thought he was a tobacco baron, you know, like Winston cigarettes? She didn't realize it was a brand, not a dynasty. She's not the brightest fairy in the forest. Turns out he's into cigarettes in a way, though. He's a pot grower. Different smokes for different folks."

She gave a little laugh. "Jan is married to Jacques Cloutier. He's descended from some French count or *comte* or whatever. No money, but she provided that and they're happy. At least that's what she says. But they don't spend much time together. Let's see. Who's next?" She paused, pursing her lips and squinting one eye. "Kathy? Been married four times, but she's single again and using her maiden name. Smythe. S-M-Y-T-H-E. Not Smith. Don't make that mistake if you want to keep on living. Then there's Linda. Hers is the sad story. Married her childhood sweetheart and he died in an accident last year. Her last name is Walters." She looked at me. "Got all that?"

I nodded. "Two of them are still married. Where are their husbands?"

"Who knows where Jacques is. You can't count on the count." She snorted a laugh at her own joke. "And Bob spends his time watching his pot grow." She broke out in a loud laugh, slapping the table.

I chuckled politely. It was better than groaning, which is what I felt like doing. With all the bad jokes, I thought she might be a little drunk. But she had confirmed what I suspected. Sheri, Jan, Kathy and Linda, a.k.a. Fireplug, Texas, Fullback and Scarecrow were there. That's why she went, "Wow."

As Heather scrolled down the spreadsheet, so was Walt Ferrier, D.D.S., a.k.a. Baron Beaton a.k.a.Wally Walrus. And, lo and behold, Jerald Steele, a.k.a. Dr. Strangelove, was also there.

"Hail, hail, the gang's all here," I muttered.

The cast of those with a motive had grown. Was it like *Murder on the Orient Express*? Had they all decided to meet on the cruise and get rid of Bix together? Had they gotten together and hoisted him over the rail with one big heave-ho?

If they had not worked together, the big question was how did they all happen to be on the ship? I could understand why the sorority Gang of Four were all onboard, but Wally Walrus and Dr. Strangelove pushed the envelope. I turned to Mindy.

"You and Bix are legally separated, so how did Bix come to be on the ship?"

"He pushed himself in. He said he was coming to see old friends." She sipped her wine. "I figured it was to put the make on old friends again. Since there wasn't much I could do to keep him away, I tried to make the best of it so as not to embarrass myself."

Something didn't add up. "But how did he know about the reunion anyway? Did you tell him?"

She paused as she was raising her glass again. "I guess I must have said something. We still live in the same house, but not the same bedroom."

I turned to Heather. "Would you email me the list of investors?" I paused. "Also how much each one invested. The higher the loss, the more the motive."

Heather started punching keys. She had located the lists of both past losers from HBM and those in Bix's latest venture, H III, who might not know they were losers as well, so there were quite a few names.

After I received the emails, I printed out copies on the complimentary printer in the suite. Then I locked my tablet in the room safe and took the copies with me as I set out to find Wally Walrus. I would wait until Heather was with me to talk to the Gang of Four because they might tell me to fly a kite, or do something much cruder to myself, if she weren't. Since we were all meeting for dinner in a couple of hours, it would make for delightful dinner conversation at the table. After my encounter in the elevator with Rex, I would make sure he wasn't around when I went to the other suite on my floor to see if Dr. Strangelove would talk to me. Or even if he could talk. It wasn't that I was afraid of him, but no reason to make things difficult. I also wanted Olav, my security buddy, to see if any of the other investors on the lists were on the cruise.

Olav was the easiest to find. I just went to my favorite bar, O'Malley's, and had the bartender contact him for me. DJ wasn't on yet, so I had to listen to fake Irish canned music and nurse a Jameson until Olav got there. While I waited, I studied the investment lists. Jerry Steele had invested the most, in the low six figures. Considering what his net worth must be, that was no surprise. Just below him was Walt Ferrier, the Baron. Judging from what I had found about the lousy area where he was living, I would imagine that his loss had taken a big bite out of his assets and given him a big motivation for revenge. The Gang of Four were quite a bit below that, with Sheri the highest at twenty grand. Having experienced Fireplug's temper, that gave her a strong motive.

Olav hadn't arrived yet, so I went down the list of Bix's investors in his new enterprise. There were no crossovers to the other list, which was no surprise. However, there was a William John Wilder. Rex's business associate was Billy Wilder. Could it be? The list was by investment date and the next name was Regis Allen Martini. Both had put five thou in the pot. I leaned back in my chair. Rex Martin was CEO of RAM Security. It could be one and the same person. After all, doesn't Rex sound much more macho than Regis? I could easily find out who were the owners of

RAM Security. It was public information, available online through the Secretary of State in the state where it was incorporated. I would start with California, since that was the address on the card Rex had given me. If I were right, two more suspects had jumped into the pool.

As I went over both lists again, Olav arrived and took a seat across from me. His short-sleeved, white uniform shirt showed off his biceps and he gave me his winning smile. Dang, he would have made a great Thor. I handed him two lists of names without investment amounts.

"Would you see if any of these people are on the cruise? I know eight, maybe ten are. It would be a great help."

He shifted uneasily and pushed them back across the table. "I am not to help you. The captain ordered me."

I took another tack. "Has the recording system been fixed yet?"

He looked at me quizzically. "Not yet. My computer operator said it is a virus. It is very . . . powerful. Why?"

"Olav, you are head of security. Without recording what the cameras are seeing, you are basically blind. One person is dead. How will you feel, as head of security, if another person dies on your watch?"

He looked away, then shook his head. I thought I'd lost until he turned back. His chin was set and his eyes firm. "You are correct. I am my brother's . . . . How do you say it?"

"Keeper?"

"Yes. I am that. I will see if any of these people are passengers." He took the list and rose. "I will have this for you this night."

"It's late. You can wait until tomorrow."

"No. I will not wait for crime to happen again." He grinned again. "I am your Watson, yah?"

I grinned back. "Yah."

Chapter 23

I finished my drink and tried to methodically search the ship for Wally Walrus and F.P., but to no avail. The ship was a floating city with streets in 3-D, running up and down as well as front to back and side to side. Plus there were dead ends all over the place. I could easily miss them and they could end up in an area I had already checked. After popping into another bar where they weren't, I almost screamed in frustration. Then I heard a voice behind me.

"Howdy, pretty lady. Got time for a drink?"

I spun around to see Disco Ghost grinning like the Cheshire Cat. Too bad he didn't disappear and just leave his grin. He was wearing cargo shorts, sandals and a neon-bright Aloha shirt covered with SpongeBob characters. Although I've never watched the show, I knew enough about it that seeing a grown man wearing that shirt made me want to barf. After giving him a latte in the lap last time we met, I was surprised that he spoke to me.

He stepped closer. "I know where sex on the beach is great." He smirked. "The drink, I mean."

I groaned. I didn't have time to waste putting him down, so I checked my watch. "Sorry. I'm meeting friends for dinner soon and have to head to the restaurant."

"Got room for one more? I don't take up much room." His smirk changed to a leer. "Maybe you could sit on my lap."

Obviously, this guy had never heard of the #metoo movement. When he stepped behind me and put his arm around my waist, I'd had enough. Nobody touches me without my permission. There are advantages to being as tall as the guy harassing you. I rammed my elbow into his solar plexus. Hard. He bent over, gasping for air.

A few people had seen what had happened and were gawking at me. I shrugged. "He says I take his breath away. I guess it's true."

As he grabbed a nearby rail to keep from falling, I headed for the restaurant. It really was time to do so, in more ways than one.

Heather and friends had decided to meet at Rick's Steakhouse Américain again, which was fine with me. I arrived a little earlier than our reservations, but Youssef remembered me and greeted me warmly.

"Ah, my compatriot lover of Casablanca. How are you this fine evening?"

He pulled out my chair and pushed it back in after I was seated.

"Very well, Youssef. And you?"

"Very well, indeed, Madame. Would you like a drink? Jameson, perhaps?"

I sighed and relaxed. "Sounds great. Make it with rocks and water."

He nodded. "Of course."

After he left, the Gang of Four showed up with Fireplug at the fore. She stood, arms akimbo, across the table from me. "What the hell gives you the right to check into my finances?"

Off to a nice, rocky start. Too bad I didn't have my drink on the rocks yet. Before I could answer, Heather and Mindy came in and Heather stepped between Fireplug and me. "Look, it's not like it sounded."

Fireplug glared at Heather, then at me. "It's exactly how it sounded. You pried into my affairs."

"No, I pried into Bix's affairs. You just happened to be a part of them. Now he's dead. Interesting, isn't it."

Fireplug's jaw worked side to side, but she didn't say anything. Then she walked to the far end of the table and plopped into a chair. The other three of her group gave me a glare and followed her.

Heather sat next to me and Mindy across, but she never met my eyes. I knew who had spilled the beans. Youssef arrived with my drink and slipped it to me, then went to the far end of the table and started taking drink orders.

"Hey," Fireplug yelled at me. "What're you drinking? Toilet water?"

"Must be. Look how flushed she is," Fullback chimed in.

Texas groaned. "Y'all startin' the Dad jokes now? I got a weak stomach, ya' know."

The gang laughed.

Heather leaned over to me and spoke softly. "It's a vodka drink."

I'd had it with Fireplug. I considered just leaving, but I wasn't going to let her win. I remembered the strange concoctions they'd ordered last night. I lifted my glass in a mock toast. "No, I leave the weirdo drinks to the weirdos. I stick with Jameson."

I turned to Heather as I stood. "I think it's time for me to make my exit before *I* kill someone."

Heather started to rise. "We'll get room service."

I rested my hand on her shoulder. "Stay with your friends. I'll be fine."

She shook her head. "You're my real friend." She paused. "Sometimes I forget that."

I kept my hand on her shoulder to keep her in her seat and leaned to speak softly in her ear. "Better that you stay here and see if you can get any information about how the Gang of Four felt about their financial dealings with Bix. I don't think they're going to open up with me around. It would really help. Okay?"

She nodded, looking like she was going to cry. "I hate how they're treating you."

I patted her shoulder and smiled. "Don't worry about it. I've had it worse. A lot worse. I've some checking on things to do. See what you can find out."

As I left my untouched drink and headed for the exit, Fireplug called out to me. "Hey, can't take the conversation, huh?"

I smiled. "No, I just hate having a battle of wits with an unarmed opponent."

Fullback started to laugh, but quickly stopped under Fireplug's withering glare.

She gave me a one-finger farewell and I blew her a kiss before turning away.

As I was headed out the door, Youssef stopped me. "I am so sorry for how that fat one is treating you. I can have dinner delivered to your room, if you would like."

"All I need to do is whistle?"

"You know how to whistle, don't you? You just put your lips together and blow." He gave a soft, Bogart-like whistle.

I laughed. "Well, I'll keep it in mind."

In truth, I was glad to be away from the catty group. Only Heather had seemed to care how I was treated. The Gang of Four had a united front behind Fireplug. Mindy had kept silent with an amused grin. It was getting late and I wanted to do a little more research anyway. But first I was going to stop by O'Malley's Pub and listen to DJ and his combo do a set so I would get in a better mood.

I found an empty table in the pub and sat down. A waitress came with some pretzels, and took my order for a Jameson and peanuts. It was a little after 9:00 and DJ and the Dukes were in the middle of a number I didn't recognize. It was a little more modern than my favorites, but still enjoyable. I leaned back and relaxed. When my drink came, I relaxed even more.

I was into my second bowl of peanuts when the band took a break. DJ came to my table, stood behind an empty chair and gave a slight bow.

"Is this seat taken, Mademoiselle?"

I gestured toward it. "Only by the handsomest gentleman in the place."

He glanced around and turned back with a grin as he sat. "Not much competition for that title, so you must mean me. So, how has your cruise been so far?"

"Great when I'm in here. Otherwise . . . ."

He sighed. "Ah, Darlin', then the men on this ship have no taste. I just wish I were ten years younger."

I laughed. "Don't tempt me. Anyway, I was wondering about the blond woman who reminded you of one of your ex-wives. Except for last night, have you seen her without a burly guy who seems to be her bodyguard? I need to talk to her without him around."

DJ leaned back in his chair. "The one built like a brick sh . . . outhouse. Wife three. Funny you ask that. I saw her wheeling some old guy in a wheelchair on my way to my gig tonight."

Nurse Bimbo and Dr. Stangelove. Why? "When was this?"

He stroked his goateed chin. "Let's see . . . . I start at eight, so maybe quarter 'til."

Interesting.

"Where were they?"

"Forward on deck 12."

"Near the elevator going up to the Grand Escape Suite?"

He held his index finger. "Bingo."

"Heading to or from the elevator?"

He thought a moment. "To it, I'd say. But I'm not sure. Why?"

"Just trying to put together a puzzle and I'm not sure if this is a piece of it or not." I hadn't seen them out any other time, so why then? Maybe just out for some air. But the suite had a nice, private balcony.

"Anything odd about them?"

"Odd?" His eyes went wide. "Are you kidding? The pair are nothing but odd. Her looking like some Playboy bunny and him like a bundled-up corpse isn't odd enough?"

"Right. Dumb question."

He glanced at his watch. "Looks like my time's up. Stayin' for the next set? I'll play *Harlem Nocturne* for you."

"Sold. Then I've got to turn in. I was up way too early this morning and I promised a priest I'd attend Mass tomorrow morning. I'm not used to getting up before the sun's been up for a few hours."

"I'm with you." He stood. "Great talkin' with you, Darlin'."

I stayed for the full set.

Chapter 24

When I got back to the room, Heather was there, dressed in red silk pajamas with a matching robe. She wrapped her arm over my shoulders. "Are you okay? Did you get any dinner?"

"Fine. I had a wonderful meal of roasted legumes." I slipped out from under her arm. I doubted she'd get that I'd only eaten bar peanuts. "I talked to one of the musicians who said he saw Nurse Bimbo pushing Dr. Strangelove around the ship earlier tonight."

She picked up a glass of wine from the table. "Maybe she was taking him out to get some sea air."

"Maybe." I poured myself a nightcap. Jameson, of course. "But they have a private deck like we do for that."

"Is that important?" She cocked her head. "You think it has something to do with Bix's murder?"

I shrugged "Hard to see how. Did you get anything from your sorority rats?"

"It's frat rats. You mean sorority sisters."

"My mistake." I sipped my whiskey.

She eyed me suspiciously. "Sure. Anyway, there was no love lost for him. He's hit on all of them at one time or another."

More reason for Mindy to get rid of him permanently. "Does Mindy know about this?"

"She does now. It was our dinner conversation."

"Sorry I missed that. Speaking of dinner, I think I'll get a snack." I went to the fridge and found some cheese from the night before. Crackers were in the cabinet. I nibbled on them. Then I looked at my watch.

"I'm going to Mass at eight in the morning? Want to come?"

"You're getting up in the morning for Mass? You'll have to get up by seven." She chuckled. "I believe I will, just to make sure you get up that early."

I gave her a small smile. "Like the song says, get me to the church on time."

She cocked her head. "What song?"

I shook my head. Definitely not a *My Fair Lady* fan. "Forget it."

WEDNESDAY

Chapter 25

All too early, my phone woke me. Groaning, I checked out the time. 7:00 a.m. I considered throwing the blasted thing against the far wall, but Apple charged far too much for a replacement. Instead, I struggled to my feet and headed to the bathroom. Why had I promised Father Tim to attend Mass?

Since I don't apply much makeup, I spend less time spend getting ready in the morning than most women. More time for sleep. But there are certain basics that are required. After my morning shower, a little foundation and some lipstick, I headed to the kitchen for a caffeine fix. Heather was nowhere to be seen, obviously not going to Mass with me.

I made it to the Starlight Theater a couple of minutes before 8:00, mug of coffee in hand. Father Tim was there, but his congregation for the Mass consisted of two very elderly ladies of the blue hair variety, dressed in matching white slacks and flowered blouses. From their identical size, facial characteristics and attire, I guessed they might be twins. They looked at me with small frowns, as if I were intruding on their private service.

However, Father Tim gave me a warm smile and motioned me to a seat in the front. "We were just about to begin the Mass. Come join us." He gestured at the two women. "Morg, permit me to introduce Lillian and Judith Grey. Lillian and Judith, Morg Mahoney, a fellow passenger. Ladies, Morg is a private detective. And Lillian and Judith were actresses."

"In silent films?" As soon as I asked it, I knew it was stupid. All movies were "talkies" by the early Thirties, which means they would be older than the century mark to have been in them. It was the name Lillian, like 1920's movie star Lillian Gish, that triggered my question. As old as they looked, there was no way they were a hundred, although Lillian's namesake just missed the century mark by a few months. "I mean, of course you weren't in the silents, but did you ever meet anyone who was?"

I could tell by their glares they didn't buy my changeup, but they managed to smile. One of them fielded my *faux pas*. "Not really. You see, we did real acting. We were stage actresses in New York, not movie actresses in Hollywood."

Then the other one added, "We are really not that old. However, we did meet Sir Laurence Olivier when he was in *Uncle Vanya* but we were very young then. A delightful man. And we were with Julie Andrews in *My Fair Lady*. She could curse like a sailor." She stifled a giggle.

Father Tim nervously rubbed his missal. "Um, shall we start the Mass, ladies?"

After the service, I decided to make amends. "Would all of you like to come up to my suite for breakfast?"

One of the ladies eyes widened. "You have a suite?"

"Actually, it's my friend who has it, but she won't mind." I hoped.

The ladies looked at each other, then at me. "Well, we wouldn't want to impose . . . ."

I raised my hands. "No imposition."

"They grinned. "Then we accept."

I looked over at Father Tim. "Will you join us?"

He brushed back his curly hair. "I could use a cuppa."

Heather wasn't there when we arrived at the suite. She'd left a note that she and Mindy had gone for a workout and breakfast. The ladies oohed and aahed as they entered. Father Tim stood still in the living room, eyes wide. After a moment, he spoke softly.

"This is quite impressive. I had no idea any cabin on the ship was so . . . grand."

I was embarrassed that they might think I could afford such a place. It was false advertising. "I'm only here because my friend is footing the bill. I'm just a simple gumshoe."

One of the ladies asked, "Like Sam Spade?"

"Actually, that's my dog. Sammy Spade is my border collie. Anyway, what would you like to drink? Coffee? Tea? A latte?" I paused. "By the way, I can't tell you apart. How do I know who is Lillian and who is Judith?"

The ladies giggled. One pointed to her floral blouse with a white background. "I love pink, so my flowers are pink. Judith likes red, so hers are red."

I looked more closely. Sure enough, the flowers were different colors, but they were so small and amidst so much greenery that I hadn't noticed.

After I finished taking their drink orders, lattes for us three women and tea for Father Tim, I picked up the house phone and gave them to Alasdair. I also got a bottle of water for Father Tim from the fridge. Then we all sat at the glass dining table to wait.

Lillian rested her elbows on the table and rested her chin on her hands. "So, tell me gumshoe, are you on a case now?"

I considered lying, but sitting with a priest right after Mass made that seem like more than a venial sin. "I am. I'm looking into the death of the man who went overboard."

Her eyes went wide. "Wasn't that an accident?"

I shifted on my chair. "Well, maybe. But maybe not."

Judith leaned in. "So, who are your suspects? Maybe we can help."

Father Tim folded his hands on the table in front of himself. "I would be glad to help as well. Perhaps I'm not Father Brown, but I am an observant person." He smiled. "'Tis part of the job."

Great. Two little, old ladies and a priest crawling around, alerting everyone who I considered suspects and making nuisances of themselves. But, then I reconsidered. Two little old ladies who were also actresses and an unassuming priest whose job included keeping secrets might be better able to check out people without arousing their suspicions than I would. What did

I have to lose? And it wasn't like I was throwing them in harm's way. A cruise ship wasn't exactly East L.A. was it?

Chapter 26

I looked around the table at their hopeful faces. "Okay, I can use some help. Ladies, there's a rather buxom woman who is with a strange-looking man in a wheelchair that I can't get close to—"

"You mean Boobsie and the Beast," Judith interrupted

Father Tim choked on his water, coughing so hard I reached over and patted him on the back. When he recovered, I continued.

"I'm concerned about a man they hired from a security company who's often with the woman. He's a big guy and not above roughing up a woman, so he's dangerous. He'll be watching for anyone following her. Whatever you do, don't approach him."

Lillian winked. "Don't worry, shamus, we'll be careful. One good thing about getting old is people often don't even see you. And don't forget, we're actresses. Pros, you know. Anyone else?"

I wasn't sure if I were doing the right thing, but I was committed. "Well, there is a would-be-prince, a little guy with glasses, and his associate, a big, out-of-shape guy with a thick mustache."

Judith nodded. "Know who you mean. Little Lord *Faux-le-roi* and Fatso. We met them. They can't be dangerous." She pronounced *Faux-le-roi* as three distinct words. I liked these ladies.

"Maybe, maybe not, but they have cause and the big one is strong enough to have done it."

Father Tim coughed softly. "I might be of assistance with them. I met them, too, and they were hinting that they might want me for some sort of coronation or investiture. I can see what I can learn from them." He paused. "As long as they don't give me any information during a confession."

I smiled at all of them. "Great. I can keep an eye on the sorority sisters.

At that point, Alasdair arrived with our drinks. He also had a platter of scones and muffins. He placed them on the table with a flourish.

"Ladies, I took the liberty of bringing some baked goods. The scones are decent and I was able to find clotted cream and strawberry jam for them."

Judith eyed him like a chocolate dessert. She winked. "You had me at 'ladies.' The rest is cream in my coffee."

Alasdair turned red. "Uh, enjoy your snacks." He backed toward the door. "I have many duties I must attend to."

"Hey, I'll take a nibble," Judith called, but Alasdair was already out the door.

Lillian rolled her eyes. "Judith, he's young enough to be your grandson."

Judith grinned. "I could use a toy boy."

Father Tim cleared his throat. "Back to the matters at hand, when and where do we meet again?"

Lillian paused while sipping her latte. "I think we should meet each morning at 9:00. I like this place, but I'd rather meet where my sister has no access to your handsome butler."

I thought a moment. "How about O'Malley's Pub? It's deserted until late afternoon. But let's make it 10:00." I paused. "I'm not a morning person."

Judith swallowed a bite of muffin. "Cool. We can be the O'Malley's Mob."

I shook my head. "I'm more into Sherlock Holmes than *The Godfather*. The Baker Street Irregulars won't work, but how about the O'Malley's Pub Regulars, since we'll be there every day."

Father Tim lifted his mug of tea. "Here's to the O'Malley's Pub Regulars."

After our toast to the Regulars, I checked my watch. "You know this is a port day for Mazatlán. Going ashore was at eight and it's almost nine now."

Lillian glanced at Judith and shook her head. "We've been on this cruise several times already and Mazatlán is not as fun as this. We'll do some investigating first."

Father Tim pursed his lips. "Well, I have never been before, but I tink I will go a little later, too."

Lillian beamed. "Great. Then we'll have our first official meeting this morning." She looked over at Judith as she stood. "We'd better get started."

Judith stood as well. "As they said in the movie, the game is a foot." She snickered. "Or a boob."

On that comment, we adjourned. I went down to deck 13, the Sun Deck. It had a great view of the pier. I could see passengers disembarking, grabbing taxi cabs that were often old minivans and vendors trying to hawk their wares before the tourists got away. I might not get ashore in Mazatlán, but I was not sure I would really miss it. I glanced to my side and spotted Olav, surveying the scene below as well. I went over to him. He grinned, a friendly Thor.

"How are you, detective? Are you not going to tourist?"

I shook my head. "Probably not. Any luck with the recording system?"

He sighed. "No. The man who operates our computer is from Scotland and he said someone was fishing. They fish much in Scotland, so he should know. But I do not understand how that would bother a computer."

I stifled a laugh. "It's spelled a little different. P-h-i-s-h-i-n-g. It's sabotage done by email."

He shrugged. "I still do not understand. English is a very difficult language." He paused. "Would you like a coffee?"

I checked my watch. I would be meeting the Regulars in about fifteen minutes, but not with a Nordic god. "Sure, sounds great. I've got a little time"

I made it to O'Malley's by 10:00. Well, almost. The three were at a small table with paper cups already as I walked in.

Lillian checked her phone and shook her head. "It's 10:07, you know."

I checked my watch. "Not in Hawaii. It's 7:07 in the morning. I'm early, Hawaiian time-wise. It's all relative."

Lillian's jaw set rigidly. "Time is not relative. It's absolute. Noon is when the sun is at its highest point, no matter where you are."

I raised an eyebrow. "Ever hear of daylight saving time? We pretend that noon is an hour before it hits its apex. And what about the distances of the time zones? It can't be noon exactly when the sun is at its zenith across the whole zone."

Judith was laughing and Father Tim was fighting a grin, but said, "Now, ladies, let us let the nature of time wait until another time." He paused and gave a wee smile. "Or not, since, as Einstein said, it's all relative."

I reached over and patted Lillian's hand. "I'm just yanking your chain. I am sorry I'm late, but I was doing research online late and I am definitely not a morning person."

Lillian smiled. "I was also, what, ... yanking your chain? After all, I am an actress."

I wasn't sure if she was yanking my chain this time, but let it pass.

Judith leaned forward. "Well, Lillian and I happened to bump into Boobsie—"

"Not literally," Lillian interrupted. "And we waited until she got off that private elevator and followed her."

Judith glared at her sister. "Anyway, we started chatting and found out we share a past career in acting."

"If you call lying on your back with your legs spread acting," Lillian added. "Not that we ever did." She hesitated. "I mean on the stage. Or for an audience. Or, uh . . . ." She quickly gulped her coffee and stared at the table, her face bright red.

Judith rolled her eyes. "Leaving our sex lives aside, Boobsie has invited us up to her suite after lunch for drinks and to talk about our thespian experiences. We're going ashore for a few hours, then we'll meet Boobsie."

I was impressed. "That was fast work. You really are pros." I paused. "Just be careful of Rex. I don't trust him. I was late because I spent a lot of time after you left researching his company. They claim to be specialists in computer security, protecting against hackers. The ship's security system has been hacked and you need to know how to hack to protect against it."

Father Tim cocked his head. "That is a very good observation. What is the problem with the security on the ship?"

I hesitated. I usually am good at not sharing too much information, but I had slipped. However, if I expected them to trust me I needed to trust them. "The video cameras are not recording. That's why we don't know what really happened to Bix. This stays among the Regulars, though. Understood?"

Father Tim nodded.

Lillian crossed her heart.

Judith raised her fingers in a Girl Scout salute. "Loose lips sink ships." She grinned. "We wouldn't want that."

Agreeing to meet again at 4:00 after the twins had chatted with Darla Darling, a.k.a. Boobsie or Nurse Bimbo, we adjourned.

Chapter 27

When I got back to the suite, Heather and Mindy were seated at the table with a couple cups of coffee.

I was puzzled. "Aren't you going ashore?"

Heather motioned to me and handed me a folded piece of paper. "We decided not to when Mindy found this. What do you think of it?"

I unfolded it. On Scandinavian Cruise Line stationery, the message was in beautiful script and read, "Stay away from me. He's going to kill you if you don't. J"

I looked up. "Where did this come from?"

Mindy sipped her coffee before answering. "The cabin attendant gave it to me today. She found it under Bix's mattress when she was stripping off the sheet."

I glanced down at it. "I assume there's no doubt Jennifer was warning Bix to stay away or Dave would kill him."

Mindy raised her eyebrows. "Not in my mind."

Heather nodded. "It's obvious."

Except it was not addressed to anyone and was only signed by "J." I sighed. Not really evidence, but good, ol' Dave just moved up a few places in the suspect derby. I needed to verify with Jennifer that she wrote it.

"I'm going to have a chat with the mysterious 'J'."

Heather grabbed my hand. "You can't go alone. He's dangerous. Maybe Bix's killer." She stood. "We'll go with you."

I considered her offer. Perhaps it was not wise to go alone, but Heather had a bad history with Dave and Jennifer, so they might not let her in the door. With her muscular biceps, Mindy looked like Barbie on steroids and could be of help if things got rough, but she was studiously sipping her coffee and didn't seem very hep on Heather's offer. With them out of the running, I considered enlisting Olav. However, since the cruise line officially pulled me off the case, it might get him in trouble. No, I was the Lone Ranger again with no Tonto.

I gently patted Heather's hand before pulling way. "Thanks, but you know me. I work best alone. Just get me the cabin number and that would be a great help."

Mindy spoke up. "It's 12512."

Heather and I looked at her. How did she know that?

Mindy shrugged. "I'm in the suite next to them, 12510. The insulation is pretty good, but I can hear him yelling sometimes."

I headed for the door. "See you later. And if I don't make it back, throw me a big wake."

Heather started after me. "Morg, I'm—"

"You're staying here," I interrupted. "That was one of my lousy jokes."

As I rode down two floors in the elevator, I hoped it was.

When I got to cabin 12512, I considered how best to approach the problem of getting to speak with Jennifer. Obviously, Dave was a control freak and likely violent. Knocking on the door and asking, "Can Jennifer come out and play?" was not an option. I took a breath and softly knocked.

"Go away."

It was Dave.

I tried to sound like one of the Filipino staff. "Oh, Señor, I have a fruit basket and a bottle of champagne for you. Open the door, *por favor*." It wasn't great. A linguist, I am not. Fortunately, Dave wasn't either.

"Just leave it by the door."

"Oh, I cannot do that. If someone else takes it, I will lose my job. I have three niños at home and I cannot lose my job. Open the door, *por favor*."

"Just a minute."

A few seconds later, the door opened. Dave, wearing only a pair of khaki slacks, looked surprised. He had a tattoo of a dollar sign just above his navel with a couple of Chinese hànzìs or

Japanese kanjis above that on his hairless torso. "Who the hell are you?" He glanced behind me. "Where's the fruit basket and champagne?"

The penthouse suite was nothing like the Grand Escape Suite. I could see the whole suite from the doorway and that was enough. Jennifer, clad only in a lacy black bra and panties, was curled on the sofa. Her head was bowed and her long hair hid her face, but I could hear her soft sobs. I could also see the bruising on her arms and upper body.

Dave was partially behind the door and I hit it hard with my shoulder, staggering him back. I hurried over to Jennifer and rested my hand on her back. "You're getting out of here."

She looked up at me, both fear and hope in her eyes. "You're Heather's friend. Is she here, too?"

Dave quickly recovered and rushed over to me, grabbing my arm. "Now I remember you. Is that bitch with you? I'd love to show her what her meddling gets her."

I glared back at him. "No, Heather's not with me. I'm all alone."

He grinned and his grip tightened. "Then I'll just have to send her a message through you."

A quick assessment of him let me know he was in okay condition, but with a bit of flab around the middle and no great muscle mass. More of a weekend golfer than a MMA fighter. Even so, probably he was he was stronger than I, so it was time to let my training take over.

Chapter 28

I had been training in taekwondo for over twenty years and Master Park at my current dojang drilled certain principles into my thick skull. Train until you do not have to think your response to an attack. However, use your brain, not your muscle, since your attacker might well be stronger than you. Let your attacker think you are weak and unprepared because the element of surprise is a valuable weapon. Do not underestimate your opponent, so make sure your defense is strong and decisive.

I pulled back from Dave, causing him to pull harder. Then I suddenly relaxed so that he almost fell backwards. He eased his grip on my arm a little to regain his balance. As he did, I jerked my arm away and stepped back from him.

If he had had any martial arts training, he might have realized I was gaining distance for my attack. But he didn't. He stood, flat-footed as I used a push kick to shove him farther back as he dismally failed at his attempt to grab my leg. Then I did a rear leg side kick.

As I turned away from him, gaining momentum and force, I thrust my heel with all my strength at his crotch. By him standing squarely in front of me, I had it easy to hit my target. With a groan, he clutched his groin and dropped to his knees before collapsing on his side on the floor. Too bad I wasn't wearing high heels.

As Dave lay curled into a ball and whimpering, I turned to Jennifer. "Get your stuff. You're coming with me."

She looked down at her husband. "Do you think we should call a doctor?"

"Are you nuts? He's been abusing you for I don't know how long and you want to help him?" I shook my head. "He'll be fine. A bit sore, but nothing serious. Now get packed before he recovers."

First Jennifer got dressed, her hands shaking. Then she pulled a couple of suitcases from under the bed and I helped her pack. After clearing out her makeup from the bathroom, we were ready to leave.

Dave had struggled to his hands and knees. He muttered something as we started to leave.

I leaned down. "What?"

His voice was more of a grunt as he gasped for air. "I'll kill you, you bitch."

I chuckled. "A lot of tougher men than you have tried, but I'm still here."

I felt like doing something that would leave a permanent impression, like breaking his nose, but decided against it. It might get me in real trouble. Instead, taking a couple steps back, I aimed a kick between his legs that I executed like an NFL placekicker. It was a field goal. Too bad I was wearing deck shoes instead of steel-toed boots. He groaned as he rolled over onto the floor again. As I turned to go, I saw a laptop on the desk. I went to it, unplugged it and stuck it under my arm.

I gestured to Jennifer. "Let's go."

She looked back at Dave with concern written all over her face, but followed me.

When we arrived at the suite, Mindy and Heather looked surprised to see Jennifer with me. Then Heather rushed over to us.

"Jen, are you okay?"

Jennifer nodded, then burst into tears.

Heather wrapped her arms around Jennifer and held her close. Jennifer leaned her head on Heather's shoulders and sobbed. I stood there, pulling a suitcase and clutching the computer, trying to figure out what I should do.

Mindy looked at me with a bemused expression. "Look what the cat dragged in."

I wasn't sure whether I was the cat or the draggee. "I didn't have a choice. Her husband has been beating her."

She shrugged. "Same old Dave. Looks like you got a new roomie."

I left the suitcase and put the laptop on the dining table. It was not even noon, but I decided to pour myself a drink. As I dropped some ice in a glass and poured in a generous shot of Jameson, I almost had to steady one hand with the other to keep it from splashing out of the glass. Sure, I'd had to get physical with an attacker before. I'd even shot a couple of people in self-defense. But it was not an everyday occurrence and my adrenaline pumping through my body gave me a case of the shakes. I added enough water to dilute the whiskey a bit, then slowly sipped it. I tried to hold my hand steady, but the ice cubes played a tune in the glass.

Mindy eyed me quizzically. "What happened? Close call escaping?'

Jennifer stopped sobbing and turned toward Mindy. "She beat up Dave. Kicked him in the . . . testicles. Twice."

Mindy started laughing and pointed at me. "You're a real ball-buster."

Heather had noticed something about Jennifer's neck. She pulled down the high neck of her top. "Is that a bruise? Did Dave do that?"

Jennifer nodded.

"She's got so many bruises it's hard to tell what her real skin color is," I added.

Heather gripped Jennifer's shoulders. "You're not going back to him. You'll stay with us and I'll get you the best divorce lawyer when we get back to California."

Jennifer looked down. "I . . . I . . . I can't. Dave's got all the money. He took my inheritance. Without him, I'm broke."

Heather shook her head. "California's a community property state and you've been married for eighteen years. You'll get half. And I'll make sure you've got plenty until the divorce. We've got to make sure." She paused. "We've got to make sure he doesn't drain your accounts first."

I pointed to the computer. "Do you have access online?"

Jennifer nodded. "Dave likes to keep track of his investments daily."

Heather grinned. "Great." She sat at the table and opened the laptop. "You don't happen to know his passwords, do you?"

"I do. He tries to make them secret, but I've watched when he didn't know it." She bit her lip. "After he'd beat me up, I sometimes dreamt of leaving him and taking the money."

Heather laced her fingers and flexed them, palms turned away from her, before poising her hands over the keyboard. "Today's the day. Let's get started."

I smiled as I sipped my drink. Dave was in for a big surprise if he thought his money was safe from Jennifer. Heather was an ace in banking and investments. The ex's in her two marriages left with no gain from her and some hefty losses. Dave was going to get his due.

Chapter 29

Heather tapped the table with her index finger and pursed her lips. "Hmm. There's not a lot, but about $18,000 in the regular checking. Less than five mil in the brokerage account, a mil in cash and the rest in stock. At least no bonds. They would make it a little more entailed. But it should get you by for a while."

I almost laughed out loud. Five million dollars would get her by for a while? On the very rare occasion I saw five figures fleetingly in my account, I felt like King Midas. A different world.

Jennifer told us that Dave had set up the accounts with Jennifer as joint tenant, just as he had filed joint tax returns. The reason had been that he had not been completely honest in a number of reportings and did not want Jennifer to be able to use that knowledge since she had also signed the returns. It made it easy for Heather to change passwords, convert the portfolio to cash and set in motion transfers to new accounts with Heather's stock broker, all confirmed with Dave's email.

When she finished, Heather leaned back in her chair. "I need a glass of chardonnay. No, make that champagne. We need to celebrate Jennifer's freedom."

As she reached for the house phone, the doorbell rang. Heather answered it and returned, followed by Olav and another Viking in a white uniform.

Olav gave me a stern look. "I have a complaint from David Wilkinson. He said you assaulted him in his cabin and stole his computer."

Heather stepped toward him, her chin jutting belligerently forward. "Now just a damn minute, bucko. You're—"

"Right," I interrupted. "And here's why." I pulled Jennifer to me. "Meet Mrs. Wilkinson." Then I pulled her top up so that her bruised stomach was exposed. "And here's why I assaulted him. There is more, but modesty prevents me from showing you." Then I pushed her top back down.

Olav's face reddened, his eyes narrowed and he clenched his fists. "He did that to you?"

Jennifer nodded, tears in her eyes.

Olav glanced back at his companion, who looked just as angry, then turned back to us. "I apologize for bothering you. We will not be back. We will have small talk with Mr. Wilkinson now."

I said, "When you do, please tell Mr. Wilkinson that it is now Mrs. Wilkinson's computer."

As the two men turned to leave, Olav grinned. "It will be my enjoyment."

Jennifer glanced at me as they walked out. "I should let him have the laptop back. It might be for the best."

I shook my head. "The hell you will. He'll change all the accounts back. Besides, I'd like to have a look at the emails. I'm still investigating Bix's death and Dave's a suspect."

Jennifer hesitated, then said, "Okay. I owe you for saving me. Go ahead and look at them."

Heather high-fived me. "This really does call for champagne. And we'll order lunch up here."

Once I'd finished my fish and chips lunch, I set to work on Dave's emails. They proved very interesting. It seemed that he had been in contact with Bix before the trip. They had been working on a joint venture real estate deal. Supposedly, it was some large warehouse in Sacramento that was going to be turned into a marijuana processing operation. Bix had a tenant lined up who wanted to lease it for that purpose and Bix and Dave were going to be landlords. The advantage was that they wouldn't be running the business, so there was no chance of violating a federal law. Plus the rent was very high, so the profit looked good. Bix had sent over pdf files of papers to sign and it looked like Dave had done so. There was even an email to his and Jennifer's broker to expect a large wire transfer, almost a million dollars. That explained why the account was so cash heavy. Then there was an email on Monday night to the broker saying the deal was off and he would be instructing him on where to invest the money after the cruise. I leaned back. That was the night before Bix took a dive overboard. Interesting timing.

I turned to Jennifer, who was in the living room, talking with Heather. Mindy had left for a workout, as if she needed it. "Jennifer, did you put a note under Bix's door, warning him about Dave?"

She blanched. "How . . . how did you know about that?"

"Mindy found it. What happened Monday night? Did Dave threaten Bix?"

"Bix made a pass at me, said he'd like to really get together again, if I knew what that meant, then winked. Dave saw it. He went ballistic. Bix and I . . . well, we did it once in college and Dave knew." She sipped her wine. Even from where I sat at the dining table I could see her hand shaking. Then she continued. "When we got back to our suite, he was so mad. He threw things, yelled at me and got a little rough. Then he went out. I wrote the note and slipped it under Bix's door. When he got back, he said he would make Bix pay, that he would regret even knowing me." She paused, eyes wide. "You don't think he . . . ."

I shrugged. "I can't say at this point. Do you know anything about a real estate deal Bix was putting together?"

She shook her head. "Why would I?"

"It seems that Dave and he were going to be partners. At least until Monday night."

"I'm surprised at that, but Dave never talked to me about investments. He said I wouldn't understand if he did."

Damn, Dave was definitely consistent. "Are you sure that Dave was in your cabin the rest of the night."

"Sure." She looked doubtful. "I mean as far as I know. I took a sleeping pill and was pretty out of it."

Very interesting. "I think I'll hang onto this computer for a while, if you don't mind."

She shrugged again. "I suppose it's okay."

I sent myself emails with all the interesting documents attached ans saved them on the cloud. Dave had moved up on my suspect list several places.

After I finished my work on the computer, I talked with Jennifer and Heather for a while. I tried probing Jennifer for more information about Dave's temper and cruelty, but she became reticent to say more, especially anything negative. At 2:45, I decided to head for O'Malley's for a meeting of the Regulars. After being late the first time, it would be nice to be the first one there to make up for it.

I locked my computer and Dave's computer in my room safe. Heather and Jennifer were going to be in the suite, but I didn't want to take any chances on Dave's computer, with all its evidence, disappearing.

Chapter 30

When I got to O'Malley's, two of the Regulars were already there. So much for being early. The sisters both had what looked like martinis. They smiled at me when I came in.

I smiled back. I wanted to be the first one here, but looks like I didn't make it."

Lillian patted my hand. "That's alright, Dear. We finished our assignment and needed a drink."

"How did it go?"

She pursed her lips. "Quite . . . unusual."

Her sister snorted. "That's putting it mildly."

I opened my arms a little, palms up, to ask for more information.

Lillian continued. "It started normally. We went to the suite. What a place. It's like yours, you know. But a mirror of it. So everything is flipped over. Darla had hors d'oeuvres and wine, both red and white for us. It was good wine—"

"Cut to the chase," Judith interrupted, then took a swig of her martini.

She sighed. "Anyway, it all started quite civilized. She told us about how she was a nurse and—"

Judith cut in. "Boobsie was a physical therapist. A PT, not an RN."

Lillian snorted. "Okay, she was a physical therapist. Jerry Steele was sent to her because of a knee replacement. She got him back on his feet and he—"

"Got her off hers." Judith smirked. "And onto her back."

"Well, that's true, I guess. She posed for his magazine, then became a porn star. But he married her, so I guess it didn't matter to him." Lillian finished her martini and waved to the waiter for another. "He promised her that he would make a legitimate movie for her to star in. Unfortunately, he had a stroke before he could. He doesn't want to go out in public much now and the movie is off."

The waiter came to our table and took the sisters' glasses for refills. I ordered a Jameson. After he left, I asked them, "Why was this so stressful that you need two martinis? You don't seem like heavy drinkers."

The sisters looked at each other. Lillian nodded to Judith, who turned to me. "Remember the goon you told us about? He was there, standing behind Boobsie. The Beast was at the far end of the room in his wheelchair, staring out the window the whole time like we weren't there. When we'd finished our chat with her and got up to leave, I decided to go see the old coot. When I did, the goon said, 'Mr. Steele does not want to be bothered.' I kept walking towards the Beast and the goon grabbed my arm and almost pulled my shoulder out of its socket."

Lillian leaned forward. "I tried to go to her rescue, but Darla got in front of me and said we should leave."

The drinks arrived and Judith took a swig. "So we got the bum's rush out of there. The big palooka jerked me out and Boobsie pushed Lillian out." She pulled up her sleeve to reveal a bruised arm. "That's what he did to me."

I saw red. This testosterone thug was not going to get away with beating an old woman, a nice old woman who was trying to help me. The last time, Rex had caught me off guard in a confined space. Not this time. I stood, but Judith caught my hand. "Where are you going?"

"His ass is grass and the lawnmower's here," I snarled. This was my fault for letting these little ladies go into the lion's den alone and I was going to atone for my sin, at least as much as I could.

"No. We'll get him, but in our own way and in our own time." Judith smiled. "Remember, revenge is a dish best served cold. We will handle this, but not rashly."

I shook my head to clear it. They were right. We would wait and plan. But he would not get away with it.

Just then, Father Tim arrived, smiling. "Ladies, it is fine to see you. How has your day been?"

Lillian returned his smile. "Most . . . entertaining, Father. Most entertaining." Then she sipped her martini and waggled her eyebrows at me.

After the ladies filled Father Tim in on their latest encounter, his face reddened and he stood, sputtering in anger. "I will have a word with those . . . those . . . ."

"Bastards," Judith interjected.

He grimaced. "I do not like that word, even when used correctly, but it is fitting. If you will excuse me, I must call them to account."

I grabbed the priest's arm. I could just imagine the reception he would get. He was shorter than I, probably close to sixty and definitely not in condition. Rex did not seem like the type to respect his clerical collar and might well harm the dear man. "Father, let me handle this later. If you alert them that we are meeting, it might clue them in that we are working together and suspect them. Please." Okay, it was weak, but I had to stop him.

He wavered, but when the ladies joined me, he finally relented and sat down, shaking his head. "It's a sad ting when a brute can attack dear ladies like you two and not suffer the consequences." He looked at each of us. "I will not let it pass if he does it again to any of you."

Lillian patted his hand. "You are such a gallant man."

Father Tim blushed.

He had nothing to report yet on his investigation and we agreed to meet again the next day at 10:00. After our meeting, I returned to the suite. As I got off the elevator, Alasdair was coming out of the other suite, the enemy suite, with a trolley of dirty dishes, glasses and remnants of the hors d'oeuvres. I considered letting him know what had happened, but decided not to get him involved. The Regulars would handle Rex in good time.

"How are you doing Alasdair?"

He nodded. "Very well. And you?"

"Fine, thanks."

"I haven't had a chance to clean up after lunch. Would it be convenient to do so after I take these below?" He gestured at his trolley.

"That would be fine. Just come on in."

"Very good, Mada . . . Morg."

With a smile, I went into the suite. When I entered the living room, Jennifer was standing by the far window, arms clasped across her chest, crying.

"What's wrong, Jennifer?" I looked around. "Where's Heather?"

"She went for Margaritas with some of the sisters." Her voice was choked. "I'm so sorry. He said he just wanted to talk, but he didn't. He's—"

"Here, you bitch," a baritone voice said from behind me.

I turned. Coming out of my bedroom was Dave. He was smirking. "Surprised? I came for my computer." He whipped his right arm to one side, expanding a collapsible baton. "That and a little payback. This time I'm ready for you."

Chapter 31

Taekwando is primarily done with the feet. The kicks help me keep in shape as well, so I try to practice on a regular basis for self-defense as well as conditioning. I'm not ever going to get in an MMA cage fight, but you never know when you might need to protect yourself. Like now.

The first time I'd caught Dave by surprise and it had not taken much to put him down. In a way, though, I was more interested in inflicting some pain that time because of what he'd done to Jennifer. This was different.

As I warily backed into the living room to gain space, he whipped the baton in front of him. It could cause some serious harm, even break a bone, so I needed to keep him from making contact.

I feigned a side kick and, when he reacted by swinging his baton, stepped in with a push kick to the gut before he could recover. I didn't get enough force into it to do serious damage, but it knocked him back. He crouched some, trying maker a smaller target. However, he stopped advancing toward me. Good. I needed to plan my defense.

Suddenly, he leapt forward and swung his baton at my head. I stepped back, blocking the blow with a high block. His baton struck my left forearm. It hurt like hell and I hoped it wasn't broken. So much for being on the defense.

Grinning, Dave swung again at my head. This time I was ready. I stepped in an snapped my left arm up in a high block again, fist clenched. But this time I was closer and hit him inside his wrist. Hard. It hurt me, but he yelped and dropped the baton. Using the heel of my right palm, I slammed his nose from below. Done with enough strength, it can drive the bone into the brain. I just broke it, blood gushing. He grabbed it with both hands. Using a front kick, I forced him back to get room. Then I did a roundhouse, hitting him in the solar plexus with the top of my right foot and knocking him off his feet. He hit the ground on his back, hard, and rolled onto his side, curling into a ball, gasping and whimpering.

I shook my left arm. The blow from the baton and using it again for the high block hadn't helped, but it didn't seem to be broken. Just very bruised.

Jennifer, screamed, as if coming out of a daze. "What have you done?" She ran toward us.

I shook my head. No doubt she would kneel and hug Dave, begging forgiveness for letting me beat the crap out of him. The battered wife syndrome. I turned away.

Suddenly, she spun me around and grabbed me in a bear hug, speaking through sobs. "You saved my life again. Are you okay?"

"I . . . uh, I'm fine." I awkwardly tried to comfort her with my one good hand, wishing my left one wasn't trapped between us.

She pulled back grabbed my shoulders. Tears streamed down her face. "No one has stood up for me before. You're my hero. You're . . . Wonder Woman." She paused. "Now I know why Dave hated that movie. He was afraid she'd come after him."

I rubbed my left wrist. "I just wish I'd had a pair of her Bracelets of Submission on." I looked at Dave, still curled in a mewling ball on the floor, and at my shaking hands. I'd bet Wonder Woman never had the shakes, even after fighting Ares. "I think I need a drink."

Jennifer broke away and went into the kitchen, giving wide berth to Dave. "What would you like? A bottle of water? Coffee?"

"Jameson on the rocks." I sat on a bar stool, trying to hide my shaking hands.

She smiled and made my drink. When she handed it to me and I took it, she wrapped both her hands around mine.

"You really are Wonder Woman, you know."

"No, I don't think she drinks any alcohol." I grinned. "But I bet I could drink her under the table, even if she's tougher than I am."

At that moment, Alasdair walked into the room, wheeling a trolley. "I came to clean up . . . ."

He looked down at Dave, who was still curled on the floor, then up to me, eyes wide.

I shrugged. "He thought he could take on Wonder Women. Even brought that to make sure." I kicked the baton far out of Dave's reach. Then I smiled. "He chose unwisely."

His eyebrows rose. "It would seem so." He bent over, checked Dave before pulling out his phone and snapping some photos of the scene. Then he walked over to pick up the baton, collapsing it and laying it on the counter. "I can dispose of the debris, however housekeeping will have to deal with the blood stain on the carpet."

Jennifer giggled. "Dispose of debris Dave. I like that." She walked over to him. "Too bad there's not a trash heap to throw him on." She leaned closer and spit on his face. "I loved you and gave you everything and you treated me like crap, a punching bag, you son of a bitch." Then she started to cry.

I walked over and wrapped an arm across her shoulders. It was not my usual way, but maybe I was getting soft in my maturity. She was shaking, delayed shock. I guided her to the couch and sat her on it. "How about something for you? A glass of wine, maybe?"

She shook her head. "Vodka rocks with lime," she choked out.

"I'll take care of that," Alasdair said.

I sat next to her. I couldn't think of anything to say. I'm not a comforting type of person. When Alasdair brought her drink, I was relieved. I handed it to her. My hand wasn't shaking anymore, but she had taken over that problem. She almost sloshed her drink out of the glass as she took it with both hands, gulped it down without a pause and handed the glass back to Alasdair with one word.

"Another."

He cocked his head. "Are you sure?"

She nodded.

I cleared my throat. "But with soda this time. Lots of soda."

He returned with another drink. Jennifer grabbed it with quivering hands.

There was a crash of breaking glass and we all turned.

While we were otherwise occupied, Dave had recovered enough to stagger to his feet. He'd grabbed an empty wine off the counter bottle by the neck and smashed off the bottom, giving him a weapon of jagged glass. The sound of breaking class had alerted me.

His face was contorted with anger and pain as he staggered toward me, brandishing his weapon.. "I'm going to cut you good, bitch."

Chapter 32

I started to rise, but Alasdair was already moving toward him. Dave made a stumbling charge at us with the jagged bottle neck held like a knife in front of him in his right hand. Alasdair moved in, blocking Dave's arm with his left forearm as he spun around, then drove his right elbow into Dave's solar plexis. Dave gasped as he dropped the bottle and sank to his knees. After being hit there two times, he must be hurting big time.

Alasdair swung his fist at Dave's jaw, but stopped just before connecting. Dave was no longer a threat, sagging until his hands were on the floor, his head down as he struggled for breath. Then Alasdair snapped more photos before pulling Dave upright. "I'll take you to the infirmary, sir. For your nose."

Dave shook his head and spoke in gasps. "I'll have your job for this. You'll be in jail."

"I do believe that security will want to know how you attacked these ladies with a deadly weapon and then one of them disarmed you. And, once again, you attacked them with a broken bottle. I may lose my position, but it was worth it. I only wish I hadn't held back after I hit you in the chest."

I stood. "You bet we'll tell security all about it and how Alasdair saved us." I pointed at Dave. "We'll see you in a Mexican jail for a long time."

Dave looked over at Jennifer pleadingly. "I was only trying to get you back. I love you."

She stared at him, eyes narrowed. "You love yourself. You did it because you didn't want me to get away, your prized possession." She got up and walked over to him. "You're nothing but a coward who beats up women. Go to hell." She turned to me with a little smile. "I think I've found my spine. It feels great."

I picked up the phone. "I'll call security and have them notify the Mexican authorities we have a prisoner for them. They have such nice jails." I paused. "Unless you had a nasty fall on the stairs and Alasdair was just helping you to the infirmary." I started to punch the number for security on the phone.

"Wait!" Dave was holding onto Alasdair's arm. "I fell on the stairs. He saved me. I'll recommend him for a citation, a bonus or something. It's all forgotten. Okay?"

Alasdair looked to me. I looked to Jennifer. Dave's eyes followed. She smiled. "Only if you never contact me again and don't fight the divorce."

"Divorce?" Dave looked shocked, then glared at me. "This is all your doing, isn't it?"

Jennifer's eyes flashed with anger. "You lousy sack of . . . ." She clenched her fists. "This is something a long time in coming. You're nothing but a bully and I'm the one who's finally had enough, so don't blame Morg. If you do anything, I mean anything, to her or Alasdair, I'll make sure you end up in a Mexican jail. Got it?"

Dave, resigned to the new Jennifer, stared at the floor. "Fine. Fine. Whatever."

I reached out and touched Alasdair's arm. "Thanks for stepping in. It was awesome."

Alasdair gave me a look of innocence. "I have no idea what you are talking about, Morg. The gentleman slipped and fell. Correct?"

I winked. "Absolutely correct;"

Then Alasdair took out a handkerchief and handed it to Dave. "You might want this, sir. You are bleeding all over the carpet."

As Alasdair helped Dave out of the suite, Heather and Mindy came in. They stared after Dave. Then Heather turned to me.

"Morg, what happened?"

I shrugged Alasdair did not want any credit. "Just practicing my Taekwando with Dave. He had a fall. Or two."

Heather's eyes grew wide. "You did that to him?"

I reached for my half-finished drink to calm my post-confrontation shakes. Damn adrenaline. "He had it coming."

Heather demanded to know the whole story and I gave as brief of an account as she would allow. Jennifer kept popping in, making it sound like I'd taken on Godzilla and saved the world. At least I'd made one friend in the sorority sisterhood. Maybe some of the others needed me to beat the crap out of their husbands. It seemed to be the cost of admission. All the time Jennifer and I were giving our account Mindy looked at me with an appraising eye. Was she wondering if she could take me? There was something about her I didn't trust.

When the tale had been told, Heather stood. "Let's go to dinner. I'll call the others and we'll meet them at Rick's." She put an arm through mine and pulled me over to Jennifer and put her other arm through hers, beaming. "It'll be a celebration."

Oh, good. Dinner with Fireplug again. I couldn't wait.

We arrived first and took our seats. Heather and Jennifer sat on each side of me and Mindy across from Heather. We ordered our drinks and they arrived at the same time as the Gang of Four. Fireplug sat across from me as Yousef set my Jameson in front of me. She smirked at my glass.

"Well, if it isn't old stuck-in-a-rut Mork."

Jennifer stood and leaned on the table. "Shut your yap, Sheri, or I'll shut it for you. You know her name isn't Mork. And Morg has done more for me than anyone here, except maybe for Heather. She saved my ass today and almost got stabbed by a broken bottle for it." She glanced back at me with a smile, then back at Fireplug with a scowl. "And after I finish with you, I'll let Morg have a go. Maybe she'll bust up your face like she did Dave's"

Mindy was ineffectively trying to stifle her laughter and Heather was smiling. She nodded her head. "Morg got Jennifer out of Dave's control this afternoon, then beat the hell out of him when he came to my suite and attacked them. I think you'd be wise to follow Jennifer's advice."

The table went silent as the four stared at Jennifer and me, stunned.

Finally Texas spoke. "Well, hell's bells, y'all. That's great news for you, Jennifer. I'll buy this round and we'll celebrate."

Heather looked embarrassed. "Uh, that's great, but Morg and I don't pay for drinks because of our . . . cabin. They're included."

Texas cocked her head and grinned. "That's fine as cream gravy. It'll save me some money and I'll have more to spend on my own."

The friendly banter had eased the tension and everyone laughed. Fireplug eyed me in a different way. I wasn't sure if it was respect or fear. Either one was fine with me.

Chapter 33

Dinner went fairly smoothly, with almost everyone chattering about Jennifer's salvation. Fireplug was unusually subdued, focused on eating, but glancing at me from time to time as though I were an oilman in a Greenpeace meeting. At least she didn't say anything. I answered any questions put to me as succinctly as possible, so Jennifer fielded most of them, gilding my lily so much that I had to get out of there as soon as possible. It was downright embarrassing. She even kept calling me Wonder Woman.

As soon as dessert was over I stood. "Sorry to have to leave, but I've got some checking on things to do. I'm still investigating Bix's trip overboard."

Texas waved bye. "Take care, Hon. And, remember, never drop your gun to hug a grizzly."

I gave her a smile as I backed away from the table. "I won't."

As I walked out of the restaurant, I wondered what the hell that meant.

When I got back to my suite, I sat at Jennifer's computer and studied the information on Dave's financial dealings with Bix. Then I went over all the information on Bix's company that Heather had downloaded on mine. I leaned back in my chair. I was sure that the reason for Bix's demise had something to do with his business dealings. His hubris had caused his bankruptcy and I saw the same attitude in his dealings since. But it was much like what I'd seen on an educational channel some years ago about the Minoans on Crete about 3500 years ago. They had a written language called Linear A and many examples that no doubt would shed light on their history and culture. Unfortunately, it had never been deciphered. So while the evidence was there, no one understood it. Just like this case.

The doorbell to the suite rang. Although I was pretty sure that Dave had no access to this floor, I took his baton off the counter as I went to answer it.

I stopped at the door. "Who is it?"

"It is Olav. I need to have a conversation with you."

Had Dave registered a complaint against me? It was a definite possibility. I sighed and opened the door. Olav stood there, looking like a very desirable Thor in his short-sleeved white uniform. "I have information for you." He smiled. It reminded me that I needed to call Robert. It would help me take my mind off Olav. "May I enter?"

I stepped to the side. "Of course. Come in. Would you like a drink?"

He stepped inside. "I would appreciate a Coca Cola, please."

I led him into the living room and dug a Coke out of the fridge and handed it to him. "So what's this information? Am I no longer investigating?"

He shrugged. "I know you are and I like it." He grinned boyishly. "Just do not tell the Captain. I thought you would want to know that I found a bar waiter who saw Mr. Maudlin get into a fight with one of the other passengers on Monday night."

"Who with?"

"It was the big man, Mr. Ferrier, who is always with the little prince, Mr. Stewart. He hit Mr. Maudlin in the mouth and then Mr. Maudlin hit Mr. Ferrier in the eye. His right eye. Mr. Ferrier grabbed Mr. Maudlin and tore his coat. Mr. Stewart started yelling at Mr. Maudlin, but did not participate in the fight. The waiter started to call security, but the men stopped fighting and just talked to each other for a few minutes. Then they left. I told him he still should have called me."

This was interesting news, indeed. And it involved someone who lost an investment with Bix. "Did the waiter give any details? What time was this? Did the men leave together?"

He sipped his Coke before replying. "Mr. Maudlin's lip was bleeding and Mr. Ferrier was covering his eye with his hand.

It was almost midnight, around 23:30. They left at the same time, but he did not know where they went."

This was interesting information, indeed. The Baron definitely had a second motive for tossing Bix into the ocean. I put out my hand. "Thanks, Olav. This is a big help. If any of the other crew saw any of the three after that, please let me know."

He shook my hand, then quickly finished his Coke. "I must leave. I have many duties."

I needed to find the Baron, if I could. He was a strong contender on my suspect list. But first I needed to make some Skype calls on my tablet.

Lois answered the first one. "Hey, Morg, having fun on your cruise? I've always wanted to go on one. Is Mexico great?"

I chuckled. Lois had two dogs herself and ran a rescue service for border collies. She'd never leave her house for more than a few hours. "It's been an interesting trip and I had a real workout today. I'll never forget it. Can you put Sam on?"

In a moment, Sam's perky face came on the screen.

I smiled at her, though I doubted she realized the image on her screen was me. "Hey, girl, have you had fun playing with your friends?"

She barked a couple of times, evidently recognizing my voice. Then she licked the screen. I leaned back in my chair. Did she actually recognize me on the screen? Then she disappeared and Lois came back on.

"Sam just went off to play with Duke and Duchess. She's having a ball. Literally. They have an old basketball out there and push it all over the yard."

"Great." Sounded like I missed her more than she missed me. "I'll talk to you later. Take care."

"You too, Morg. Don't drink too many margaritas. Bye now."

"I promise I won't. Bye, Lois." Then I disconnected. I shook my head. I missed Sam, but did she miss me?

I needed to make one more call. Hopefully, it would make me feel better. Skype rang, but no one answered. Robert wasn't home. I checked my watch. We were on the same time and it was eight at night. Where was Robert anyway? Maybe visiting a dead or dying parishioner. I grimaced when I realized I'd rather someone in his congregation be dead or dying than him out with another woman. It showed how deserted and alone I felt. Even though Heather and Jennifer considered me some sort of hero for what I had done, they hadn't left the dinner party when I did. They hadn't asked if they could help me in my investigation. I was Wonder Woman, not a friend.

I sipped my whiskey.

Chapter 34

It was almost 9:00. I wasn't in the mood to be here when the gang returned to the suite, so I headed for O'Malley's for some cool jazz. DJ was on a break when I arrived. There was more of a crowd than previously, but still a lot of empty tables. I was headed for one when someone called to me.

"Hey, Shamus, you too good to sit with us poor folk who can't afford a suite?"

I turned to see Lillian and Judith at a table. Lillian was wearing a pink frilly blouse and Judith had a matching one in red. Lillian gave a wave and Judith raised a glass in salute. I grinned and went to join them. As I sat, a waiter came to me for my order

"Jameson on the rocks with a splash." I nodded to the ladies. "And whatever they're having next is on me."

Lillian touched her lips with her forefinger. "I really shouldn't . . . ."

Judith rolled her eyes. "Make it two champagne cocktails." She smiled at me. "We do appreciate it. I hope you know that the crack about the suite was a joke."

"No problem."

Lillian leaned forward. "I'm glad you came here tonight. We have some information for you."

She paused dramatically, looking from side to side as if making sure we weren't being watched.

Judith snorted. "This isn't some Sam Spade movie. It's a cruise ship, for goodness sake, Lillian."

Our drinks arrived, so we took a brief pause as the waiter served us. Their drinks were served in champagne flutes with a sliver of lemon rind on the rim. Judith lifted her glass in a toast.

"Look out teeth, look out gums, look out liver, here it comes."

I stifled a laugh as we clinked glasses and took a sip.

Lillian set her glass on the table, looking very serious. "We followed that bully, we call him T-Rex, and he met with another man, not nearly as big as him. Much nicer, too. We got to talk to him after T-Rex left."

Judith rolled her eyes. "We only got to talk to him because of me. I *accidently* bumped into him and made him spill his drink on me. He was so sorry that we got him to sit with us. His name's Billy Wilder, just like the director. But he said he's no relation. Anyway, we found out he's one of those it guys—"

"She means eye-tee guys," Lillian interrupted. "Not like an 'it girl.' They prance around town in skimpy clothes and make sure the press sees them in nightclubs."

"Anyway, he works a lot with computers, whatever that makes him." Judith glared at her sister. "The important thing is, you know how you told us the ship's TV cameras are down?"

I nodded.

"Well, we started talking to him about how people mess up other people's computers. I asked him how hard it would be to mess up the ship's computers. He said he could do it in a heartbeat."

Lillian shook her head. "He said a 'heartbleed.' We bought him a couple gin and tonics and told the waiter to make them triples." She smiled. "He must've done what we asked, 'cause Billy was looser than a goose. Bragged about how he could hack anything, given enough time. Said if you've got a rear door, it made it a lot easier."

"I think he said a back door. But he clammed up quick when Lillian asked him about messing up the security TV cameras. Suddenly decided he had an appointment and left." Judith cocked her head as she looked at me. "That's important, right?"

I nodded. "Very."

Things were making sense. Dr. Strangelove, a.k.a. Jerry Steele, had been angry because he lost money with Bix. He had hired RAM Security to have Billy stop the video recording of the security cameras, then had Rex toss Bix overboard. Rex had shown himself to be a ruthless person when he attacked me and I could well imagine he was not above doing worse. Yet, murder was a step beyond. It also meant Billy was involved in murder. Was he the type? I didn't know. Still, there were things that didn't fit. How did Dr. Strangelove know Bix would be aboard? He and Nurse Bimbo weren't exactly in the sorority set. And wouldn't it be a lot easier just to put a hit out on Bix, have someone gun him down while Dr. Strangelove made sure he had an airtight alibi? Had he wanted to confront Bix, watch him die? I wondered if anyone had seen him in his wheelchair about the time Bix took his swan-song dive. I needed to talk to Olav.

I came out of my reverie with Judith tapping on my hand. "Earth to Morg, are you there?"

I shook my head, to clear my mind. "Sorry, just running through what you said. Did you get a read on Billy? I mean, messing up a security system is a long way from being a part of a murder, doing a killing for the money. Do you think he could do that?"

Judith and Lillian looked at each other, then back to me.

Lillian shook her head. "No, I just don't see it. He's a nice young man, not a murderer."

Judith pursed her lips. "I've met some cold-blooded men in my time, men who had killed someone. They have cauterized their sense of morality, seared it off from their existence. That's not Billy. If he had been a part of it, the guilt would be eating away at him. I think he's guilty, guilty of sabotaging the cameras, but not of murder."

By that time, DJ was back on stage, so we stopped to listen. He had his quartet with him, but also a trumpet player and a young, black woman in a red satin dress with spaghetti straps. She was attractive, while not stunning, but the dress made her very sexy. She seemed nervous, her eyes darting around the room as she clutched her hands together.

Being a jazz lover, I immediately recognized the first song: Duke Ellington's *Creole Love Call*. After the opening bars, the woman stepped up to the mic stand. When she opened her mouth, the most incredibly pure soprano tones filled the room with the haunting melody. With no words, the song made the voice into an instrument and the singer's was exceptional. She hit every note perfectly and smoothly, then dropped to the raucous, raspy section before a silky finish.

The small crowd there went wild with applause. I had to restrain myself from pounding the table in approval. The song that made the Duke world famous had long been a favorite of mine and I'd listened to it in many versions, from Duke's first recording with Adelaide Hall to one by Kathleen Battle. This young woman who looked to be maybe twenty had nailed it better than anyone I'd ever heard. No vibrato and clean, pure tones. She should go far.

As soon as the applause started to die, DJ went up to the singer and whispered in her ear. She nodded, then hurried off the stage and toward the door. The trumpet player started to follow when DJ stepped in front of him and put a hand on his chest. The trumpeter was a head taller than DJ, probably weighed twice as much as the sax player and was about half his age, but the bigger man just glared at him and stepped back. After a few moments, DJ let him pass, saying something as the trumpeter walked past. DJ turned to his band, nodded, and they started playing Coltraine's *In A Sentimental Mood*.

While the next selections were very good, I wanted to know about the lady in red. When the next break came, I waved DJ over. "You are a great player, DJ, but that singer blew me away. Who is she and why only one song?"

He sighed as he sat with us. "She's a friend's daughter. He was one of my mama's students and he's an English teacher now because of her. We keep in touch and he told me about Leona and her so-called manager, the Jack with the trumpet and no lip. I told him I'd keep an eye on her."

"I got the idea you and the trumpeter weren't on great terms, but that doesn't answer why only the one song."

He shook his head. "Because I don't want her to get used to singing in bars. She's already been getting hit on by drunks and pervs. She's got incredible pipes, but is way too nice for the life and still a child, just eighteen. She's a church singer and that's where that lowlife heard her and convinced her he could make her a star. He's a hack, no musician and no manager, but he thought he'd use her as his way to promote himself as her partner. So she got me to get them passages as a members of the band, her and lipless. I've talked to her a lot since then and she's going back home. She's going to go to college, major in music and see if she can get into opera. She's got the voice for it. If not, she'll teach and sing in the choir. So, on the ship she sings one song or two in one of our sets every day and that's enough for me to say she's in the band."

I chuckled. He was her protector, a role he probably wasn't used to playing. "So what did you tell the trumpet player?"

He looked up to the ceiling. "That if I saw him bothering her, I'd cut him good."

My eyes widened. "You don't exactly seem the type to get in knife fights."

He looked up and grinned. "Darlin', the only thing I cut with a knife is my steak. But don't tell lipless. I've got an image to maintain." Then he turned to Judith and Lillian. "Now, we've been rude and ignored these lovely ladies. They look like movie stars. Introduce me."

They both giggled. I smiled. It was turning into a fun night after all.

Chapter 35

DJ was a real charmer, asking the ladies about themselves while not talking much about himself. After finding out that they were former actresses, he gestured toward me. "And how did you meet this Darlin'?"

Lillian beamed. "We're her O'Malley's Pub Regulars. We do the dirty work in her investigations."

"Oh, really?" DJ glanced at me with a raised eyebrow. "Tell me more."

I gave a weak smile. "They are helping me investigate the death of the man who fell overboard. But I'm not having them do anything dangerous."

Judith snorted. "If you call being roughed up by a thug not dangerous."

Nervously, I cleared my throat. "I didn't expect that. I mean, all they were doing was having tea with, uh . . . ."

"Boobsie," Judith chimed in.

"Yes. I mean no." This was getting out of hand and DJ was looking at me funny. "With Darla Darling, a fellow actress. It seemed safe enough."

"Until the goon roughed me up." Judith rubbed her arm. "I can show you the bruise. But Morg's going to kick his butt like she did the wife-beater's husband. Right?"

I was rocked back by that. I hadn't told them what happened with Dave. "How did . . . ."

Lillian grinned like the Cheshire cat. "I was on a film shoot in the Philippines in the 60's and I learned Tagalog. I'm very good at languages. We had dinner at that Casablanca steakhouse tonight and I heard the wait staff talking about you. The women you're with were talking about it and they overheard. Very few Americans speak Tagalog, you know, so they had no idea I understood them. They said you're called Wonder Woman."

I needed to get the conversation away from me and my martial exploits. "So, what movie were you in on the Philippines? I'm an old movie buff, so maybe I saw it."

Judith chuckled. "It was pretty bad. Ever see 'Guerillas in Pink Lace'?"

I shook my head. "Sorry, never saw it." Or heard of it, even.

Judith grinned. "Don't think more than a couple dozen people have."

Lillian sniffed. "You're just jealous because I got to act with George Montgomery." She turned to me. "He looked a lot like Clark Gable, you know."

I shook my head. "Ladies, let's get back to your investigation. Jerry Steele is definitely an odd duck. It's been impossible to talk to him." I turned to DJ. "Have you seen him? He's in a wheelchair and his wife is the top-heavy blond I asked you about."

He stroked his goatee. "Funny you should ask. Yeah, I saw him. His wife wheeled him in here about an hour ago. They only stayed a couple of minutes, though. That's the only the second time I've seen him. Except for when you were here when she sat by the guy who's dead, same for her. Never talked to either of them. Not the friendly type."

That puzzled me. Why come here if it weren't for the music? A couple of minutes weren't enough to hear anything. Did it have anything to do with Bix?

DJ checked his watch and rose. "Time for my next set."

After he left the table, one of my not-so-favorite people walked in. Disco Ghost. I groaned and he looked around, saw us and headed to our table. "Fasten your seat belts, it's going to be a bumpy night."

He pulled out a chair and plopped on it. The topless hula girls on his pink Aloha shirt shimmied as his belly hit the table. He grinned at me, nodding at my glass of Jameson. "Well, my feisty friend. No coffee this time?"

I glared. "I can order some."

He leaned closer, his back to Judith and Lillian, ignoring them. "Look, we got off to a bad start. What say we split and have a stroll on the deck?"

I smiled. "I'm very happy with my present company."

Judith tapped him on the shoulder. "She means us, you rude buffoon."

He sat back in his chair and sneered at my companions. "You mean arsenic and old lace? Let's ditch the old crones and have some fun."

I considered spilling my drink on him, but hated wasting good whiskey. However, Judith had no such qualms. She threw her cocktail in his face and, after just a moment's hesitation, Lillian followed suit.

Sputtering and wiping his face with the back of his hand, he stood. He raised his right hand. "I oughta knock you bitches—"

I threw my drink in his face. "You touch them and I'll twist your head off and spit in the hole. Got it?"

Okay, I'd used that threat before with him, but I was ready to do it this time.

He grabbed a cocktail napkin and wiped his face, glaring at all of us. "You're a bunch of lez bitches, that's what you are." Then he stomped out of the bar.

DJ was heading for us, and almost to our table and stopped. He started laughing loudly, bending over and putting his hands on his knees. Then he stood up and motioned the waiter over. It took a minute for the waiter to react. He was standing, staring at us, eyes wide. DJ motioned again and the waiter came over, standing a little back as though we might bite.

DJ put his arm across the waiter's shoulders. "My man, I want you to refill these fine ladies' drinks, on me."

I started to protest, but he waved his hand. "I insist. That was one of the best shows I've seen in a long time and it was well worth the price of admission." He turned to the waiter. "And wipe off their table. It's a mess."

When our drinks arrived, DJ was into his next set. Judith raised her glass.

"To the bitches. Don't mess with us."

Lillian raised hers. "Or the pack will make you wish you hadn't."

I raised mine. "To the pack."

We clinked glasses. I leaned back and sipped my Jameson. It had been quite a day.

Chapter 36

As I got off the elevator on my floor, the door to the opposite suite was open. Rex was just inside, yelling.

"After all I've done for the two of you, you've got a hell of a nerve, that's for sure. I've got a mind to let everyone know. Then you'll find out that you still need—"

He suddenly seemed to realize I was there. He turned and scowled at me.

"You got something to say?"

I shrugged. "You seem to be saying it all."

He took a menacing step toward me. "What's that mean?"

I considered my options. I might take him. He wouldn't be expecting me to fight back after our last encounter. But he was ready for a fight. While I don't often follow the adage, discretion is the better part of valor. There would be another time.

I gestured toward the door to my suite. "I'm just going to my cabin."

"Then get the hell in there."

I bit my tongue and went into my suite. But I left the door open just a crack. Being such a hothead, I hoped he would keep up his rant and not notice. I was in luck.

"You think you can fire me like some gardener at your mansion, well, you'll pay."

I couldn't hear the reply, but he seemed calmer when he spoke again.

"Okay, then. That's better. I want to be fair, but you owe me."

Again he waited for a reply, then continued.

"That's better. I'll go for that. Make sure the money is wired to my account when we get back in port."

The other door clicked shut and I quietly closed mine. I stood with my back to the door for a few minutes, then cautiously opened it. The hallway was empty. Rex had left.

This was an interesting bit of information. It sounded incriminating, very incriminating. From what I had heard, Dr. Strangelove had fired Rex and he wasn't happy about it. Had Rex dumped Bix overboard for him and wanted hush money or he would tell? But if he had done the dirty deed, wouldn't he be guilty of murder himself? Still, he must have done something that Dr. Strangelove did not want made public and was going to get paid for not talking. If not murdering Bix, then what? I needed to think this over when I wasn't so tired.

The place looked like there had been a toga party, or whatever sororities have. Food remnants and half-empty glasses were on every flat surface. I was glad I had been out all night.

I went into my room. Someone was snoring. I took out my phone and used the light to check. I walked over to my bed. Fireplug was in my bed, under my covers, snoring. She rolled over, pulling up my sheet to block the light. She snorted, then resumed snoring.

I wanted to pull her out of my bed, drag her out of my room and throw her out the suite's door. But the only way she could be in the suite in the first place was if Heather let her in. Let her take my bed. What was going on? Should I wake Heather and find out? I went to her door and stood outside her room. I grabbed the doorknob, but stopped. Did I want to start a war? I was tired and I just wanted to get some sleep.

For the second time that night, within just minutes of the first time, I let things slide. Jennifer was in the only other room. I went back into my room, grabbed the spare blanket and headed for the couch. It was plenty big enough to sleep on. I threw the blanket on the couch, stripped down and crawled under it.

This had been a day of questions. Tomorrow was a day for answers. A lot of answers.

THURSDAY

Chapter 37

My first reaction to the noise was to reach for my gun on the nightstand. But as I reached out, there was no gun and no nightstand. As the fog cleared in my sleep-dazed brain, I realized I was lying on a strange couch. Then I remembered I was on a ship in the Pacific and the noise was Heather and Jennifer talking. I sat up, looked over the back of the couch and saw the two of them by the doors to their rooms, looking like a couple of fashion models in track suits. I dropped back on the sofa, but it was too late. Heather had seen me.

"Morg, what are you doing on the couch?"

"I was sleeping, but you took care of that."

She walked around to the front of the couch, looking down at my clothes tossed on the coffee table. "What are you wearing?"

I reached for my clothes. "The same thing I always wear to bed. My birthday suit."

She looked confused. "Why didn't you sleep in your bed?"

"Because Goldilocks is in my bed." I paused. "Actually it's her ugly stand-in."

Heather looked confused. "What are you talking about?"

"Firepl— I mean Sheri is in my bed."

Fire was in Heather's eyes as she stomped to my room and flung open the door. "What the hell are you doing in that bed?

I couldn't make out the reply, but Heather stood there, arms akimbo.

"Get out now. You've overstayed your welcome."

By the time I had dressed, a bedraggled-looking Fireplug came out of my room. Her slacks and blouse obviously had been slept in, her hair was a mess and so was her make-up. She glanced over at me and mumbled, "Sorry."

As she went out the door of the suite, Heather came over to me and hugged me.

"I'm so sorry, Morg. Everyone came over after dinner and we had a girl party. Jennifer and I decided to go to the gym this morning with Mindy before going ashore, so we put in earplugs and went to bed while it was still going. I guess Sheri got so drunk she passed out on your bed. It won't happen again."

I patted her back and pulled away. "It wasn't your fault." I smiled at her, relieved that she cared so much. "I thought about kicking her out of my bed, but was afraid I wouldn't stop there. But I have a request."

"Name it."

"Make sure the housekeeper changes the sheets and towels. At least she didn't barf in my bed." I caught something in Heather's eye. "Did she?"

She shook her head. "Not in your bed, but in your shower."

I groaned. "Better have the whole place fumigated. What time is it anyway?"

"Almost seven. That's when we're meeting Mindy."

I groaned again. At least I could go to Mass with Father Tim and confess my many sins in thought, word and deed. "Do you mind if I use your bathroom to get ready this morning?"

She hugged me again. "Of course not."

When I walked into the Starlight Theater just after eight, Father Tim and the twins greeted me with smiles. After we exchanged greetings, Father Tim handed me a missal and we began. There was something comforting in confessing my sins and receiving the Eucharist. I felt cleansed and ready to get on with my day. After the benediction, I turned to the group. I hadn't had time for my morning coffee.

"Shall we get a latte or are you going ashore in Puerto Vallarta?"

Lillian smiled at me. "Maybe we'll go ashore later, but a latte would be lovely now. Then we can get going on finding your killer."

I held up my hand. "Whoa, there. You've done enough. We'll just enjoy our morning caffeine fix."

Judith gave me a hard stare. "Whoa yourself sister. You're thinking because the goon grabbed my arm, we're too old and fragile to risk it. We're tough old birds and we're in this whether you want us or not. Got it?"

Lillian's jaw set with determination. "Yeah. We bitches stick together, you know."

I held up both hands in surrender. "Okay, but you don't do anything I don't approve. Got it?"

They both nodded.

Father Tim looked confused. "Well, I'm not a female canine, but I would like a cuppa."

I chuckled. "Then let's grab our beverage of choice as we head to O'Malley's."

After we were settled around a table as the sole occupants in the semi-lit pub, I told them of my latest encounter with Rex.

Father Tim nursed his tea before responding. "I agree that the man would not have been so vocal about killing, if he had done so. It would be nice to know what services he performed for Mr. Steele, see if they had anything do with Mr. Maudlin going overboard."

Judith leaned forward. "Lillian and I will be glad to have a go at him. He doesn't scare us."

I shook my head. "No way. Remember my conditions for continuing? Anyway, your other research gave me an idea. The weak link is Billy."

"Great." Judith took a sip of her coffee. "Then we'll have a go at him."

"I will have a go at him. You two will keep an eye on Nurse Bimbo and see if she does anything suspicious. From a distance, mind you."

Judith rolled her eyes, but nodded.

Father Tim set his tea on the table. "I did have a chat with the Baron and the Prince, to use their own titles for themselves. They came on the cruise because they received an email that Mr. Maudlin was going to be on the cruise and wanted to confront him. They did have an altercation with him, or should I say Mr. Beaton did. I got the idea that Mr. Stewart just observed so as not to sully his royal image." The sides of his mouth twitched as he stifled a smile. "However, when it comes to murder, I do not tink that the Baron has the, uh—"

"Cajones," Judith interrupted.

Father Tim reddened. "Ah, yes, to put it rather graphically. That being said, I also got the distinct impression that they were not giving me the full story."

I leaned back in my chair. "Like maybe they didn't kill Bix, but were involved."

He cocked his head. "It is possible, but it will take more investigation before I would say that."

"So who sent them the email that Bix was going to be on the cruise?"

"They have no idea." He pulled a piece of paper and glasses out of his pocket. After putting the glasses on, he looked at it. "I knew I would not remember this, so I wrote it down. The sender was mlhawthorne1620@gmail.com and the subject was 'Bilked by Bix.'" The priest looked at me over the top of his glasses. "Supposedly, there were a number of those who lost their investments with Mr. Maudlin on the cruise. They said they were to meet in one of the conference rooms tonight." He gave me a wry smile. "I would imagine that any meeting is now cancelled. The two gentlemen stated they were not attending."

This was getting interesting. "So no one knows who sent it, so I suppose it was a dummy account. Who all got the email?"

He shrugged. "They did not know. The Baron said something about the names being hidden with 'bcc'."

Blind carbon copy, hiding the recipients from each other. I wished I could see that list. If Dr. Strangelove got it, then it gave him a very good reason to be on board.

Father Tim continued. "I'll see if they have any more information when I meet them later for tea." He glanced down at his cup. "At this rate, I should change to decaffeinated, but I hate the taste."

Judith lightly slapped the table with both hands. "Then we all have our assignments. Shall the O'Malley's Pub Regulars meet again at three?"

We all agreed and left as soon as we finished our drinks.

Chapter 38

I set off to find Billy. It was a big ship, but I eliminated things like the water slides, go-karts and paint ball gallery. He just didn't seem the type. I wandered around, from deck to deck for over an hour without results. Then I finally saw him out by the pool. Unfortunately, he and Rex were sitting together at the outdoor bar by the pool drinking some pink drinks in fancy glasses with wedges of pineapple on the rims. As I stood, hidden from the two men, thinking, I saw Olav walking past the pool. He was in his white uniform, muscles bulging in his short sleeves. I shook my head. I needed to talk to Robert to take my mind off that Viking god. Meanwhile, I had an idea. I waved to Olav and he headed my way.

He smiled when he got to me. "How is Miss Sherlock Holmes?"

I returned the smile. "Still working on the case. Have you got the recording going again on the cameras?"

His smile drooped. "No we have not. The captain is not liking it."

"I have an idea that might find out what happened to it, but I need your help."

His eyes widened. "You know what is cause?"

"Maybe. But I need to get more information. I want to talk to one person, but alone. He's with the big guy at the bar." I pointed at Rex. "He's—"

Olav scowled at him. "I know who he is. He has been calling me incontinent. He told captain he should run security." He turned to me. "I will remove him."

"Thanks." I didn't tell him that Rex had probably called him incompetent instead of commenting on his bladder control. "Oh, and you should know he grabbed a friend of mine, a little old lady, so roughly that he bruised her arm."

Olav's eyes narrowed, making him look like an angry Thor. He marched over to Rex. He said something that got Rex to his feet. Then he motioned like he was hurling his hammer for Rex to come with him and they left. Billy sat, watching them leave. I headed towards Billy. We had much to discuss.

I sat on the bar stool next to him. "What's that? A Shirley Temple?"

He turned to me with a dazed look. "Huh?" He looked at his drink. "No, it's a Vallarta Viper. Would you like one?" He paused. "Wait, you're that Morg person, the one who's a snooper. Rex told me about you."

"Actually, the term is P.I. and I'll pass. I'm not into frou-frou drinks." I smiled. "So you're the I.T. guy who screwed up the ship's security cameras."

Billy was sipping his drink and started choking.

I slapped him on the back a few times. "Better take it easy on that strong stuff."

He wiped his face with a napkin, coughing before he regained his voice. "I don't know what you're talking about. We do security, that's all."

"That's not what I heard when he left Jerry Steele's suite last night. He was yelling that they would regret firing him when he let the authorities know you guys had messed up the recordings for them. But they offered him money, a lot of money, to keep it quiet." I stood. "I thought it might be worth something for me to keep it quiet, too, but I was wrong. Guess I'd better find that blond giant and let him know. I'm sure he would be interested."

He grabbed my arm, panic in his eyes. "Wait! Don't do that." He gulped. "I'm not saying we did anything like that, but it would be, uh . . . embarrassing for the company if you made any wild accusations." He managed a weak smile. "We might be willing to give you something to forget anything you heard."

I smiled again. I didn't hear anything, but he swallowed it hook, line and sinker. "Let's talk about what else you did for them. Like tossing Bix overboard."

He looked truly surprised. "What the hell are you talking about. We never did anything to him."

I sat back down and sipped my whiskey. "But you know exactly who he is."

"Uh, yeah. Sure. He's the guy who fell overboard."

"Look, I know you and Rex, or should I say Regis, invested heavily with him, you two have good reason to get revenge. So, how do you know he was the guy who went overboard?"

"Uh, I heard someone talking about him falling off the ship." His eyes darted around. "That's all. I swear."

"Who did you hear talking?"

"One of the guys working on the ship." He nodded. "Yeah, a couple of the waiters in a bar were talking and I overheard."

"I raised my eyebrows. "You speak Tagalog?"

"Huh?" He looked confused. "What's that?"

"It's a lot like pig Latin. You know, like upidstay isay atchingcay."

He furrowed his brows. "Like what?"

"Forget it." I stood. "I've got to run."

"Wait." He grabbed my arm again. "How much do you want to, uh, forget anything you heard."

"We'll talk later, after I figure what it's worth." I shook off his hand. "Oh, and I wouldn't tell Rex."

"Why?" Then, the elevator reached the top floor. "You didn't really hear Rex at all . . . ."

I patted his hand, which was clutching the bar edge like it was a lifeline. "I did hear Rex getting fired, but . . ." I grinned. "You seem like a nice guy, so I'll give you some advice. Never play poker with me, Billy-boy."

He was finishing his drink in one gulp as I walked away.

That had been a fruitful meeting. Luckily, Billy was not good at hiding his emotions. I was now sure that he had sabotaged the security cameras and that Jerry Steele had hired him to do it. Then he had confirmed my suspicion that Rex Martin was really Regis Martini and that they had invested with Bix. He also knew that Bix was the guy who went overboard, even though it had never been made public by the ship's officers. However, he did not seem to have been involved in tossing Bix into the drink. That didn't mean that Rex hadn't done it, since he definitely was not as nice as Billy. How could I find out without asking him? While I doubted Billy would risk Rex's wrath by telling him that I'd tricked him into spilling the beans, I'd better be ready if he did Rex did not strike me as a forgiving fellow.

Chapter 39

I went back to the suite. I wanted to do a little more online research. And maybe take a nap. I hadn't slept very well last night and getting up at seven two mornings in a row hadn't helped. The room attendant had cleaned up the debris from the "girl's night in" and Alasdair was restocking the depleted bar, looking dapper in his white shirt, vest and bow tie. He gave me a smile as I entered.

"Not going ashore, Ms. Mahoney?" he hesitated. "I mean Morg. The other ladies have. Looks like all of you had a bit of a party last night."

I shrugged. "I wasn't there, but I guess it was. Not sure if I will go ashore later. I've got some things I need to check on." I paused. "By the way, where did you learn that move you did with Dave yesterday? Special Forces or something?"

He chuckled. "Or something. Liverpool pubs. I grew up Merseyside and was a bouncer for a couple of clubs there before entering service. You learn to handle yourself or suffer for it. Broken beer glasses and bottles are a favorite weapon of yobs like him."

I laughed. "Remind me never to go at you with a bottle."

He grew serious. "That would never happen. You, Ms. Mahoney are a lady. I have been in service for some years now and I can tell. It's not money or title that makes a lady, it's character." He reddened and turned back to his work. "I've said too much. I'd better finish this restocking."

When I had been in England almost two decades ago, I'd found most men to be much more reserved with women than the average American male. Obviously, Alasdair was that type and felt he had been too forward. I smiled and touched his arm.

"Thanks for the compliment. And it's Morg, remember?"

He grinned. "Right, Morg."

I noticed Bix's laptop sitting on the table. There were some things I wanted to check on. I remembered his password from when Mindy had accessed the info on Bix's company. I sat down and opened the laptop. First I opened the emails. Nothing of interest, nothing personal. Mostly the emails were to and from unhappy investors with Bix trying to put them off. Some were threatening, but about lawsuits rather than bodily harm. A number were from old buddies setting up tee times. A few were Bix looking for more capital. The "trash" file had been emptied.

Next, I opened Word. There were quite a number of documents and I started opening all of them in turn. Almost all were business letters, again either communicating with unhappy investors or many looking for new investors for his failing company. One was quite different. The file was named simply "Junk." It started out:

> *My Darling Mindy,*
>
> *I know things have not gone good with us lately, but I hope we can change it. I love you now as much as when I first saw you at the Kappa kegger years ago. You were hot then and still are. I know I got a roaming eye and fooled around a few times, but that just shows I apreciate hot women like you. I always come back to you. I know you want a divorce, but I can't do that. I love you to much. When we married, it was until death do us part. I will stay with you as long as I live and my love won't never die.*
>
> *Your ever-loving guy,*
> *Bix*

I had to laugh. What a romantic. I mean Byron's "She Walks in Beauty" paled by comparison. Junk was a good heading for the file, especially with the poor grammar and spelling. But Bix's determination to die before divorcing was interesting. I wondered if he had ever sent it to Mindy. I checked the date on the file. It was one week before the cruise sailed. Interesting. I took a photo of it with my phone and sent it to me by email, erasing the evidence from Outlook Express after I did. Best not to show my hand, just in case.

Finally, I went to the web browser and checked the history. Nothing. All deleted. I checked the cookies, cache and saved password files. Gone. Someone had wiped out everything.

While I'm no computer whiz, I do know a few tricks, especially since it was a Windows computer using Internet Explorer 9. I went to System Restore, but the back-up files were gone. I had one more chance to find the search history. I went to Settings then Control Panel and finally Folder Options. I clicked the View tab, then went to Advanced Settings and clicked on Show Hidden Files and Folders, unchecked Hide Protected Operating System Files and clicked OK.

"Now let's see what someone is trying to hide," I muttered, as I went to My Computer and used the search tool to find all instances of index.dat in the C drive. Empty. Someone had wiped the past clean, very clean. I leaned back in my chair and sighed. A pro might have other ways of restoring the lost data, but I had shot my bolt.

I mulled over who might have done this. Bix? But why leave all the files on his failed companies there and unprotected? And Mindy seemed to think he was an amateur with computer security. The killer? Mindy? Of course, the last two could be one and the same. But why leave incriminating company files and a love letter on the computer while eliminating browsing history? To show what a louse Bix had been? If Mindy had killed Bix, she would want the suspect pool to be as large as possible and maybe she had emailed some sort of threat to him. Since the love letter was buried in a slew of business letters, she might easily have missed it. Then again, Billy the I.T. kid could be the culprit, hired by Dr. Strangelove for the same reasons. I shook my head. I far preferred following footprints in the snow. They were much clearer clues.

I stood up and stretched. This had taken some time and lunch was soon. I needed to get a little excitement. It was time to grab a stick and stir up a hornets' nest. I went to the suite next to mine, Dr. Strangelove's. Rex had been fired, so I would only have to cope with an old man in a wheelchair and a pneumatic former porn star. I wasn't worried about that. I pounded on the door. No answer. Possibly she had gone ashore, but it wouldn't have been with Rex this time. I pounded again. Nurse Bimbo opened it, looking very perturbed and wearing a terrycloth bathrobe.

"What the hell do you want?"

I gave her my winning smile. "I'm your next door neighbor and I wondered if I could borrow a cup of sugar?"

Okay, it was weak. Pathetic, really, but I had no firm plan in mind.

Without answering my polite request, she started to slam the door. But I blocked it with my foot.

"Actually, I wanted to talk to you about RAM Security."

"I don't know anything about them." She pushed against the door to close it, but I kept my foot against the bottom. "Anyway, I fired them."

"I fired them?" That was interesting.

"WE fired them. My husband and I." She kept shoving. "Now if you don't let me close the door, I'll call security."

Time for a frontal attack. It had worked with Billy. "Ask for Olav. He'll want to know why you hired them to mess up their security cameras."

She looked startled, but not surprised. She should have taken a different kind of acting lessons. "I don't know what you're talking about." She was a broken record.

"You can also explain why you had them wipe Bix's computer clean. Was it to cover why you murdered him? I know your husband invested heavily with him."

Her expression went to smug. "Go ahead and tell your Olav all that. We own a lot of stock in this cruise line, so if he bothers us it will cost him his job. Since it's all lies anyway, we can sue you then." She shoved harder. "And if you don't let me close this door, I will sue you."

"Let me talk to your husband first. If he confirms everything, I'll leave." I tried to see inside, but she was blocking my view.

"Go to hell!" She slammed her body against the door and my foot lost traction. The door slammed closed.

Fortunately, I had not put my foot between the door and the jamb nor worn sandals. Still, my toes felt like I'd kicked a rock. Silicone must have given her extra bulk for that last shove. I hobbled back to my suite.

With ice on my bare foot instead of in a nice Jameson, I mulled over what Nurse Bimbo had said. And not said. Her look when I said they'd been behind the security camera problem had been like a kid with his hand in the candy jar: guilt and fear. But when I'd blamed her for Bix's computer being wiped clean, she hadn't blinked. Maybe Billy hadn't done the computer. Then again, maybe he'd done it on his own after he and Rex tossed Bix over the side. However, I had to keep an open mind to someone else having erased both the computer and Bix himself. Pushing down one path with blinders on would not be wise.

I flexed my toes. No permanent damage, just a little bruising. I put my shoes back on. Although there would be no physical evidence, I decided to go back to the scene of the crime, deck 8 by the lifeboats. Although I could use the exercise of taking the stairs, I saved my foot by taking the elevator.

Chapter 40

There were only a couple of people on the deck. There was not much to see except the boats and most people were also ashore. I studied the scene. The scratch on the rail was gone, repainted already. I leaned on the railing, staring out at the water. What was there to learn about what had happened here just a few days ago? The only thing I knew for sure was that it was a lonely place, great for shoving someone over the rail without being seen, especially with security cameras not recording.

I turned to leave. I was now the only person on that small area near the lifeboats. Except for Rex. He was standing in the doorway to the interior of the ship, staring at me.

"I understand you've been asking Billy a lot of questions about my work for the Steeles. Things that aren't any of your business."

It didn't sound like Billy had told Rex that I'd played him into pretty much admitting he'd sabotaged the ship's camera system. I smiled disingenuously. "I have no idea what you mean. What did I ask him?"

He took a step toward me, his eyes cold and hard. "You know exactly what I'm talking about."

I considered my options. I owed him for what he'd done to Judith. He needed to be taken to task for pushing around a sweet old lady. Well, a feisty old lady. But he was not like Dave. He was bigger, stronger and, while I didn't buy his Navy Seal story, likely he had martial arts training. He was also ready for me. But, while the odds were not in my favor, there was no way I was going down without a fight. If he were planning on shoving me overboard like Bix, he'd have a lot of physical evidence on him showing that he'd done it.

I set my stance for balance. Like a boxer's, my back right foot was back at and ancle to my left with my knees slightly bent.

I brought my hands to just below my shoulders, elbows slightly bent. I would only have one shot at him, so I needed to be ready for any opening Rex gave while not looking like it. There was not room for a roundhouse kick. My best bet would be a back or side kick, but it would be hard to pack enough power to do any real damage with one kick. I would need a combination.

He walked slowly towards me, eyes locked on mine. He paused, glancing through a doorway to the side. I tensed my muscles, but he was not close enough. If I tried and did not connect solidly, I was dead meat. He turned back to me and slowly walked closer. Then . . . .

"Oh, Matt, I think we're lost," a feminine voice said with a laugh.

A middle-aged woman and a man about the same age came through the door behind Rex. They were both pudgy, wearing straw hats, T-shirts, shorts and sandals, but not matching. Her pink shirt said "Hot Stuff Has No Age" in white lettering and the red lettering on his white one said simply "Cerveza Por Favor." She held a couple of bags, evidently the spoils of shopping in Puerto Vallarta.

The women looked surprised to see us. "Oh, did we interrupt something?"

The man waggled his eyebrows. "Hey, we'll get out of here and let you do whatever you're doing."

I stepped around Rex and took the woman's arm in mine. I was dressed in white Bermuda shorts and a blue and white horizontally striped knit shirt, so I looked like I might be on staff. "Let me guide you out. It can be confusing."

The woman looked down at my hand on her arm. "Uh, that's okay. We'll figure it out."

I raised my free hand. "Oh, I insist. We'll even buy you a drink because of your troubles."

The woman shook her head. "We really —"

"Let the woman do her duty, Jane," Matt interrupted. He turned to me. "Can we order any drink?"

I gave him my ship's staff smile. "Anything you want."

He grinned back. "Yeah! I wanted to try one of those big Piñata Piña Coladas."

I cocked my head. "You got it."

As we went out the door, I glanced back at Rex, standing and glaring at me. He mouthed, "This isn't over." I knew I would have to stay in populated areas for a while.

After buying my two saviors Piñata Piña Coladas in souvenir glasses, I headed for the dining room for lunch. Because of many passengers being ashore, it was easy to find a table. I sat at one for four that was empty. I didn't want any company. I ordered a Jameson on the rocks. When it arrived, the cubes played a tune when I held it. Damn adrenaline rush again.

I needed to let Olav know that RAM Security was responsible for the ship's camera problems. I had no proof, but maybe the way he felt about Rex would be motivation for putting pressure on him. Maybe that would keep Rex occupied enough to leave me alone. I would get my revenge, but in my own good time. Trying to rush it would only turn out badly for me.

After lunch, I went to the purser and asked him to contact Olav. After unsuccessfully trying to do so, he asked me if I wanted to leave a message.

"No." Then I thought again. "Actually, I do. Tell him it's from Morg. Please have him come up to the Grand Escape Suite. I have some very important information for him."

After leaving the message, I wandered around the ship a little before I headed for the suite, hoping to spot Wally Walrus and FP, but had no luck. They probably were still ashore. I was thinking about how I was going to convince Olav that RAM Security was behind his camera woes as I took the private elevator to my floor, room card in hand. As the doors opened, Rex stepped in. He slammed me against the wall and shoved his forearm against my throat, almost choking me.

Grabbing my room card from me, he smiled like a snake viewing a mouse. "Why don't we continue our chat in your room?"

Chapter 41

In those tight quarters, I was in a worse place than when we'd met before. Sure, I could try to knee him in the crotch, but that's a lot more difficult to do accurately and with enough force to stop a male aggressor than movies would have you think. I decided to pretend to be the weak woman and hope for an opportunity which, considering I was having trouble breathing, was not that big of a stretch.

With a gurgling noise, I rolled my eye up so only the whites showed and let my knees sag. I had been hoping Rex wasn't trying to kill me and I had been right. He relaxed his arm against my neck, allowing me to catch my breath as I launched myself upward, slamming the heel of my right hand under his chin. There was a pleasing sound of his lower teeth jarring against his uppers, maybe even chipping a couple of teeth. I had caught him by surprise and he staggered backwards. Before he could recover, I hit him in the nose with a back knuckle strike and set him back with a side kick to the knee.

I hadn't been well planted when I kicked and, while it pushed him back farther in the elevator, it had not done more than that. Before he could recover and close in on me, I backed out of the elevator. In the elevator, I was at a distinct disadvantage and, as much as I would like to have pushed the attack, knew I needed to get some room between us. His superior strength was definitely a trump card if he got his hands on me.

From the way he recovered from my attack, I knew I was in trouble. Rex wiped his bloody nose with the back of his hand and smiled. "You're tougher than I expected. Good. I like it rough."

"You're softer than I expected." I glared at him as I slowly backed down the hallway. "I'll make it a lot rougher than that."

Sure it was an idle boast, a taunt. But if I made him mad enough, maybe he would make a mistake again and give me another opening. Then again, it would only make things worse if he got hold of me. I had to make sure he didn't.

He came out of the elevator in a defensive stance, feet parallel to each other with his right well ahead of his left. His fists were clenched, but they weren't held high like a boxer's, but lower like a karate fighter. Unfortunately, it looked like I was correct in assuming some martial arts training. The elevator closed behind him, cutting off that meager hope of escape.

As he slowly advanced toward me, I just as slowly circled away. I had to be careful not to let him back me into a wall, though. I would literally be dead meat if I did. My best hope would be for someone to show up like they had the last time. Obviously, he didn't want to be seen beating up a woman. I didn't think anyone was in our suite, but I had to try.

"Help!" I yelled at the top of my lungs. "I'm being attacked."

He laughed. "These places are pretty well insulated, so even if anyone is in, they probably won't hear you."

"Help!" He was right, but it didn't hurt to try. "Rape!"

He gave me an evil grin as he took another step towards me. "I'm not planning to, but don't tempt me."

From the corner of my eye, I saw the door of the other suite open slightly for a moment, then close. I could expect no help there. Rex had my key, so even if I got to my door quickly enough to get inside, there was no hope. I set myself for a front kick. I could see that he was ready for me, but what hope did I have? With enough speed, it was my only chance. As he took another step toward me, I set to launch my attack.

With a soft swish, the elevator doors opened. I hesitated. Would it be Heather? Would he attack her, too? Rex turned slightly to see who it was. I acted, using the front kick since the limited space made any spin or other fancy kick impossible. But Rex still had an eye on me and blocked it with his right arm. He turned his attention back to me.

What sounded like "Why hey vita" boomed behind us. It was Olav. Or should I say Thor. His face was contorted in rage. I swear fire shot from his blue eyes.

Rex spun around and stepped back from him. His hands came up shoulder high, with open palms facing Olav as if in surrender. "It's not what it looks like. She attacked me and I was just defending myself."

In a flash, Olav was right in front of Rex, leaning down so his face was inches from Rex's. "Then I attack you like she did. Defend yourself."

Rex stepped back again, hands still raised. His voice quavered. "Hey, man, I got nothing against you. This was a personal dispute."

"Personal?" Olav stepped closer. "You attack a woman. This is personal to Olav." He slapped Rex's cheek. He did it with enough force to knock Rex's head sideways. "I will fight like a woman. Now you attack me."

Rex stepped back once again and I got out of his way. In spite of Olav's insult of female fighting techniques, I was enjoying this. Rex looked back for a second, his fear obvious. Typical bully.

"Look, I made a mistake. I'll get out of here and won't bother her again."

Olav slapped him again, harder. "I am fighting like a woman. Attack me."

Then Rex made a bigger mistake. He threw a punch. It was a boxer's punch, a right cross. Olav made no attempt to block it, turning his head as Rex connected. But that was his only reaction. Except for a small smile.

Moving so quickly that I wasn't sure what he did, he speedily ended the fight. Rex was on the floor, loudly gasping for air. Olav stepped over him and took my hand.

"Are you okay, Morg Mahoney?" Worry was in his eyes.

I patted his hand with my free one. "Thanks to you, I'm more than okay. Seeing Rex put in his place was great."

He glanced down at Rex, who was still on the floor. "I do not want to hit people, but he made me very angry. You told me about your friend and now he attacks you. I cannot let that happen."

"There's more you need to know. Rex and his partner at RAM Security, Billy Wilder, are the ones who sabotaged your camera system. They did it with a virus in an email."

Thor's look grew darker as he stared at Rex, who was now on his hands and knees, still gasping. "Why did he do it?"

"I'm still working out the details, but I'm pretty sure Jerry Steele had him do it."

Thor grabbed Rex by the back of his shirt and pulled him to his feet. He looked the still gasping Rex in the eyes. "We are going to talk to the captain. We will see who is incontinent."

I suppressed a laugh. I didn't have the heart to correct him, but I hoped he wouldn't use that word with the captain. "I have a question. What was that you said when you got off the elevator? It sounded like 'why hey vita.'"

"Ah, it is Norwegian." He thought a moment. "I think you would say 'What the hell?'"

"Yeah, I guess I would." I did something I don't usually do and gave him a hug. It was like hugging steel. "Thanks, Olav. You are a life saver. Literally."

He blushed. "I am happy I could save you, Morg Mahoney." He paused a moment as though he were going to say more, then decided not to. "I must talk to the captain now."

"Before you do, Rex took my room key."

Thor grabbed Rex's hand and squeezed. Rex yelped and held out the key. I took it and smiled at him.

"Thank you, Mr. Martini."

Then Thor started marching toward the elevator, dragging Rex with him.

After they got on the elevator and left, I headed to my suite. I saw the door to the opposite suite was ajar and an eye was peering out. I gave a one-finger wave as I opened the door to the suite and heard the other door slam shut.

Chapter 42

I went inside and closed the door. My hands were shaking. I went to my bathroom sink and turned on the cold water. I splashed it all over my face. Makeup be damned, I needed to calm my nerves. I looked in the mirror. I could see a red welt on my neck. I hoped Rex was hurting from Olav's blows. My doorbell rang and I answered it. Alasdair was there, looking very concerned.

"How are you, Morg? Olav called me and told me what happened."

"I'm okay. Really. Just a little shaken up." I walked over to the bar.

He followed, stepping ahead to pull out the Jameson Black Barrel. "Neat or rocks and water?"

I wanted neat, but needed to pace myself. As shook up as I was, it would be too easy to drink myself blotto. "Rocks and water."

He poured my drink and handed it to me. My right hand was shaking so much I used my left to steady it, but it was shaking too.

Alasdair steadied my hands. "This will not happen again." He took out a business card and wrote on the back before handing it to me. "This is my private mobile. If that beast even looks at you again, you call me. I'll handle him."

I smiled. I didn't have the heart to tell him that Rex's martial arts were probably more than a match for Liverpool pub training. "Thanks. Once Olav tells the captain what happened, I'm sure Rex will be in the brig for the rest of the voyage."

He looked me in the eye. "Still, you keep the card and call me any time of the day. I'm here for you."

Suddenly the door to the suite banged open and a stink of sorority sisters stumbled in. That may not be a recognized collective term for such a group, but it fit. They were stinking drunk and laughing like a cackle of hyenas.

Heather was the first through the door. She grinned at me.

"Hey, you missed a great time at Señor Frog's. They have margaritas by the yard." She spoke very slowly and distinctly, a sign that she was past her limit and trying not to show it. She paused and frowned. "I mean the glass is a yard. You know, three feet long. I mean tall."

Then she noticed Alasdair and wove her way to him.

"Alasdair, would you make a pitcher of margaritas for us? No, make that two pitchers." She glanced back at the rest of the sisters, six of them, most of whom were plopping on the chairs and sofa. "No, we need three pitchers." She held up three fingers and studied them. "That's it. Three." Then she giggled.

He gave a half nod, half bow. "Yes, madam. I will need to get some more supplies first."

Fireplug staggered over to us. She was wearing a blue T-shirt that snugly fit her stout body that had a green frog holding a drink with the message "Normal is Boring . . . Señor Frog's." If that were the case, she didn't have to worry about being boring. It looked like she'd missed her mouth with her margarita a few times and hit her shirt. She looked at the whiskey in my hand.

"Looks like you got a head start on us." She spoke with a slur. Then she grabbed my glass and took a hefty swig. She started coughing and spit part of it back in the glass, making a face. "What's this crap?"

I stared sadly at my polluted Jameson in her hand. "It used to be the good stuff. Something way out of your league."

Alasdair gently, but firmly, took my glass out of Fireplug's hand and poured my drink down the sink. "Miss Mahoney had a rather unpleasant experience with a brutal man just before she came here. He physically attacked her. I poured her the whiskey to calm her nerves."

Heather seemed to suddenly sober up and hugged me. "Are you okay? What did he do? Who did it? Where is he?"

Jennifer, who was slouching on the sofa and seemed to be having trouble not sliding off, tried to stand, but gave up. She pointed at me with an unsteady finger.

"I bet you kicked his butte." She paused. "I mean butt. Kicked his butt."

I shook my head. "Actually, he just about kicked mine. It was Rex, the guy Heather and I met the first night aboard. Thor, . . . I mean, Olav from security took care of him, though."

Heather pulled back. "Your neck. It's all red. Did he do that?"

I touched it gingerly. "He did. But I got him back. His nose is sore and maybe he lost a tooth or two."

She took my arm. "We're going to the infirmary. It's on the bottom deck."

I shook loose. "I'm fine. Really." I glared at Fireplug. "But I never got to try my drink."

Alasdair handed me a fresh whiskey in a clean glass. "Here you go, Morg."

"Thanks, Alasdair." I took a sip, then checked my watch. "I have a meeting soon, so I've got to get going." I took my drink with me.

Fireplug snorted. "Don't leave on my account. I won't touch your awful drink again."

"Don't flatter yourself. I've got a meeting." I paused and gave her a death stare. "Just stay out of my bed."

Heather reached out, almost touching my neck, then pulled her hand back. "You sure you're okay? Would you like some lotion? Or makeup to cover the bruise?"

"I'm fine." Leave it to Heather to worry about how I looked. "And if anyone says anything about the bruise, I'll tell them I'm a real redneck."

Texas roused in her chair. "Yeehaw! You tell 'em, pard."

I laughed, gave Alasdair a sympathetic look because I was abandoning him to the stink of sisters, and left. I was over an hour early for my meeting with the O'Malley's Pub Regulars, but

I had to get out of there. Watching seven drunken women getting drunker is not my idea of fun.

Chapter 43

As I took the elevator down from the suite, I thought back to the morning Bix was first missed. A question I didn't ask then nagged me, a piece of the puzzle that needed to be found. I went to the purser's desk. Freya was on duty again and her icy smile let me know she remembered me from before. She glanced at the drink in my hand and raised an eyebrow.

"Yes? You want me to page Olav?" She paused dramatically. "Or would you like a drink for your other hand?"

I returned her smile in kind. "Neither. I just would like a little information." I paused. "If that's not too much trouble."

She shrugged. "It will depend on what *information* you want."

I so wanted to reach across the counter and shake her. But I needed her help. So instead I tried a little tact, something I'm not used to doing. "Look, for the record, I'm not after Olav. I have a boyfriend . . . man friend in California. He is helping me with my investigation. Period. So, can we start again? I apologize if I've offended you, but it's been a difficult case."

She seemed to thaw a bit. "I was having a difficult day, too. I will try to give you any information you want."

"It rained on Tuesday morning. Can you tell me when? Need to know when the storm hit the ship to as close to the minute as possible."

"I do not know how accurate I can be, but I will try." She started tapping on her keyboard, gnawing on her lower lip as she concentrated on the computer screen. She would pause her typing, shake her head, then start typing again. Finally she stopped typing and sighed. "I have checked our location then and used weather charts from several sources, including your Noah, but can only give you an approximate time."

"Noah?"

She gave me a slightly condescending smile. "National Oceanic and Atmospheric Administration. N-O-A-A. Noah."

"Of course. I didn't know you could tap into them." It was true, but that was because I had had no idea who they were. I'd seen the initials before, but I still didn't know exactly what they did.

"It is not difficult." She looked back at her screen. "The best I can do is say it was between two and four in the morning." She looked up at me with a smile of regret. "I am sorry I cannot do better."

I returned her smile. "Thanks for trying. I appreciate it."

As I turned and headed for the elevators I considered how fantastic Freya and Olav's kids would look if they got together. Totally unfair to the rest of the human race.

It was close enough to my meeting with the Regulars that I went to O'Malley's. I was the first to arrive and easily found an empty table. A waiter came up to me, but stopped when he saw my whiskey in my hand.

I looked down at my glass. "I came prepared."

As he backed away, the twins arrived and sat at my table.

Lillian motioned the waiter back. "I'll have an iced tea. A real one, not one of those Long Island things."

Judith thought a second. "I'll have a Diet Coke. Make sure it's Coke. I hate Pepsi and I can tell the difference."

The waiter nodded and smiled before leaving. I felt like the token lush. Maybe I should cut back. I mentally shrugged. Tomorrow.

Lillian excitedly leaned forward. "So, we talked to Billy and—"

Judith slapped the table and glared at her sister. "Wait until Father Tim gets here."

Lillian gave her a hurt look, but perked up as Father Tim came to the table and sat.

"Can I tell them now?"

Judith rolled her eyes. "Go ahead."

Lillian folded her hands in front of her. "Well, we talked to Billy. He said that they were fired by the Beast because Rex got too familiar with Boobsie. He was always putting his hands on her. She told him she was no slut and to get the hell out. Her words, according to Billy." She giggled. "I guess the 'me too' movement has come to the porno world."

The reason for Rex's dismissal was no surprise, considering how he had been acting with the woman when they were getting off the ship at Cabo. It showed that Nurse Bimbo wasn't looking to fool around on Dr. Strangelove with Rex, but it didn't help me solve the case.

She shook her head. "He clammed up quick when we asked what they did for the Beast. Said just some security stuff."

I leaned back in my chair. "Thanks, ladies. You've done a great job."

Judith snorted. "The hell we have. He wouldn't let us buy him a drink this time. We tried everything but flashing him to loosen him up, but he didn't say much. It was like he'd been warned against us."

"Not against you, but against anyone. I had a run in with Rex a little while ago and Billy seems to have told him we'd been pumping him. My guess is that he's afraid of Rex and rightly so."

Judith peered at my neck. "I almost didn't notice how red your neck is in the dim light here. Did he do that?"

Lillian touched her fingers to her lips. "Oh, my word. Are you okay?"

"I'm fine." I shrugged. "But you should see the other guy. Rex. He made the mistake of going up against Olav, the head of security. Now he's in the brig, or whatever they call it on a cruise ship." I winked at Father Tim. "So you won't have to deal with him for me."

Father Tim raised an eyebrows. "I suppose they will properly handle that cad." He leaned over, concern in his look. "Child, you need to go to the ship's doctor to make sure you have no hidden injury."

I held up my hands in front of me. "Please, everyone, I'm really okay. Let's stick to what you've learned since our last meeting."

The ladies' drinks arrived and we paused as they were served. Father Tim ordered his usual hot tea with milk. Since my hands were no longer shaking, I restrained from having a Jameson and ordered coffee. After the waiter left, Father Tim adjusted his glasses and smiled.

"I tink I have some interesting information. The Baron and the Prince were very talkative when we met. I do believe they are worried for their own safety. And it's because of Mr. Maudlin."

At that point, the waiter brought Father Tim's tea. Instead of continuing with his story, he poured milk in his cup and then the tea. He frowned at it.

"I should have let it steep longer."

I leaned forward. "Why are they afraid?"

"Oh, that." He set his cup on the table and laced his fingers together. "After their, ah . . . altercation with Mr. Maudlin, they met again. This time he was much friendlier. He told the two gentlemen that he might be able to give them a down payment on the money he had . . . . How did he put it? Misappropriated. Yes, that was it." He poured a little more tea in his cup and sipped it. "Much better."

I tried to keep my impatience out of my voice. "And?"

He set his cup back down. "Mr. Maudlin said that he had $50,000 with him. He was going to purchase illegal narcotics from a person on the ship who was part of a Mexican drug cartel. He could sell them for a rather large profit. With that money, he planned to recover his losses and start regaining his good name by remunerating those who had lost money with him previously."

The whole thing sounded quite farfetched. I doubted that he could have made enough money to pay everyone back, even if the story were true. But then I remembered a car maker who had been caught trying to buy drugs to sell in order to help his struggling company. What was his name? John DeLorean? Yes, that was it. Could it have been a drug deal gone bad?

"If Bix were involved in some drug deal, why are FP and Wally Walrus in danger?"

Father Tim looked at me quizzically. "FP and Wally Walrus?" Then he nodded. "I see. That is what you call the Prince and the Baron. Why?"

I waved a hand. "Not important. What is important is why the two of them think they are in danger."

He rested his hands on the table. "Because Mr. Maudlin was going to tell his drug supplier from the cartel that he could only buy $40,000 in merchandise and give $10,000 to the Prince and the Baron. He told them to meet him by the lifeboats at 3:30 and he would pay them. But when they got there, they saw his jacket lying on the deck and left. They tink the supplier got angry and killed Mr. Maudlin. So now he will be looking for them since they know about the deal."

That part of the story sounded as fishy as a StarKist cannery. It was more likely that Bix promised them money to get the pair off his back, but I could see Bix getting killed in a drug deal that went south. Then I remembered the night before Bix went overboard, when I had seen him here, in O'Malley's. Nurse Bimbo had come out of the bar before I went in. Rex had followed her. Bix had left as I entered. It had looked like he left as soon as he saw me. He had spoken to the Latino with a mustache who was coming in as he was leaving. Both men had turned my way, then left. What had the Latino man looked like? At the time, I had had no reason to take notice of him. I racked my brain, but only remembered vaguely that he had had a mustache and black hair. I closed my eyes to concentrate, but it didn't help.

Chapter 44

Somebody snapped their fingers and I opened my eyes. It was Judith, leaning close to me and looking concerned. Lillian and Father Tim were watching me with the same look. I gave them a smile.

"I saw Bix with a Latino the night before he died. They were here, in this bar. It might be the drug dealer and I was trying to remember what he looked like."

Judith rested her hand on mine. "We were worried about you. After all you've been through, we thought you had fainted."

I laughed. "Not my style. No, just thinking." I looked around the table at my Regulars. "You've all been a great help. Maybe I could get Olav to help us on this. If there's nothing else to report, I'll go look for him."

They looked at each other, then back at me.

"I think that's it," Judith said. "Meet at ten again tomorrow?"

I nodded. "Sure, sounds like a plan."

As we stood to leave, Father Tim asked me, "Will you be at Mass tomorrow morning?"

I cringed. "If it were a couple of hours later, I would. I'm just not a morning person."

He gave me a small smile. "We can't have the Starlight Theater at a later time. But it was grand having you for the ones you made." He made the sign of the Cross. "Dominus vobiscum, Morg Mahoney. And try to be careful. We don't want for anyting to happen to you." He paused. "Again."

I chuckled. "On that we do agree."

After leaving O'Malley's, I wandered around the ship, eventually ending up by the lifeboat where this case all began. It was one of the few quiet places on the ship and good for thinking. I was alone, looking out over the port of Puerto Vallarta.

Although I had said I was going to find Olav, there was no way I could ask him to see if he could find a Latino that I could only say had black hair and a mustache who might be connected with a drug cartel and also might have killed Bix. Talk about racially profiling with no shred of evidence.

So again I let my mind go back to the night I had seen the Latino and Bix together, see if I could conjure up what the man looked like. If I did that, maybe I could remember if I had seen him since. In a ship of over 2,000 passengers, not seeing him didn't prove he wasn't still aboard.

I was having problems getting a firm mental picture of the man with Bix. Then one thing in the picture hit me. I had completely forgotten about the missing gym bag. It had not seemed important and I had let it slide. Had the cash for a drug purchase been inside it? Had the seller decided to kill Bix and keep the money? If so, it explained the missing bag. The only way to know would be to find the man Bix bumped into at the bar. Good luck. Not only that, if he had killed Bix and taken the cash, why would he stay on the ship after the first port? Father Tim's clue brought about more questions than solutions.

My reverie was cut short by someone speaking behind me.

"Thought I might find you here again. For some reason, you seem to like this place."

My blood ran cold as I slowly turned to face Rex. A gauze bandage covered his nose and he had swollen, black bags under his eyes. He grinned.

It took me a moment to recover from the shock of seeing him here. "How the hell did you get out of the brig?"

"My former employer vouched for me. Since she rehired me, I should say my current employer. She told the captain you attacked me. Since I got the worst of it in our last tango, he believed her." He took a step forward. "You broke my nose. You owe me big time."

I quickly scoped my escape options. There were two doors, heavy ones, with one behind Rex and one behind me. While I might make it to the one behind me before Rex could catch me, there was no way I could get it open and go through it before he did. Flight was not an option, so it was fight.

Although I'd started Taekwondo years ago because I'd dated a cute Korean guy who was a fourth *dan* black belt, I'd stayed with it after our five-week relationship had ended. After a few years shy of two decades in it, I could kick as high as a Rockette. Unfortunately, that was great for keeping in shape, but many kicks are lousy for close-quarters combat. I had learned punches and strikes as well as kicks, however, there are martial arts disciplines that are better for those than Taekwondo and probably Rex was trained in one of those. Although I'd been learning Muay Thai as well, which was very good for close fighting, I was far from adept at it yet. Add that to no longer having the element of surprise and I was burnt toast.

With my left foot ahead of my right, I set for his attack. If I were lucky, I'd get a good strike or two in before he closed on me and I was going to make them count. Whatever the outcome, I was going to make sure I used every bit of skill I had. I glared at him, determined to not show any fear.

"You had it easy when you killed Bix. Now you're going to find out what fighting tooth and nail means."

Chapter 45

I needed for Rex to make a mistake and he did. He hesitated, looking uncertain. As I started a front kick, aiming for Rex's hurting nose, the door behind him slammed opened with a bang. Startled, I jerked and my kick merely grazed his shoulder instead. I stumbled to recover. But he didn't take advantage of my momentary disadvantage as we both turned to the door.

Thor stood there, looking like he was ready to kill someone and it wasn't me. His eyes were narrowed and his jaw was set. He flew through the doorway at Rex and slammed him against the metal wall. The back of his head hit the wall with a loud clang.

Thor spoke through gritted teeth, his forearm pinning Rex to the wall. "I told you to stay away from her."

Rex's eyes were wide, like a fearful prey caught by a lion. "I wasn't going to hurt her. I just wanted to talk."

"Talk is over. I see you near her again, I will break your arms." Thor leaned closer to Rex. "Understand?"

Rex's voice was choked, barely audible. "You'll lose your job if you hurt me."

"Then I lose my job." He leaned even closer, his face almost touching the other man's. "I asked you, understand?"

Rex nodded. His voice cracked. "I understand." His eyes darted from side to side. "Can I go now?"

Thor removed his arm from Rex's chest and stepped back. He motioned at the door like he was swatting a fly. "Go."

Rex didn't hesitate, rushing inside as he rubbed the back of his head. He left a small smear of blood on the wall behind him. I wondered if he had a concussion. Couldn't happen to a better guy.

Thor became Olav, looking at me with concern. "Are you okay, Morg Mahoney?"

I smiled. "I am, thanks to you. Hope you don't lose your job over me." I paused. "It sounds like Rex pulled a few strings. I'm surprised, considering he and his cohort sabotaged the ship's security."

"I do not think the captain believed you attacked that man. I told the captain that I know what happened, that it was not as the woman told him, but he is afraid of that old man, the one in the suite across from yours. He has much power with the company. Rex Martin said he did not ruin the cameras, but his friend will fix them." Olav shook his head. "Now his friend is working on our computer. I do not trust him." He looked at me quizzically. "Why are you here? When the captain let Rex Martin go free, I tried to find you, to warn you. When I saw him walking to here, I followed him. He is a bad person."

"I'm glad you did. I don't think I would have fared too well in this encounter." I almost hugged him, but refrained. Not my style. I patted his forearm of steel. "By the way, I wonder if you could try to get me some information. I want to know as accurately as possible when the squall hit on Tuesday morning. Freya tried to do it on her computer, but being as the ship is at sea, there was no way."

"You want to know when a squaw came on this ship?" He cocked his head. "I do not think I understand this word."

I was unable to stifle a short chuckle. "Not squaw. Squall, with an 'all' on the end. It means small storm. Just a hare-brained idea I have that I need to know when the squall hit the ship to know if it is possible."

"Ah, squaw-all." He grinned. "I did not know that word either, but have learned it. Now you have hair on your brain? What does that mean?"

This was going nowhere fast. Time to move on. "Right. I have hair on my head. Can you find out the exact time the rain hit the ship on Tuesday morning?"

"I will try." He looked dubious. "Is that all?"

"Yes." A thought hit me. "No, I might have one other request. Good hotels have a record of key entries to rooms. Do you have that for the cabins?"

"We do."

"I would like the records between, say, midnight Monday and six Tuesday morning for several of them. Let's start with Bix's cabin. I've got a list of suspects as well, so you might want to write them down."

He pulled out a small notebook and pen, then gave me a nod. "I am ready."

"Okay, Jerry Steele, Rex Martin, that Baron guy . . . Ferrier's his last name, I think, Dave Wilkinson, and ah . . . ." I wanted info on Fireplug, Texas, Scarecrow and Fullback, but only remembered their first names. I also really wanted to know the whereabouts of the Latino man from the bar, but didn't even have his first name. "Do you know if there's a guy from a Mexican drug cartel on board?"

By his shocked look, I figured he didn't. I waved my hand. "Forget that last one. It's a hare-brained idea anyway."

He cocked his head with a puzzled expression. "You have hair in your brain? Is it not on top of your brain, on top of your head?"

"Right. It's hare, not hair and . . . . Forget it. That's one of those strange American expressions that's not worth learning. If you can get me the info on when cabin keys were used by those people, it would help. I might have some more later."

He put his notebook and pen in his pocket. "I will work on this." He paused. "I am very sorry that Rex Martin was let free."

I patted his forearm again. It was a nice forearm to pat. "Thanks. I'm sure he won't bother me now."

Thor returned. "He had better not. If he bothers you again, I will make him very sorry."

I grinned. "I think he already is."

Chapter 46

Olav walked me to the elevator. The ship sailed at five and it was getting close to that. A last sailing party was scheduled on the Sun Deck, the last of the cruise. Since the only one I had attended had been when we left on Sunday and I had not been to any of the ports, I decided to go to the last hurrah for the cruise. Tomorrow would be a day at sea and the next day we disembarked in the morning, so this was it.

I got off the elevator and went to the suite. At the bottom of the door to our suite was a small box, wrapped in gold paper with a gold bow. I picked it up. It had an envelope attached that said "Morgana Mahoney" in flowing script. I pulled a card out of it. All it said was, "Enjoy this little gift."

Curious. Why would anyone give me a gift? It had to be someone who had access to this floor. That narrowed down the prospects and made it even odder. There was no one with access who I could imagine would give me a gift. I took it inside, fearing the disaster the wild women might have inflicted on the suite. No one was there. Everything had been tidied up and the place looked great. Alastair, no doubt.

I peeked in Heather's room. She was in bed, softly snoring. I closed the door and went to the room Jennifer was using. She was asleep as well. With a sense of dread, I opened my door. No one was in my bed. I checked the bathroom. Empty and no smell of vomit. Good. I set the package on the dresser. I would open it later, after I did my swan song on the Sun Deck. I opened my closet and took out the nautical outfit I had worn when we had sailed. I shook my head. The cruise had not exactly lived up to my high expectations. This was its last chance.

I hit the Sun Deck with my wide-brimmed, 1940's style white straw hat rakishly dipped just above one eye. With my navy blue dress and red wedge sandals, I didn't exactly fit in with the T-shirts, baggy shorts and flip-flops that abounded for males and females. Yeah, looking out at the crowd gathered for the last sailing party, I was again way overdressed, but so what? I liked the outfit and had spent too much of my hard-earned money to not wear it one last time on the cruise.

So many people were milling around that it was hard not to be jostled, which violates my personal space. You'll never find me clubbing with the mobs of boozers spilling drinks on my basic black dress, especially since I only owned one. I carefully wove my way through the masses without anyone spilling anything on me until I found an empty space by a railing and took it, leaning against the rail as I waited for departure. A waiter in an Aloha shirt and white jeans came up with some weird drink in what looked like Mason jars with handles. On it was the red Scandinavian Cruise Lines logo with "SCL" in white lettering and "Let 'er Rip" in blue. Classy, I mused. The drink itself was layered with red on the bottom, yellow in the center and blue on top, garnished with a wedge of pineapple. The waiter offered me one.

I looked at it, askance. "What is it?"

He smiled at me. "La Cucaracha Cocktail. Very good."

I laughed. Naming a drink after a cockroach? "So what's in this concoction?"

It took him a moment, but then he grinned and nodded. "Grenadine, pineapple juice, Galliano, Blue Curacao and vodka." He winked. "Much vodka."

The sound of the sickly sweet drink made me nauseous.

"I'll pass. Bring me a Jameson." Wait, this was the last sailing of the cruise. "No, make that champagne."

After he took my cabin number, he left, pawning off his cockroaches on cruisers as he went. I wondered what he would have done if I had katsaridaphobia? But then, fearing the real thing is not the same as fearing the drink named after it.

As I leaned on the railing, I watched the people. It was entertaining. Some were definitely showing the effects of a few too many cockroaches or other libation. After the ship's horn blasted, a mariachi band started playing *La Cucaracha* over the loudspeakers. A few couples tried to dance in the press of people. Others locked lips, oblivious to their surroundings, evidently overcome with amorous emotions aroused by the romantic music in spite of the lack of privacy. Riiight. One or two looked like they wouldn't make it back to their cabins before things got more serious. Then I spied him.

On the opposite side of the ship, the Latino man I had seen at O'Malley's with Bix on Monday night was standing with his arm around a stunning Latina. Even though I had only seen him the one time, I was sure that it was he. He wore a classy-looking white guayabera and slacks. The woman was probably an inch or two taller than he, with long, raven hair and a slim, yet buxom, figure. Dressed in a red off-the–shoulder blouse and white shorts, she looked like a movie star. They were the perfect image of a Hollywood drug lord and his trophy wife or mistress. Sometimes even Hollywood gets it right.

I started working my way through the crowd, avoiding getting any drinks spilled on me as I kept my eye on the couple. Suddenly, I stopped. Two men approached the couple and started talking to them. It was FP and the Baron. The same ones who had told Father Tim they feared for their lives because they thought Bix had been killed by his cartel connection. Now they were chatting with him like an old friend? Something wasn't right.

I moved back, finding cover in the gangs of people as I watched the scene in front of me. I did not want them to spot me. My waiter was over where I had been standing, looking bewildered with a glass of champagne on a tray. I caught his eye and motioned him over. I took the flute of bubbly and thanked him, adding a nice tip to the tab. Considering that I had been working most of this cruise, I did not feel badly about having Heather pay it. I sipped it. Even I could tell it was the cheap stuff. Definitely not as good as Jameson, but it would have to do. When I looked over at the odd quartet, I got another surprise. In the short time my eye had not been on them, they had been joined by another person. Mindy was greeting the woman with a hug.

This made no sense. I needed more information, like who this couple was. I headed for the doorway so I could secretly watch for them when they left and follow them to find out their cabin number. As I pushed my way through the revelers, I passed my old antagonist, Disco Ghost. Dressed in a fuchsia Aloha shirt with topless hula dancers, he reached out and grabbed my arm, almost knocking the champagne out of my hand.

I glared at him. "I'm in a hurry or I would break your arm for that. Get your damn hands off me."

He'd evidently had a few because he was swaying a bit, but not drunk enough to not understand that he was in imminent danger of bodily harm. His eyes went wide and he released me, raising his hand as he did.

"Sorry. Just got caught up in the moment and wanted to feel some flesh."

Not sorry enough, I decided. I didn't want the rest of my barely-touched champagne anyway, so I tossed it on one of his naked ladies. He gasped and stepped back, but wisely didn't say any more. As I turned and continued on my way, I planted the empty glass on a passing waiter's tray. I only wished I been drinking hot coffee again.

Chapter 47

I lurked near the door, watching the quintet surreptitiously. Mindy left first, fortunately heading away from my hiding place. The other four stayed for a while longer. The stunning Latina looked bored, having a couple of the specialty drinks as she gazed toward the departing shore. Finally she said something to her companion and they started my way. I turned to look at a diagram of the decks as they walked behind me. Since we had never met, I had no fear of them recognizing me, but didn't want to appear to be interested in them. I sauntered behind them, catching the same elevator. The man punched the button for deck 12, the next one down. I reached over as he was selecting his deck, then pulled back like I wanted the same one.

We all watched the doors as the elevator descended, the usual way to keep from acknowledging that anyone else was on the elevator. When the doors opened, I took a moment to look in my purse for my cabin key, then followed them out. I stopped at a cabin door and watched as they went to one of the owner's suites at the end of the corridor. After they went inside I checked out the number, 12502. It was next to Dave and Jennifer's cabin, which meant it was also near to Mindy's. While I could ask Mindy who they were, if she were involved with them in Bix's death, it would only tip my hand without getting the real story. Maybe Olav would give me some info on the occupants.

I looked for Olav for a while without any luck. I left a message with the purser that I needed to speak with him, but this time a young man I didn't know was manning the desk and did not show much interest in my request. I hesitated to say it was urgent since it wasn't. I didn't want to be the big girl who cried wolf. Tomorrow was a day at sea, so no one could escape until I got the info I requested from Olav. Maybe it would help me make some sense out of all this mess. I headed to the suite.

When I arrived, Heather was up. Dressed in a bathrobe, she was sipping a cup of coffee as she sat with legs curled under her on the sofa and looking out the large windows at the Sun Deck below. She turned to me.

"How's your neck?"

I self-consciously touched it, but felt no pain. "Fine. How's your head?

"My head?" She smiled. "Ah, the drinking. I stopped after you left and took a nap. I'm fine." She paused. "Not so sure about the others. Jennifer's still asleep and everyone else was gone when I woke up."

"So, everyone had a great time." I tried to act casual. "Was the whole gang there?"

"Yeah. Well, almost. Mindy decided to work out instead." She sipped her coffee. "She's such a fanatic. She's into that martial arts stuff like you are, too."

Hmmm. All the easier to knock you overboard, my dear. "I thought I saw her on deck for the sailing party and figured she must not have made the Señor Frog party." I hesitated, thinking of how to phrase my question without getting Heather suspicious. "Does she know anyone else on board. I mean, besides your Southern Belles."

"I don't think so. Why?"

I shrugged. "No reason. Idle curiosity. Since a lot of Bix's former clients are on the ship, I wondered if she knew them. It might help me learn more about them. Probably not, though."

Heather studied me. "Didn't you already ask her that?"

"I guess I did." I hoped that if Heather asked Mindy about knowing his clients she wouldn't mention I'd seen her. Time to change the subject. "I got a gift from someone. It was outside our door. Know anything about it?"

"No. Who was it from?"

"The note was unsigned. I'll show you."

I went into my room and retrieved the package and card. This time I used Kleenex when I handled it. Something was very wrong about this. I brought it back to the living room.

Heather reached for the package. "That's pretty."

I gently slapped her hand. "Look, but don't touch. At least until I've checked it out."

I got a knife from the kitchen and cut the ribbon, then used it and another knife to undo the wrapping paper. Next I opened the gold box with them. Inside was a perfect-looking chocolate truffle.

Again Heather reached for it. "That looks scrumptious. You're going to share, aren't you?"

Again I slapped her hand. "I will when I feel it's safe."

I carefully took the truffle out of the box with the Kleenex and looked it over. On the bottom, the smooth chocolate surface had a smear right in the center. I turned to Heather.

"Do you have any powder with a soft brush, like a compact?"

She seemed puzzled. "I have some foundation powder, great stuff. It's by Clé De Peau. Want to try some?"

"Please." I picked up the house phone and called room service. "Would you bring up some cocoa powder please?"

"You want a hot cocoa?"

"No, just the powder. Don't put it in milk."

"You want cocoa *powder*, not cocoa?" The man on the phone sounded confused.

"You got it. And a pair of latex gloves. Please send them up as soon as possible."

I hung up. I did not want to explain. Not my thing.

Heather was staring at me like I was from Mars. "What are you going to do with that?"

I smiled and used a wise-sensei-like voice. "Patience, Grasshopper. You will understand in time."

Heather rolled her eyes. "What are you trying to be? Yoda?"

"Not really. It's a phrase from a TV show from the 70's, *Kung Fu*."

"You weren't even alive then."

I slowly shook my head. "Ever hear of reruns?"

She threw up her hands. "Whatever. I never saw it. I'll go get the foundation powder." She paused as she was turning to go. "Just don't put any cocoa powder in it. Going blackface is not cool anymore."

"With cocoa powder, I think it would be brownface."

She rolled her eyes again. "Whatever."

Heather brought out a square compact that had a fine, wide brush and flesh-colored powder. I would have liked white, but it would do. Alasdair soon arrived with the gloves and cocoa powder. I put the powder in a saucer and donned the gloves before sitting at the table with the box in front of me. I picked up the truffle and gently brushed some of the foundation powder all over it. It covered the chocolate in a light beige. I studied it carefully, then set it down. Then I used the brush to apply the cocoa powder to the box, wrapping paper, ribbon, envelope and card. The brown powder revealed only what I knew was there. I realized Heather and Alasdair were on each side of me, looking over my shoulders as I sighed and set the brush down.

I leaned back in my chair. "Bummer."

Heather picked up the brush and studied it with a frown on her face. "Bummer what? Besides making a mess of my brush and your truffle, what were you doing?"

Alasdair patted my shoulder. "She was checking for fingerprints. Very ingenious. Did you find any?"

I shook my head. "I found fingerprints where I handled the package and the card, but nothing else. No doubt they're mine."

Eyeing her cocoa-coated brush, Heather frowned. "So you didn't find out who your secret admirer is and wasted my brush for nothing. " She looked down at the truffle. "Are you at least going to share that with me?"

"Not unless you want to be poisoned."

Chapter 48

Heather's eyes widened. "It's poisoned? How awful. How do you know that?"

"I don't for sure, but someone went to a lot of trouble to get rid of any fingerprints. That with the smudged chocolate on the bottom of the truffle that looks like someone messed with it and tried to hide it makes it very suspicious." I picked up the truffle and offered it to Heather. "Want to try it and find out?"

She backed away. "No way. What are you going to do with it now?'

I studied the truffle in my hand. "I guess save it until we get off the ship and have a lab test it."

Alasdair leaned over, looking at the truffle. "If it is acceptable with you, I would like to cut it in half. I will test it for poison, although I will not be able to tell you what kind. Then you can take it to a laboratory after we dock in San Pedro."

"How? Give it to a crewman you don't like and see if he survives?"

A smile tugged at the edges of Alasdair's mouth. "In a way, yes. One of the engine crew has a rat that he captured. For a few dollars, I'm sure he'll let me experiment with the little stowaway. But you must keep it hush-hush. The officers would get their knickers in a twist if they heard there was a live rat on board."

Heather gasped. "You get rats on the ship?" She nervously looked around. "Think there are any in here?"

Raising a calming hand, Alasdair shook his head. "I can assure you that you are quite safe from the little buggers. Very few get aboard and they are found most quickly. Any entry points are heavily covered with traps. That's how our test case was caught. He, or she, should have been exterminated immediately."

I set the truffle on the table. "Then let's give him a little treat and see what happens."

Heather calmed visibly and looked down at the truffle. "Well, if it is poison, at least he'll die happily. Everybody loves chocolate"

I chuckled. Leave it to Heather to find a silver lining to rodenticide.

After Alasdair left, I gathered up all the debris from the package and bagged it in one bag, the remaining half of the truffle in another and the note in a third to give to a lab for analysis when we returned to California. Heather cleaned her compact's brush at the sink, grumbling as she did.

"Hey, Heather, I'm sorry for messing up your brush, but I was hoping for some fingerprints to know who sent the truffle."

"It's okay." She studied the brush. "It looks like it will be fine."

"You know, I forgot the last names of uh . . . Sheri, Jan, Kathy and Linda." I said it as nonchalantly as I could. Fortunately, I had caught myself before I said Fireplug, Texas, Fullback and Scarecrow. "I remember one of them was the same as a cigarette and another was Smythe, not Smith, but I forgot who went with what name and the other two. Also, if you know their cabin numbers, that would be great, too." I could check out their names on Bix's computer, but I really wanted the cabin numbers for Olav to check on.

She eyed me suspiciously a moment before replying. "Like I told you already, it's Sheri Winston, Jan Cloutier, Kathy Smythe and Linda Walters. Why do you want their cabin numbers?"

I hesitated. "Oh I don't know. Maybe in case I want to invite them to coffee, or have a drink." Lame, I knew.

Heather put her hands on her hips. "You'd rather eat a bat than go anywhere with them. Spill."

I sighed. "Alright. I'm getting a readout of when everyone who might have a reason for bumping off Bix used the key for their cabins late Monday night and early Tuesday morning. Just don't make me go out for a drink with them." I grimaced. "Or eat a bat."

"Well, I don't think they had anything to do with it, so I'll give you their numbers to prove it." She took a piece of ship's stationery and wrote them on it, then handed it to me. "Are you checking me out too?"

I took the paper and looked at her askance. "Sure. The person who is afraid of spiders is going to off some guy for no reason. Plus I was here with you."

She shrugged. "I'm not afraid of spiders. I just . . . have a healthy respect for them."

I grinned. "Riiight."

There was a knock at the door and I answered. Alasdair stood with a grim expression. Without a word, he walked past me and looked around the suite. Then he turned to me.

"You haven't let anyone in here since I left, have you?"

"No. It's just the two of us still. Why?'

"The rat died."

I started to make some smart-ass comment about at least it wasn't the rabbit, but Alasdair's worried expression made me change my mind. "So someone tried to kill me. Unless there was enough to kill the rat but not me. I weigh a little more." I looked down at my stomach. "Especially after this cruise."

Heather came up and wrapped her arms around me from behind. "This is not funny Morg Mahoney. Someone's trying to kill you and it's all my fault for getting you involved in all this." She looked over at Alasdair. "Did you tell the captain? Does he still think she's wrong about Bix's death?"

"I don't know, but he's informed security about the poison and Olav will be here soon." He looked uneasy. "The captain has told me to tell you that you are not to do any more investigation. It's too dangerous."

I pulled away from Heather before turning. "Sorry, but danger is my middle name." Trite, I knew, but I liked it. "Besides, now it's personal. While I wasn't a big fan of Bix and wasn't that upset that he died, I get a little angry when anyone tries to kill me."

Heather gave me that look. "Morg, don't you think you should—"

But she was interrupted as the door flew open and Thor stormed in, followed by another Norseman in a white uniform. The other fellow was red-headed and shorter, but his biceps were actually bigger than Thor's. Thor's eyes flashed with anger that changed to concern.

"What happened, Morg Mahoney? Are you okay?"

I shrugged. "Some idiot tried to poison me, but it didn't work." I patted my chest. "See? Still alive and kicking."

"We will protect you." He gestured toward the redhead. "Svein will stay with you for the rest of the cruise."

I waved him off. "I don't need a bodyguard. I can take care of myself." I paused. "Besides, all bedrooms are occupied."

His chin jutted forward. "He will stay with you. He will use the sofa. And the captain wants the sweet that is poisoned."

First he doesn't believe me and now he wants the evidence? Hah! "Eric the Red can sleep on the couch, but I'm keeping my truffle. Got it?"

Olav looked abashed. "I . . . I will tell the captain. I must go now. I am to investigate who tried to kill you." He pointed at the redhead. "His name is Svein, not Eric." He paused and grinned. "Ha! Eric the Red. That was a joke. Very funny."

"Before you go, I've got a few more cabins to add to the list I gave you." I quickly added the cabin for the drug lord to it. Well, possible drug lord. Then I handed it to Olav. "I don't know the name of who is in the last cabin number, so I would greatly appreciate it if you would give me that with where they live."

He studied the list a moment before answering. "You think one of them killed Mr. Maudlin and tried to kill you?"

"I really do. I believe it was one or more of the ones on the first list I gave you or of these. I'm only guessing at this point, but knowing when these people went in and out of their rooms would be a big help to know who is guilty."

He folded the paper and slipped it in his shirt pocket, tapping it afterwards. "I will have this for you in a few hours."

Chapter 49

After Olav and Alasdair left, I sat at the table with my truffle half. Wearing my gloves again, I carefully took it out and studied it. With the latest information from Alasdair, I could see that the bottom had been cut out and put back on, hence the smudging to hide the fact. Cut in half, it showed a dark chocolate filling. But something looked off.

"Heather, could I borrow your reading glasses?"

Most people didn't know she had reading glasses since she wore contacts with one lens for distance and one for reading. Her vision was so bad she still struggled to read menus, so often she had the waiter suggest something or her date order for her to cover. But I knew.

Heather glanced over at Svein, who was sitting on the couch, but he didn't seem to have heard. "I'll get them. Just keep your voice down."

I shook my head. Vanity, thy name is Heather.

When she returned with them, I put them on to study the truffle. Since the lenses are strong, they were like a magnifying glass when I put them low on my nose. I could see white specks in the chocolate. I returned the truffle to the bag and leaned back in my chair."

Heather was looking over my shoulder. "Well? See anything interesting?"

"I can't know for sure by looking, but I'd guess either strychnine or cyanide. I'll have to wait for a lab test to know."

Her eyes went wide. "Where would anyone get that?" She put her hand to her lips. "Was it one of those professional hit men? Like a John Wick? Oh, Morg, did he kill Bix and now there is a contract out on you?"

"I'd be dead if John were after me." I chuckled. "He's way above my pay grade. No, about anyone can get poisons online. Even on eBay."

"Then who would give you a poisoned truffle? Is it because you know who killed Bix? Did the killer want to shut you up before you could tell?" She grabbed my shoulders, staring into my eyes. "Who did it?"

Before I had a chance to say I didn't know, the door to our suite suddenly opened and Mindy walked in. Svein sprang like a watchdog and was at the door before I could react, blocking her entrance.

She held up her hands. "Whoa, big guy. It's just little ol' Mindy. I'm here to see if they want to go to dinner."

He glanced back at me and I nodded that she was okay before he let her pass. She walked over to the table and looked down at the truffle.

"A little before dinner snack?" She eyed my waistline. "Don't you think you should watch the sweets?"

Heather let go of my shoulders and stepped in front of me. "Back off, Mindy. It's poisoned. Someone tried to kill Morg to keep her quiet and she's figuring out who."

"But she survived." Mindy raised an eyebrow. "And who did it?"

I studied her. "I've got a couple of ideas, but nothing I can prove yet."

Heather brandished the plastic bag with the gift card. "All we know for sure is that he or she sent it with this card."

Mindy took it and studied the card for a few moments before speaking. "Huh. No name on it?"

I shook my head. "Just what you see."

She tapped the card against her other hand, looking closely at me, then handed it back to me. "Not much to go on, is it?"

"Not much." I took the card. There was something missing from the table. "By the way, did you take Bix's computer?"

She shrugged. "What if I did? It's community property. Why are you asking about it?"

"I think this tale of the tainted truffle will get whatever authority's in charge to take another look at Bix's death. I'd like to take a look again before we get back home."

"Sure, sure." She gave a dismissive wave of her hand before looking at her watch. "I made reservations at Rick's at six. I made them for eight of us, but Linda, Kathy and Jan said they're not feeling great. Sheri's in the same suite as Jan and I guess she's snoring like a congested hippo. Is Jennifer here?" She scanned the room.

I stifled a laugh. While I wasn't sure how a congested hippo sounded, I liked the analogy.

Heather headed for Jennifer's room. "I'll see if she wants to go with us."

She returned in a minute. "She's not coming. I think she has what Linda, Kathy and Jan have." She paused dramatically before continuing with a grin. "Margarita-itis."

Mindy snorted with disgust. "Well, we'd better go if we don't want to miss our reservation."

As we headed to the door, I was at the tail of our group and Svein was right behind me. Mindy glanced back at him.

"Is he coming?" She sneered at me. "You think you need a bodyguard just to go to dinner?"

Heather dropped back and looped her arm through his. "He's my date." She gave Mindy a hard look. "Any problems?"

She shrugged. "I guess not, as long as I'm not paying for his dinner."

When we got to Rick's, Youssef ushered us to our table. He wore a double-breasted white dinner jacket, black bow tie and no fez. Not only that, he had shaved off his mustache. After we were seated and he handed us our menus, he took our drink orders. He gave me a Bogart smile, which wasn't as much a big smile as curling back his top lip against his teeth so that they showed.

"When I heard you were coming tonight, Sweetheart, I got dressed up."

I assumed my best Ingrid Bergman-as-Ilsa voice. "A franc for your thoughts, Rick."

He pulled a silver cigarette case out of his jacket pocket, opened it and took out an unfiltered cigarette, putting in his mouth without lighting it. "Of all the gin joints, in all ships, in all the world, she walks into mine."

Without another word, he turned and walked away, his right hand casually slipped into his trousers' pocket.

I laughed, but noticed the other two women were looking at me like I had been speaking in Arabic. Svein had no reaction, but was slowly sipping his water as he scanned the room.

I sighed. "We were doing lines from *Casablanca*. He was doing Rick and I was doing Ilsa. This place was named after Rick's Café Américain from the movie."

Heather turned to Mindy. "It's an old movie Morg likes."

Mindy glared at her. "You told me before, remember? Since I've never watched it, I had no idea what that was all about." She gave me a sidelong glance. "And I can't say I really care."

Cocking her head, Heather looked nonplused. "That's harsh."

"Sorry." She shrugged. "I'm just getting weirded out with this whole trip. I mean, first Bix was killed and then someone tries to poison your friend. It was supposed to be a fun reunion. Instead, I'm having dinner with only one of my sisters, a Wonder Woman wannabe, and The Norwegian Hulk."

If that was an apology, I missed it. Svein appeared unphased, his eyes roving the restaurant as he sipped his water. Maybe he liked being called The Hulk. Maybe he had no idea what Mindy was saying.

Heather drew back and stared at her. "What's with the bitch mode?"

Mindy raised her hands in surrender. "Sorry. I'm getting bummed out and need to vent. But I'll be little Miss Sunshine for the rest of the dinner. Promise." She crossed her heart with her index finger.

The drinks arrived and I sipped my Jameson and Heather her chardonnay. Mindy knocked back her vodka martini in a few minutes, then waved the waiter over for another. She caught Heather and my surprised looks and gave a weak smile.

"I guess it's all finally hitting me. Bix and all. But a couple of drinks will lighten my mood."

Heather raised an eyebrow. "Whatever works."

But her three martinis didn't work. Our conversation was desultory, with Mindy saying little. She seemed to find her martini glass very interesting, spending most of the evening studying it. When our dinners were served, she poked at hers like a kid with cold oatmeal. Heather tried to enliven things, but failed. Only Svein looked like he was enjoying the meal, probably much better food than he was normally served aboard. We didn't linger for dessert.

Chapter 50

As we walked out of Rick's, I smiled at Youssef and he returned his Bogart-style one.

"We'll always have Cabo, Sweetheart."

I tried to sound like Ilsa. "Here's looking at you, Kid."

That was Rick's line, of course, but it got a laugh from Youssef and lightened my mood. When the four of us got to the elevator, Mindy pushed the button for the deck two below our suite and turned to us.

"I'll get Bix's computer and bring it up to you in a few."

Heather gave her a smile. "Great. We can have a drink and relax. I can order some hors d'oeuvres. Or maybe dessert."

Mindy shook her head. "I'm not in the mood right now. I'm going to work out."

"I can be ready in a few minutes and join you. I need to work out, too."

She shook her head again. "I'd rather be alone right now."

Heather looked hurt. "Sure. Whatever you want."

After Mindy got off, we continued to our suite in silence. Once inside, Svein planted himself on one of the barstools that had a view of the entry door. Heather paced the kitchen.

"I don't understand it. Mindy was fine earlier today. What could be the problem?"

"I don't know." I picked up the note from the truffle box. "It was after I got the truffle. She didn't seem to want to let go of this card."

Heather looked over my shoulder, then grabbed the card. "I don't believe it." She went into her bedroom and returned with a piece of paper. She handed both to me. "Mindy gave this to me Wednesday. What do you think?"

It said, "Meet at the gym at 7? M." It was in a flowing script that looked a lot like the truffle card, especially the capital M's.

I whistled softly. "Very interesting. I need to think about this."

"Do you think—"

Heather was interrupted by a knock on the door. Svein sprang up and answered it. It was Mindy. I went to the door.

She handed me the laptop. "Here. Give it back to me when you finish."

Without waiting for a response, she turned to go. The door to the other suite opened and Rex came out. Nurse Bimbo came to the door and stood there, her face contorted in anger.

"I told you that I'm not interested. It's time for you to go. Now."

He put his hands on his hips, speaking in a snarl. "Well, have it your way. But you still have to pay me for what we did for you."

"Fine. Give me the total bill and I'll pay the whole thing. Happy?"

His hands dropped to his sides and his tone softened. "Look, Darla, can't we just—"

Before he finished what he was about to say, she slammed the door shut. He turned and jolted when he saw we had heard everything. Then he strode to the elevator as if nothing had happened.

Mindy stood just outside the door, not moving.

I cleared my throat. "You okay?"

She shook her head. "Yeah. Fine." She turned back to me and hesitated. "Uh, just feeling a little funny. Mind if I get a glass of water?"

"Sure." I stepped aside.

As she walked by the dining table, she stopped and steadied herself by leaning her hand on it.

Heather rushed to her, putting her arm around Mindy's shoulders. "Are you okay? Want me to take you to the doctor?"

Mindy straightened up and shrugged off Heather's arm. "I'm fine now. Just a momentary thing." She turned back toward the door and started toward it.

"Are you sure?" Heather gave her a concerned look. "I'd be glad to go to the doctor with you."

"I'm fine. I'll see you later," she said as she waved with one hand and slipped the other into her pants pocket.

Once she left, I closed the door. Being the suspicious type, I went to the table to check on the truffle and note which were close to where she had rested her hand. They were still there. Still, she had acted oddly. With a shrug, I put the computer on the table. Then I sat, opened it and turned it on. After it booted up, a quick scan of the files confirmed my suspicion.

As I leaned back in my chair, Heather tapped my shoulder. "Well? What do you think?"

Although she hadn't completed her question before Mindy's arrival, I knew what it was. Had Mindy written the note with the truffle and, therefore, tried to poison me.

I leaned over with my elbows on the table, interlaced my fingers together, and rested my chin on them as I stared at the list of files. "I don't know, but it doesn't look good. There was a letter from Bix to Mindy. Bix wrote that he loved her and would never give her a divorce."

"That's not good, is it?"

"It's worse than not good. The letter was deleted while Mindy had the computer."

"You mean . . . oh." Heather went to the bar and pulled a bottle of chardonnay out of the wine cooler. "I'm not ready to think of her as a killer. A killer who tried to kill my best friend. I need a drink." She poured herself a full glass and took a healthy swig before sitting at the table with me. 'What are you going to do?"

"Nothing yet." I turned off the computer and closed it. "Having a note in what looks like Mindy's handwriting and a love letter deleted that only I saw is hardly proof. I need more." I remembered something Father Tim had told me. "Do you know Mindy's email address?"

"Just a sec."

She went into her bedroom and returned with her iPad. After a couple of minutes on it, she handed it to me and pointed at an email. It was from **mlhawthorne1620@gmail.com**. "Mindy's maiden name is Minden Laura Hawthorne, after her grandmother."

"And the 1620 is because she had an ancestor on the Mayflower." I stood and went to the bar, pouring myself a Jameson.

Heather set her tablet on the table. "That's important, isn't it?"

I nodded without a comment, then sipped my drink. "Why?"

"Because people who lost money with Bix got an email with the subject 'Bilked by Bix' from that address that said he was going to be on this cruise. I don't know all who got it or how many of those came on this cruise because of it, but I know at least two did."

She collapsed on a dining chair. "So Mindy was setting Bix up to be killed by sending that to people who hated him. And one of them killed him."

"Possibly."

She looked up at me, pleading in her eyes. "But she didn't use them as a cover to kill him herself, did she?"

"Possibly."

She buried her face in her hands. "I wish I'd never come on this cruise."

I sipped my drink. "Ditto here."

Chapter 51

While Heather took her third glass of wine out on the private deck, I stayed at the table with a pen and pad of paper, writing down everything I knew about Bix, Mindy and anyone else who had a reason to make him disappear. I included everything I'd seen or heard. That was a lot. Before long I had several handwritten pages. Then I leaned back and reread what I had written, mulling over each point. But I had no provable conclusion.

My reverie was interrupted by a knock at the door. It took Svein a moment to rise and go to the door. I wondered if he might have been dozing. It was nearing ten.

Olav came in and handed me a few sheets of paper. "These are the times when the people you wanted me to check on went into their cabins with a key."

I did a quick scan of the information. "What does one or two mean?"

"Key card one or two for the cabin opened the door. I do not know who had which card."

I gave him my most winning smile. "Thanks. This should help a lot. No luck on when the rain hit Tuesday morning?"

"I am still working on when the . . . squaw-all came." He cocked his head. "Did I say that right?"

"Just great." I looked down at the sheets. "I'd better get on this."

He backed toward the door. "Let me know if I can help with anything else."

I nodded, already finding some interesting data.

After he left, Svein double-checked the door before settling on the couch. He looked tired. Unfortunately for him, I was a night owl and was finally able to crunch some important numbers. He would have to tolerate me tonight.

After a while, Heather came inside, mumbled something about bed and headed for her bedroom with a little stagger to her step. I waved goodnight before getting back to circling important numbers. The Gang of Four looked like they were all in the clear since none of them used their keys to enter their rooms after two in the morning. As expected, the Baron and the Prince opened their door at 3:46, using key number one. Jerry Steele or his missus opened theirs at 2:58 with key number two, too early if Bix went overboard at 3:17, but interesting. What were one or both of them doing out so late? However, the last four on the list were even more interesting.

Key two had opened Bix and Mindy's door at 2:25 and at 3:46. The first time was when Alasdair took her to her cabin, but the second time? Key one had opened Dave and Jennifer's door at 3:45. Odd. Why had someone opened the door at that hour? Key one had opened Rex and Billy's cabin at 3:31. Possibly bumping off Bix was part of what he'd been hired to do. That needed more investigation. Key one had opened 12502 at 3:51, the suite of Ernesto and Julia Ortega of Torrey Pines, California.

I softly whistled. Although I don't keep up on the real estate market, since I don't have enough money to buy anything in Southern California, even I knew Torrey Pines to be among the most expensive communities in the San Diego area, even the whole state. It's famous for great coastal views, stunning golf courses and homes starting at a million dollars. If you'll settle for a townhouse with no view. But then, drug lords have lots of ready cash. However, being a wealthy Latino is no indication of nefarious dealings, much less involvement in the drug trade, any more than being Italian is indicative of being in the Mafia. They were both nasty stereotypes and I would never have thought that way if not for what Bix had told FP and the Baron about making a drug deal and me seeing him with Ortega the night he disappeared. I needed to dig deeper.

The Internet is like The Force in the Star Wars saga: a neutral power, with the ability to be used either for good or evil. Although those who feel privacy is sacrosanct, something that should not be violated no matter what the stakes, might consider some programs I use to be evil, I only use them for what I consider good. However, my travel tablet does not have most of those programs since the authorities would take a dim view of them if it were ever inspected.

One I did have could do sort of a reverse search of California corporations where I could find out if a person was an officer in any corporation or partnership. Since it basically hacked into the California Secretary of State's data base, it wasn't really legal to use. I had done so when on a case that took me to the Silicon Valley in pursuit of a pervert who made kiddie porn and had forgotten to take it off my tablet. I entered the names of Ernesto and Julia Ortega individually, then looked for companies that had both of them listed. It was a common practice for a husband and wife to both be officers on closely-held corporations and partnerships.

I sipped my Jameson while I waited. After about fifteen minutes, I hit paydirt. There were three Limited Liability Corporations and one Limited Liability Partnership. The partners on the LLP were one of the LLCs and an Ortega Family Trust. From the filings, the LLC that was a partner in the LLP listed its type of business as "real estate investments." The other two LLCs listed "business investments" as their activity.

My program also let me search all county records in California for property owned by an entity, the LLP in this instance. That would take longer to run, but I sent it off like a hound following a scent. I had some time, so I decided to talk to someone who liked me and had nothing to do with the Greek reunion. Since my computer was occupied and I did not want to slow it down, I picked up my cell and went to my contacts, selecting the one I wanted. Although it was late, I needed to chat. He answered on the second ring.

"St. Nicholas rectory, Father Bruce speaking."

"Hey, there. Did I wake you?"

"No, I had to get up to answer the phone anyway." He hesitated a moment and sighed. "Just kidding. I just got in a few minutes ago from a nursing home. I've been with a dear lady from the church every night this week. This was the last one, though. She died from cancer tonight."

Guilt slammed me like a punch to the gut. When he hadn't answered his phone on Wednesday night and I'd been hit with a twinge of jealousy, I'd hoped he'd been visiting a sick parishioner instead of out with someone else. Now I found that he had been with a parishioner and she died. Be careful what you hope for.

"I'm so sorry, Robert. It must have been hard. Did she have any family?"

"No, Violet was an only child. Her husband died a couple of decades ago and they had no children." He paused. "She was ready to go. The fight against the cancer wore her down. It had gone into remission after chemo, but came back with a vengeance. Before she passed she told me, 'I'm tired, Father. I want to go now and see Jesus and Daniel.' That was her husband. Then she asked me to pray for her. I said the prayer for a person near death from the Ministration at the Time of Death in the Book of Common Prayer. She died while I was saying it. It was peaceful. I finished the service alone. She would have wanted that." His voice had cracked and he paused again. "I'm sorry to be such a downer. Why did you call? You're on a cruise with Heather, aren't you?"

My problems seemed trivial now compared with Robert's. I hadn't even liked Bix. "Yeah, I'm on a cruise. I just had a question, but it wasn't important."

"It is to me. Look, I was feeling very low after tonight, even though I know everything ended as Violet wanted. It's the hardest on those left behind and I guess I'm the only one she left behind. But hearing your voice is a big help. Please, I want to talk to you right now. What can I do to help you?"

I hesitated. I had previously given him advice when he had looked into suspicious deaths in his parish that he had gone on to solve. He had a sharp mind. But how could I explain all that had happened in the last few days succinctly?

I took a deep breath. "Well, something happened on Tuesday. It looks like the husband of one of Heather's friends was murdered, shoved overboard. I've been investigating. There's way too much to go into on this phone call, but I have a theory based upon everything I've seen and everything people have said. But it's like I'm putting together a puzzle and some of the pieces just don't fit. Normally, I look at physical evidence for that, but there really isn't any. I've come up with a theory, but with no proof. I'm wondering if I'm right. I really don't know what to do next."

Okay, that was very vague. What else could I add? If I was right, I could do a dramatic revelation like a Miss Marple mystery. If I was wrong, I would look the fool and maybe have far worse consequences, like a lawsuit that would break me. Tough choice.

Robert was silent. I began to wonder if I had been disconnected when he finally spoke.

"Morg, you helped me with your insight when I wasn't sure about murders in my small town. What you've told me obviously isn't enough to help in the same way, but you're having self-doubts. In that, I can help. You are the most intelligent person I have ever met and you have great instincts. My advice is to go with your gut." He paused. "And if you're wrong, don't blame me. But I will give you a job here in Buggy Springs as the church secretary."

I stifled a laugh. "If I became your church secretary, the bishop would excommunicate you. But you've made up my mind."

"Are you sure I've helped? I didn't say anything profound."

"You definitely helped. Now get some sleep."

"Well, if you're sure I can't give some real help, I'll do just that. I'm wiped out. Good night, Morg."

"Good night, Robert. Sleep tight."

After he disconnected, I stared at my phone. I had one more thing to say. "I think I love you."

Chapter 52

My results for the property search had come in. The LLP owned property in San Diego, Venice Beach and San Jose. A quick search on Google showed they were office buildings. Not high rises, but not strip malls. If there had been a warehouse in San Ysidro, a place that could have a convenient tunnel to Mexico and store drugs, I would have been very suspicious. The buildings the LLP owned would provide a nice income, but did not look like candidates for drug trafficking or money laundering.

The other two LLCs were for a cosmetic company that was headed by the former model Julia E and a company that recycled dental gold. My guess was that Julia E was now Julia Ortega. As far as I knew, recycling dental gold was not normally a way to launder drug money, but tracing whether gold was from dental scrap or other sources might be a laundering opportunity. I could find nothing to tell me except that dental gold was 10 to 18 carat and would need refining to be used for other purposes. Not much help.

I tried a web search of Ernesto Ortega, but there were far too many results to check out in a reasonable time. It was far too common a name. Adding Torrey Pines to the search didn't help. I found no usable data.

I was considering my next step when I heard a soft knock at the door. I had thought Svein was asleep, but he sprang up and went to the door. He stooped down and picked up a paper, then handed it to me. He opened the door and looked around, then closed it and gave me a shrug. No one was there.

I unfolded the paper. It said, "Rain started after 0245 was over before 0300. I can not find any better information. Olav"

I sat at the table and picked up my glass, taking a drink. So it definitely wasn't a suicide. I realized why the pieces of the puzzle did not seem to work together. Two puzzles were thrown together to be confusing. But I had the key pieces for the real puzzle and saw how they fit. There were some important details I didn't know yet, however I hoped I could figure them out if I confronted the killer. It wasn't going to be easy, but I had to get the captain to go along with me. If I was right, it would all be solved in the morning.

"Svein, I'm going to bed. Would you like a blanket and pillow?"

He shook his head, then laid on the couch with his head on the arm. "I am fine. It is warm in here."

Those were the first words he had spoken to me. I had almost thought he was a mute. He had a resonant bass voice with a Norwegian accent, but was very understandable. It took me a moment to recover from my surprise and respond.

"Well, if you want anything, let me know or go ahead and get it for yourself."

"I will be fine."

I wished I could do something to make him comfortable, but he did not want me to. I turned out the lights as I went into my bedroom. It was after one in the morning. I should go to Mass in the morning with Father Tim and the ladies, but I was exhausted both physically and mentally. I set my phone to wake me at nine. I didn't want to sleep too late. It was time to wrap this case up.

Friday

Chapter 53

When my phone alarm went off, I jerked awake. It took me a moment to orient myself to where I was. I slowly crawled out of bed and headed for the shower. I needed to be alert for the coming events. Once dressed in my nautical white trousers and blue and white horizontally striped knit blouse, I went out to the kitchen. Svein was up, of course. He had red stubble and his white uniform was rumpled. I gave him a smile.

"Why don't you use my bathroom? You can take a shower and use one of my razors. Sorry that they're pink, but a razor is a razor, no matter what color."

He shook his head. "I am to make sure you are safe."

"I won't open the door for anyone." I looked around. "I assume Heather and Jennifer are already gone, so it's just the two of us. Or you could call Olav and have him relieve you. I need to talk to him anyway."

Svein pulled out a small walkie talkie and had a conversation in Norwegian. Then he turned to me.

"Olav will be here in a few minutes. I will leave then." He sniffed under his arms and grimaced. "I do need a shower."

"Yeah, you do." I laughed. "Just kidding. You're fine. And I appreciate you staying here last night."

He grinned. "I was happy to guard you. But do not get too close or you will faint."

After Olav arrived and Svein left, I made a cup of coffee and set out to win Olav to my plan.

"I need you to convince the captain that we need to make Jerry Steele talk to me. I can almost guarantee it will solve this whole mess and you'll have your killer."

He looked dubious. "You say 'almost guarantee.' But that is not the same as guarantee, is it?"

I was pleading, but I had to get him to help me. "No, I can't totally guarantee it. However, I've worked it out and my idea fits perfectly with everything that happened and what people have said. Nothing else does. Sherlock Holmes said, 'Once you eliminate the impossible, whatever remains, no matter how improbable, must be the truth.' Every other solution is impossible when you look at the whole picture. It is what Sherlock would say. Trust me."

"Sherlock Holmes agrees with you?" He pondered that, then gave a quick nod. "I will go with you to the captain. We will talk to him."

I had hoped that Olav would handle it without me since I wasn't even supposed to be working on the case, but beggars can't be choosers. Maybe almost being killed myself would give me some credibility. I finished my coffee in a gulp. "God hates a coward. Let's go see the captain."

As we exited the suite, the housekeeper was opening the door of Jerry Steele's suite. We headed for the elevator, but were stopped in our tracks by a shrill scream. I spun around to see the housekeeper backing out of the door, hands clamped over her mouth.

With the speed of Thor, Olav was at her side. She pointed mutely at something inside the suite, her eyes as wide as an ostrich's. By that time, I had reached them and looked at where she was pointing.

Chapter 54

Like my suite, the door opened to a hallway with a wall three feet away. Olav and I stepped inside. From there, we could see the living room. There weren't any bodies, but a couple of chairs at the table were knocked over and a glass-top of an end table was shattered. More importantly, there were splotches of dark red all over the blue carpet, with a couple of very large ones. Cautiously, we crept up the hallway to the room.

I knelt at the biggest splotch of red, about three feet at its widest, and touched the edge and then the center of it. The edge was crispy, but the center was still wet. I sniffed it. There was a metallic odor to it. I stood, took a tissue out of my pocket with my clean hand and wiped it off. It was too bad I hadn't gone back for my latex gloves, but I'd wash my hands when I finished.

Olav looked at me questioningly. "Is it blood?"

I nodded. Then I stooped again, studying a full bottle of champagne, with the cork and foil still on it, lying by the splotch. There was blood on it. There was blood splatter on a nearby wall and on the floor. It was safe to assume the bottle had been used as a weapon.

The room was very warm, but the glass door to the deck was propped open with a chair. There were a few bloody footprints as well, two different sets. One was bare feet and looked like a man's. The other ones were from what looked like athletic shoes, probably a woman's from their size. A trail of blood led from the pool of blood out the open door to the private deck. Edging past the trail, I went out on the deck. There was dried blood on the solid railing as well.

Olav followed me out, looking stunned. "What happened? Did the wife kill the man in the wheelchair?"

I mulled over what I had seen. "No, a third person killed them, then tossed the bodies overboard."

"The same person who killed Mr. Maudlin?"

I shook my head. "I very much doubt it. Two different people killed Bix and Jerry Steele." I paused. "You'd better let the captain know."

"Yes, yes." He grabbed his walkie-talkie and started speaking in Norwegian.

I slipped back inside. I checked the three bedrooms, using my tissue to open the doors. The bed in the master bedroom had been used, but none of the others. I went into the master bedroom.

The bathroom had all the normal makeup a woman would ever want, plus some. The only men's toiletries were an electric razor, a comb and deodorant. The clothes in the closet were almost all a woman's. A woman with very slutty taste, in my opinion. The few men's clothes were fitting for Dr. Strangelove: dark, long-sleeved shirts and trousers. The black shawl was on one hanger and the black floppy fedora and gloves were on a shelf above. So much for tropical wear for him. Also on the shelf above was a large box. I took another couple of tissues out of my pocket and brought it down, setting it on top of a trash can.

The box itself was basically a cube of about twelve inches. There was a mailing label from "*crea fx*" with an address in Firenze, Italia. It was addressed to Frank Abagnale at a P.O. Box in Sacramento. The name was familiar, but I couldn't place where I'd heard it. I opened it. Inside was a Styrofoam faceless head like wigs are stored on. Nothing else. Interesting.

Leaving the box, I checked the nightstands. Except for a pair dark sunglass, a tube of K-Y gel and a box of tissues, there was nothing of note on one of them. The other had something far more interesting. It was a white bottle with a blue cap like for vitamins or medicine, but it was neither. This was from a chemical company and the label said it was potassium cyanide. It wasn't the rat poison available on eBay or Amazon. It was serious poison normally seen only in laboratories. But with enough money, it could probably be found on the dark web. And it was in the master bedroom nightstand. Very interesting.

Using a tissue from the nightstand I picked it up and put it on top of the box from the closet. Both of these needed further investigation. I sensed someone behind me and turned. Olav was standing in the doorway.

"We must leave now. The captain has sent for the United States Coast Guard to investigate. He does not want us to touch anything."

I held up my index finger. "Just let me take a few photos."

He shrugged. Be very quick. I do not want to get in more trouble."

I went through the suite, snapping photos of everything I thought might be important. I looked longingly at the box and bottle that I knew I couldn't take with me. It galled me that I had to leave physical evidence there and I had to leave without a thorough search. I wasn't sure how expert the Coast Guard was in crime scene investigation either, but I didn't have much choice.

Olav came to my side and reached out his hand. "Come. We must leave."

With a sigh, I followed him out of the suite, careful to avoid stepping on any spots or spatters on the carpet. Once we were outside the door, we found the housekeeper still standing there.

From her appearance, I assumed she was Filipino like most of the workers. She was only about five feet tall and very thin, with grey-streaked black hair pulled back into a bun. While she no longer was panicking, she still looked shaken.

Olav gently patted her shoulder and looked down at her. "How are you feeling?"

She looked up at him blankly.

I raised an eyebrow. "I don't think she understands you." I smiled at her. "*Hablas español?*"

She shook her head.

Since I only knew a smattering of Spanish, it wouldn't have been that great of a help is she did. I turned back to Olav. "I don't suppose you speak Tagalog."

He looked at me quizzically. "I do not know what Tagalog is."

"It's one of the main languages of the Philippines. So is English, but in some back areas it's not spoken. Maybe a quarter of the population doesn't understand it. Unfortunately, I don't speak Tagalog either." I looked into the woman's eyes and pointed at her chest. "You okay?"

She smiled a little and nodded. She probably had a smattering of English words she understood.

Olav smiled at her. "Good." He pointed at the door to the suite. "Don't do any cleaning in there. Okay?"

She gave a little shrug and shook her head, not understanding.

Olav spoke slowly and a little louder, still pointing. "No clean, okay? No clean."

Her eyes widened a little and she shrugged again. "Okay."

He turned to me and took a breath. "Now we go to the captain and you can tell him what happened to Mr. Maudlin. Then maybe he will have you help find out what happened to Mr. Steele and his wife."

It was no longer the time to talk to the captain. I needed to figure out these latest murders, which I was sure they were. I had an idea, a very good idea, what happened, but I needed some more information before I could lay it before the captain. I checked my watch. It was almost ten.

"Looks like that will have to wait. I have a meeting with some friends at ten and I can't miss it."

He gave me a strange look. "Should we not see the captain first?"

"I'd love to, but I can't keep my friends waiting. I headed for the elevator with Olav following. As we got inside and I pushed the button, I saw the housekeeper talking on her walkie-talkie.

Chapter 55

When I got to O'Malley's, it was just past ten. the Regulars were already there and seated at a table. I sat down, wishing for another cup of coffee. Since the bar wasn't open yet, there wasn't any chance of that. Father Tim, dressed in black with his clerical collar, was holding a paper cup. The ladies were in flowered blouses, Lillian in pink and Judith in red. Or so I assumed.

Father Tim smiled at me. "We missed you at Mass."

Guilt washed over me like the California surf. "I should have been there." I hesitated. "There's been an unexpected development. It looks like Jerry Steele and Darla Darling were killed this morning."

Father Tim jerked like he'd been slapped, spilling his tea. The ladies gasped almost in unison.

Judith leaned forward. "What happened?"

Still missing my coffee, I explained the events of the morning as quickly as I could through many interruptions. When I finished, we sat a few moments in silence. Finally Judith spoke.

"So, you think it was the same killer who offed Bix?"

"No. I think I've pretty much figured out what happened to Bix, Jerry and Darla, but I have no way of proving it." I tapped my index finger on the table, thinking. "When you were in the suite with Darla, when you went to talk to Jerry, Rex grabbed your arm and stopped you?"

Judith rubbed her upper right arm. "Sure did. I've still got the bruise. Want to see?"

I shook my head. "No, I believe you."

"Is it important?"

I smiled ruefully. "Just another piece of the puzzle that I now see where it goes."

Father Tim set his tea on the table. "What can we do to help?"

"Right now, nothing." I stood. "I'll let you know if you can. There are a couple of people I need to interview."

Lillian rested her hand on mine. "Do be careful, dear. Will we meet at three today?"

"Sure." Why not? Even if it had nothing to do with the case anymore, I enjoyed the company of the O'Malley's Pub Regulars.

On the way back to the suite, I saw Olav ahead of me and called to him. "Hey, Olav, how was the meeting."

He turned and stopped. He looked like a scolded puppy. "It did not go well. I told the captain what we saw and that I thought you could help. He said to keep you away from everything. He is so unhappy with all these people dying he might dismiss me."

That rubbed my nose in the kitty litter. I felt like going to the captain and telling him that he was a big horse's patootie. However, that would get Olav fired for sure. No, I needed to end this case before the Coast Guard arrived. I grabbed his arm of steel.

"Can you get Rex Martin and Billy Wilder into some sort of an interview room?"

"Why?"

"Because we are going to give this case all solved to the captain, wrapped up with a big red bow."

He stepped back. "The captain said the United States Coast Guard was to handle it." He paused. "I do not think the captain even likes red bows."

"Then we'll make it blue. Just set up a meeting and scare the crap out of those two when you to take them to it."

He looked at me like I was loco. Maybe I was. But he nodded, his chin jutting forward. "Why not? If I lose my position it will not be because I did not try to do my job." He thought a moment. "Meet me in the Stockholm Room on deck 12. It is being remodeled and no one will be there." He pulled a ring of keys out of his pocket, took one off and handed it to me. "I will find them and bring them there." He grinned. "I will not be gentle." Then he hurried away.

I whistled tunelessly as I headed to the Stockholm Room. I had unleashed Thor on Rex and Billy. God help them if they resisted.

Chapter 56

Olav was right about the remodeling. It was dark when I entered, but I found a couple of floodlights on stands and turned them on. Although no one was working then, there was no carpet on the floor, the walls had patches of paint in various colors and wires were hanging out of the ceiling instead of chandeliers. Supplies and parts were stacked against the walls. There were a few folding chairs that workers must have used, metal ones. It was perfect for my purpose. I started my phone recording and put it in my pocket.

A few minutes after I arrived, the door opened and Rex and Billy stumbled in, followed by a grim-visaged Thor. I motioned to a couple of chairs I had positioned under one of the lights.

"Gentlemen, have a seat."

Rex sneered at me. "I don't have to do anything. When Jerry Steele hears about this, you'll be in the brig and your bully buddy will be out of a job."

I stroked my chin. "That might have been true yesterday, but Jerry Steele and Darla Darling are dead. Murdered. And you two are our prime suspects, especially after the agreement I heard outside their suite last night. Now sit."

Rex's jaw dropped so much I thought it would hit the floor. Billy turned to Rex with pleading eyes. Good. Rex was the alpha dog. And I was going to break him.

"I said sit. Next time, Olav is going to make you sit so hard that it will crack your teeth."

Olav glared at them and cracked his knuckles. We were bad cop and badder cop. They sat in the chairs, blinking at the floodlight.

I strolled over in front of them. "Now, you gentlemen are going to fill me in on everything you did for the two deceased, starting with sabotaging the camera system and finishing with the poisoned truffle. Care to start, Billy? Tell me what you did with the cameras. I already know you sabotaged the cameras. Why? Was it to cover throwing Bix Maudlin overboard?"

Billy looked over at Rex, who gave a resigned shrug. He turned back to me. "Mr. Steele was paranoid about being watched. He thought the government was trying to find a way to put him in jail. That's why he wanted them off, so he couldn't be watched. At least that's what he told me."

"Jerry told you himself?"

He shifted uneasily. "Uh, not directly. His wife told me and he would nod. He's had a stroke, you know, so his words sort of slurred and didn't always make sense."

Interesting. "What about the browser history you cleared on the laptop? Whose laptop was it?"

His eyes went wide. "How did you know that?"

"I'm asking the questions here. Answer." I was enjoying being bad cop.

"That was on Monday night. I went to the suite and did it for her, Darla."

"Did you see any of what you erased?"

He shook his head. "The history had already been deleted. I just made sure it couldn't be recovered, that and all the deleted emails and stuff in the trash bin. I used a shredder that's so good that even the FBI couldn't recover them." His voice sounded proud.

I gave him my death stare. "You'd better hope they don't or you'll end up in a federal prison. Now tell me about the email you sent to Bix's investors, the 'Bilked by Bix' one."

He gulped. "I didn't send it. That was someone else. Rex got one too." He turned to Rex. "Didn't you?"

Rex nodded. "So what?"

It was his turn in the hot seat. "So you had a good reason to kill Bix, didn't you?"

"He sneered at me. "Stuff it, bi—"

Before he could finish, Thor gripped his shoulder, squeezing. "Apologize."

As Thor's grip tightened on Rex's trapezoid, Rex grabbed his fingers and tried to pry them off. His pain showed in his eyes. I was about to call Thor off when Rex nodded as best he could. Thor released him and Rex sagged in the chair. Fear was in his eyes as he turned to me and his voice was hoarse. "Sorry."

I was reminded of the fictional Vulcan Nerve Pinch from the Star Trek franchise. Although Rex hadn't passed out like Nerve Pinch victims did, he was far outmatched by Thor's strength. The Security Chief was definitely the badder cop. It was a side that I'd never seen. But it was sort of sexy. I shook my head to clear my thoughts, then asked the question again.

"You had good reason to kill Bix and you came on this cruise to do it, didn't you?"

He shook his head violently. "I only had a few thou with him. It cost more than that for this cruise. I was only here because Jerry wanted me here. I was Darla's body guard. She'd gotten an email from some perv who got obsessed with her porn films. He said she would be his or no one's."

I thought about this. "So, were you following her when she went to O'Malley's on Monday night?"

"Nah. I was making sure she wasn't followed."

Considering he'd missed me, he wasn't too good at that. "So who do I talk to about the potassium cyanide?"

Billy gave Rex a sidelong glance, but Rex stoically stared straight ahead. I went for the weak link.

"Billy, did you get it on the dark web?"

He jerked when I asked him. I'd hit a nerve

He glanced again at Rex. "Why would I do that? Most of the stuff on the dark web is drugs. That and kiddie porn. I'm not into those. Scammers put up stuff like poisons, but they don't deliver after you pay. It's for suckers."

"You sound like you know from experience. So where did you get it? I know you did, so you might as well save yourself a lot of trouble and pain and tell me now."

Thor took a step towards him.

He nervously glanced at Thor, then Rex and finally back to me. "One of our accounts is a medical lab. We have extra security on drugs and poison. We told them there was a malfunction we needed to fix. While the system was off, Rex got the cyanide." He turned to Rex. "Sorry, it would come out one way or another."

Rex glared at him, but said nothing.

I stepped closer to Rex. "Shall we have a chat? Why did Jerry want poison?"

He looked at his feet. "It wasn't Jerry. She wanted it. She said they had a rat problem."

"And you believed that?" Before he could answer, I did. "Of course you didn't. So why get her the poison?" And then it hit me, their argument last night. "You thought she was going to poison Jerry. You'd been wrinkling the sheets with her and thought if Jerry were gone, she'd marry you and make you rich. But last night she made it clear nothing like that was going to happen. You were her sucker."

He said nothing, staring at the floor.

"So after she fired you last night, you went ballistic and killed her this morning. After all, you had already killed for her. That's why you didn't get back to your cabin until after 3:30 the morning Bix went overboard."

He looked up, shocked. "No way. Darla called me that morning, woke me up, and asked me to come up to her suite. She said she needed to talk to me. When I got there, she brushed me off. Said the old man was awake and I should beat it."

I had one more question, but I knew the answer already. "Did you poison the truffle and put it by my door?"

His jaw dropped and he stammered. "I . . . I . . . I bought a truffle in the shop, but she asked me to. I gave it to her. She said it was a parting gift for someone. I thought . . . ."

"You thought it was for Jerry. That she was going to finally poison him and you could have her." I chuckled. "You really were her chump." I turned to Thor. "They can go now."

He looked confused. "They killed Mr. Steele and Miss Darling, yes?"

"No, they did not." I pulled my phone out of my pocket and shut it off. "But they did a lot of other bad things, which they confessed to."

Rex sprang up. "That's not legal. I'll sue."

I snorted. "Like I care. Heather's the one with money. I'm broke. But after this goes on the Internet, along with how Regis Martini is a fake Seal, you won't be able to get a job as a security guard at a preschool." I paused for effect. "Unless you keep your mouth shut about all this."

Rex stood, clenching and unclenching his fists at his side. Then nodded. "No one talks and no one gets in trouble."

"Sounds like a plan."

He held out his hand to shake.

I looked down at it. "Don't push it. Just get the hell out of here."

Billy and Rex almost fell over each other getting out the door.

Olav turned to me. Thor was gone. "What do we do next?"

"Well, is there any chance we could take a quick look in Jerry Steele's suite?" I raised my hands before he could object. "I won't touch a thing. Promise."

He hesitated, obviously torn, before his jaw set with determination. "We will go into the suite. You are Sherlock and I am Watson, yes?"

"You betcha." I grinned.

"Wait outside while I turn everything off."

I stepped out the door and almost ran into Disco Ghost. He wore another Aloha shirt, this time with no naked ladies, and cargo shorts. In his hand was some orange-colored drink. He glared at me.

"Well, if it isn't the broad who likes to pour drinks on me. Guess what? Payback is a bitch."

With that, he tossed his drink on my face and clothes. Unfortunately for him, Olav was just coming out of the door of the Stockholm Room. Thor took over.

In an instant, Disco was pinned against the wall, Thor's huge hand holding him by the throat as he gasped for breath.

I pulled Thor's hand away. "It's okay, Olav. This man spilled his drink on me and is going to buy me a replacement outfit." I turned to Disco. "Aren't you."

Eyes wide with panic, he nodded. "I . . . I . . . Can I just give you a couple hundred and we call it even?"

I thought about how much I'd overspent on the outfit at Nordstrom's "I think five will work. You can give it to Thor . . . I mean Olav and he'll get it to me. What's you're cabin number?"

'It's a . . . It's a . . . ." He pulled out his key card. "I can't remember right now, but this is my key."

Thor snatched it from his hand and glared at Disco. "Wait here." He paused. "I'll be back."

Olav turned to me and handed me a clean, white handkerchief.

I wiped off my face and, as best I could, my ruined clothes. I stifled a laugh as we turned to go to the suite. I wondered if Olav knew he'd used the famous *Terminator* quote. I glanced back at Disco. He was standing still, staring after us. The crotch of his shorts was dark. He may have dumped his drink on me, but Olav made him wet his pants. I chuckled. Yeah, payback was a bitch.

Chapter 57

Before we went into the murder suite, I asked Olav to wait. I went into my suite for my latex gloves. The plastic bags with the truffle and note were still there, but no gloves. Had the housekeeper tossed them? I grabbed some more tissues and went back to Olav outside the murder suite. He opened the door and we stepped in. Both of us came to a quick halt. The place was spotless. There was the smell of ammonia and bleach in the air.

Then the elevator reached the top floor and I turned to Olav. "When you said 'no clean' to the housekeeper, she thought you were saying the room was dirty and needed cleaning." I looked around. "And she did a heck of a job cleaning it."

He smacked his forehead and groaned.

I patted him on the back. "It's okay. Miscommunication is easy when you don't speak the same languages." I started for the master bedroom. "Let's see if anything is left."

When I walked in the bedroom, my heart sank. I had set the mystery box and the poison on the trash can, not expecting anyone to clean the place up. I had been wrong and both items were gone. I checked the nightstand. The K-Y gel and sunglasses were still there, which would have fingerprints. That was some consolation. Nothing else in the bedroom or bathroom had any interest to me. As I exited, Olav met me in the hall.

He shook his head. "There is nothing in the kitchen. Did you find what you wanted to find here?"

"Unfortunately, the poison and a box I wanted to keep went out with the trash,"

He quickly grabbed his walkie-talkie and spoke what sounded like Norwegian into it. He held up his index finger for me to wait and not say anything. After a few minutes, he spoke again. We waited for a few more minutes. Then he spoke once more and put away his walkie-talkie. He did not look pleased.

"The garbage has all been dumped. The ship wants to dispose of all of it before entering American waters. I am sorry."

I sighed, disappointed. "You win some and you lose some. You tried."

We went back to my suite. At the door, I stopped him from entering.

"Look, the person who tried to kill me is dead. Rex got the poison for Darla and brought her the truffle. She tried to kill me and she's dead, so I'm safe now. You can get back to your duties."

He looked hurt. "We do not know who killed anyone. Are you not Sherlock and I am your Watson? We can solve this."

Could I tell him? Not yet. "It's not over. Give me your cell number and I'll call you when we're ready to finish our investigation."

He took out a pen and notebook, tore out a page and wrote his number on it. He handed it to me, holding my hand a moment when I took it. "Call me when the game is a foot." Then he turned and left.

I entered his number in my phone before I went inside. Heather, Jennifer and Mindy were there.

Heather came up and hugged me, saying, "I heard what happened next door. Isn't it horrible?"

Then she pulled back and looked at my clothes. "What happened to you?"

"Someone spilled a drink on me. I'm going to go change." I headed for my room.

After I washed my face and repaired the little makeup I wear, I put on a white polo, jeans and sandals, work clothes for me. Then I checked through the photos I'd taken of the Steele's suite. Next I opened my tablet and booted up. I did a web search for "crea-fx," the sender of the box in the murder suite. When I saw it, I almost shouted "Yes!"

I understood why Nurse Bimbo and Dr. Strangelove had gone to O'Malleys Wednesday and hadn't stayed long. They wanted to be seen and not talk to anyone.

There was a knocking at the door. "You okay?" It was Heather. I realized I had shouted.

"I'm fine. I'll be right out."

I turned off the tablet. I didn't need to search for Frank Abagnale. I remembered why the name was familiar. I called Olav.

"Stay on the line, but don't say anything. Just listen."

When I went out of my bedroom, I found the Gang of Four had joined the group. I was the only one not wearing shorts and some colorful blouse. I didn't mind not conforming. I was glad not to look like part of the sister-hoods.

Heather came up and took my arm. "Mindy heard something last night. She thinks that security guy, the brute who attacked you, did kill those people. Probably killed Bix and tried to kill you, too. It makes sense, doesn't it?"

"It does make sense." I turned to Mindy. "What did you hear?"

"He was leaving the other suite and having an argument with the woman. He said something like she would regret throwing him out. He'd make her pay big time."

"Interesting."

Heather pulled me towards the door. "We're all going to our last lunch together. Well, the last one on this cruise." She grinned at the others. "It's so good to be a group of friends again."

I pulled away. "I'll be there in a bit." I looked at Mindy. "I've got a question about something on Bix's computer. Could you stay a minute?"

She shrugged. "I guess so."

Heather stopped. "We can all wait."

Mindy waved her away. "No, you save us seats. I'm sure this won't take long."

No doubt she thought I'd ask about the missing love letter. She'd deny erasing it or even seeing it. It'd be her word against mine, but she would not want all the rest of the clique to witness it.

Fireplug spoke up. "I'm starving. If they want to play around on a computer, let them. I want to eat."

I stifled a smile and held back on making a comment about her not exactly wasting away. Or waisting away. I wanted them gone. And they did finally leave.

While they were going, I booted up Bix's computer and went to the crea fx website, making sure Mindy could not see what I was doing. I set my phone on the table by the computer and went to the bar, pouring myself a Jameson.

Mindy rolled her eyes. "Don't you think it's a little early? Ever consider joining AA?"

I added water and ice, then gave her a half smile. "Ever consider joining MA"

She looked at me quizzically. "What's that?"

"Murderer's Anonymous. You killed those people in the other suite."

Chapter 58

Mindy snorted. "You're crazy. I didn't even know them. Why would I do that?"

I sipped my whiskey. "You knew at least one of them. And revenge is the why."

Her expression changed suddenly. Her eyes narrowed and her jaw set. "Who did I know?"

I spun the computer around so she could see the webpage. It was a company that made high-end silicone masks, ones so realistic that they could fool people at a few feet away. "Bix. Or should I say, the fake Jerry Steele."

She couldn't hide her surprise. Her eyes went wide and her mouth opened, but she didn't say anything.

I continued. "I figured that he had faked the scene of his going overboard. It was all too phony to be real. The broken watch at a certain time, blood on the rail and his coat with his wallet conveniently dropped on the deck. I had no doubt he was not the type to commit suicide. Either he had been murdered or, more likely, had faked his death. I followed both avenues. However, I did not find anyone with enough of a reason to kill him except for you."

"Why would I kill him for faking his own death?" She looked me in the eyes, trying to seem truthful. "Whether he was dead or had disappeared from my life forever, either way it was good for me. He was a leech and I was glad to get rid of him."

I set my drink on the table. "Until you found he was trying to frame you. Sure, he set up a couple of red herrings that didn't point the finger at you, but the big ones did. He used your email account to send out the 'Bilked by Bix' email to get unhappy clients on this ship. Then he left a letter to you on his computer, one you deleted, that said he'd be with you until death. I'm guessing he never actually sent it. Finally, he forged your writing on the note with the poisoned truffle. I remembered that you said that he forged your signature on some documents and did so very well. Aside from this being a private floor with no public access and the truffle poisoner having to have a key, how did you know Bix was playing Jerry Steele?"

She studied me a moment. Then she gave me a hard smile. "You can't prove any of this, so it's fun to have you know and not be able to do anything about it. It proves I'm the real detective here."

I didn't say anything about the emails and photos I'd saved, figuring she'd want to prove how great she was.

"I didn't know Bix was disguising himself as the old man or even hiding in the suite next door," she continued. "It was Darla that tipped me off. I recognized her voice when I heard her last night. She called me about a quarter after three the morning he disappeared, pretending to be someone on the ship's staff. She said that he'd been injured on the boat deck and I needed to go there. Even called a second time to see if I was coming. I was half drunk, so I got dressed and started to go there. Then I thought, 'Why am I doing this? I couldn't care less if he's hurt. Or dead.' So I went back to my suite."

She gave a harsh laugh. "She sounded as Norwegian as Beyoncé. I guess her acting ability is limited to saying, 'Oh, oh. Deeper, deeper. Yes, yes.' I knew it was the same person when I heard her last night."

I had already guessed a connection between Darla and Bix. Time to see if it was true. "Why didn't you recognize her when you saw her? She was Bix's physical therapist when he hurt his knee, wasn't she?"

She raised her eyebrows. "I didn't expect you to know that. I guess you're better at your job than I thought. Darla was Bix's physical therapist, but under a different name then, and I caught her in my kitchen wearing only her panties when I came home unexpectedly. I'd seen her only that one time, eight years ago, but didn't recognize her at first. She looked a lot different then. Short, brown hair and skinnier. Smaller boobs, too. Guess those got pumped up for her porno films. But she did look familiar when I saw her last night and I finally figured it out when we were at dinner."

"So, what time did you go to their suite this morning? Four? Five? The blood wasn't totally dry, even though you turned up the heat and opened the door. Some of it was still wet at nine-thirty. Your footprints were dry, though, so the authorities can do a match on them." She didn't need to know the room had been cleaned and evidence destroyed.

"It was a little after four, when there aren't many people awake. I pounded on the door and she answered." She winked. "And my shoes went overboard with Bix and his slut."

"And the Jerry Steele mask." I raised an eyebrow at her surprised look. "You missed the box from crea-fx it came in. Pretty amazing how good they are, but they're not cheap. However, next time you kill someone you should make sure you're better on clean up."

She paused. "That wasn't my plan, you know. I just went to talk to them. I thought Bix was hiding there and I wanted him to stop trying to incriminate me. I was glad he was gone. But they were the ruthless murderers. They killed the old man, her husband. She attacked me with the champagne bottle and Bix came at me, too. I was defending myself."

I shook my head. "I might have believed you if you hadn't stolen my latex gloves off the table last night, when you faked being dizzy." I smiled at her surprised look. "I didn't realize it until this morning. You had every intention of killing everyone in the suite, of getting revenge. The only reason you didn't kill Jerry Steele was because he was already dead and dumped over the side. I think I have enough circumstantial evidence to get you charged and, hopefully, convicted."

She started edging around the table. "But you're the only one who has all the information, aren't you?"

I slipped off my sandals. "How do you know I didn't record everything?"

"If you did, I'll find it and destroy the recording." She edged closer. "You're supposed to be some hot-shot martial artist. Let's see who's better. I know I'm stronger."

Chapter 59

I knew if she got too close the advantage would be hers. I moved slowly away from her, keeping the table between us. I didn't know who was better. I guessed I would find out soon. Maybe if I could keep her talking, Olav would realize I could use some help.

"Out of curiosity, how do you know Ernesto Ortega, Walt Ferrier and David Stewart?"

She stopped and cocked her head. "Ernesto used to be my dentist until he made so much money in gold recycling and his wife made hers in cosmetics that he retired. I have no idea who the other two are. Why?"

"I saw you with them at the sailing party last night, all talking together."

She laughed. "You mean the fat Baron and the wimpy Prince? The so-called Baron's a dentist and knows Ernesto professionally. I don't know anything about that Prince guy except he's a little twerp who thinks he's important. What a couple of clowns."

She started moving toward me again and I backed into the living room to have enough room to kick. A good technique for a woman is to feign inexperience, lull your opponent into a false sense of superiority. However, Mindy already knew I had some ability, so that wouldn't work. I had to watch for an opportunity and strike with enough force to disable her.

We had similar stances, mine with my left foot forward and her with her right. She was a leftie, something I'd noticed before. Suddenly, she stepped in, trying to get close enough to use a hand strike. But I was ready. I caught her with a push kick to the gut, forcing her back, following quickly with a front kick to the face, using the ball of my foot. She blocked my leg to the side with her left arm, then struck with a back fist with her right hand before I recovered. I pulled back as she did, but she still connected with my left cheek. Although it was not her dominant hand, it still dazed me momentarily and I circled back to gain time and distance. I'd have a nice bruise if I survived this fight. But I had caught the side of her face and her lip was bleeding.

She gave me a slight smile as she wiped the blood off her face. "You're better than I thought you'd be. I won't make the same mistake twice."

I kept eye contact with her. "Ditto."

I continued slowly back and she matched my moves, keeping closer than I wanted. As quick as a cobra, she moved in with a roundhouse kick aimed at my chest that I blocked by dropping my forearm. I was surprised how much power she packed into her kick. My arm tingled. As she followed her kick by closing in with a half-knuckle strike to the throat, I blocked it to the side with the knife edge of my left hand and stepped in, hitting her with a solid right elbow strike that connected with her chin. She grunted and staggered back, shaking her head as she brought her hands to a defensive position. This time she moved back away from me. She was far from down, but I could tell by her reaction that I had hurt her. I then knew I could defeat her, even if she was stronger than I was. I could see in her eyes that she realized it, too.

Suddenly, the door burst open and Thor charged in at a full run, followed closely by Eric the Red. As she turned to meet Thor's charge, he hit like an NFL tackle and she went down like a sacked quarterback. Eric positioned himself between me and the other two like a blocking lineman. My Vikings to the rescue, whether I needed it or not. The Rams could use these guys.

As Thor flipped Mindy onto her stomach and trussed her hands together with a couple of zip ties, she called him every foul name I've ever heard and then some. I guess not being in a sorority limited my education. When he pulled her to her feet, Eric relaxed.

Olav dragged Mindy over to us. He was panting heavily. "I am sorry we did not get here sooner. We were on deck 3 and could not get an elevator, so we ran up the stairs. How are you,

Morg Mahoney?" His eyes widened as he looked at my face. "I will have Erik take you to the infirmary."

I waved him off, disappointed that I hadn't been the one to take Mindy down. "I'm fine. It looks worse than it is. I'll put some ice on it."

Mindy was so angry she was spitting. "What are you doing, you son of a bitch. She attacked me. I'll sue all of you. I'll own this cruise line."

I went over to my phone and raised it high. "Did you get it all?"

Olav flashed a satisfied grin. "We recorded it. It will be good when she is tried for murder."

"Hah." Mindy sneered. "Just try to use it in any court in California. You can't record me without me knowing it."

Olav chuckled softly. "I do not know California law, but I had to learn maritime law to be head of security. We are still in open sea and are registered with Panama. We can send you there for trial."

Her eyes shone with panic. "You can't do that. I'm an American."

I slipped my phone in my pocket. "And on foreign soil. You can appeal to the embassy in Panama, but good luck with that."

Olav tugged her toward the door. "I am arresting you for murder. Do not say anything you do not want used at your trial."

He opened the door and pulled Mindy out with him. Svein and I followed. The elevator doors opened as two young men in blue short-sleeved shirts, blue trousers tucked into black lace-up boots and blue ball caps stepped off. On the ball caps and above their left pockets were the words "U. S. Coast Guard." One of them stepped forward.

"I'm Lieutenant Grant and this is Chief Petty Officer Juarez. We're here to investigate a murder on this ship."

Olav raised an eyebrow. "There were three murders. All of them are solved." He nodded toward Mindy. "This is the suspect for two of them."

Lieutenant Grant reached toward Mindy. "I'll take the prisoner and conduct my own investigation."

Olav pulled Mindy away from Grant's grasp. "The investigation is finished. We are in international waters and under the Panamanian flag. We will keep the prisoner."

Grant hesitated. He was about six feet tall and maybe 170 pounds. Juarez looked to be about my height, five nine, and 160 pounds at most. "Your captain asked us to conduct the investigation. Please comply with his wishes."

"I am Chief Security Officer Larsen and I will take the prisoner to the brig before I talk to the captain. Deputy Security Officer Nilsen will take you to the captain until I can meet you there." Olav headed past Grant for the elevator and Svein stood in front of the Coast Guard men, blocking them.

Mindy struggled in Olav's grip, looking back. "I'm an American citizen. I demand you free me from these thugs and take me with you."

Grant uneasily eyed Olav and Svein. "Sorry, ma'am. He's right. This is open sea and we're on a ship under a foreign flag. We have no authority here."

As Olav and Mindy got on the elevator, Mindy yelled back. "You cowards! You're nothing but a couple of damn cowards!"

The doors shut, blocking the rest of her comments about the Coast Guard men.

Svein walked up to the second elevator and pushed the button. When the doors opened, he gestured to enter. "Gentlemen, if you will accompany me."

The three of them entered and the doors closed.

I went back into the suite and picked up my drink. My hand was shaking so badly the ice in my drink made it sound like a maraca. I tried to steady it with my other hand, but it didn't help. I sighed. I would have to wait until the adrenaline rush subsided.

Somehow, meeting the sorority sisters for lunch and explaining how I got one of their clan arrested didn't appeal to me. I called Alasdair and he came to the suite.

"How may I help you, Morg?"

"I could really use some fish and chips."

"I will order them for you." He started for the door and paused. "Are you okay? I cannot help but see you've been hurt. And I saw the security officer with one of your friends. It looked like she was in restraints."

"She's Heather's friend, not mine. And you're right, she was in restraints. It's a long story and, if it's alright, I'll tell you later."

He inclined his head. "Of course, Morg." He started to leave, but stopped. "I noticed you are low on Jameson. Would you like me to replenish your stock?"

I gave him my warmest smile. "That would be lovely."

"I will bring a bottle with extra ice." He paused again. "Would you like it in an ice pack?"

"Yes. Alasdair, you think of everything."

I looked in a mirror after he left and grimaced when I touched the bruise on my cheek. The ice should help take down the swelling. It looked like I'd need to borrow Heather's make-up as well. Her supply was much better than mine.

Chapter 60

I had a leisurely lunch alone. After some research online, I chose a foundation and concealer from Heather's mobile cosmetic shop. I applied it heavily and hoped it would cover. Then had online video chats with the lady who was taking care of Sam and with Robert. I told Robert all about how I solved the three murders. He congratulated me on my success.

"You had faith in yourself. Good for you." He smiled at me. It was great to have video chatting so I could see him as well as hear him.

"You helped, telling me I was good at detection and to go with what I felt was correct. Thanks." I reached out and put my hand on the screen.

Nothing to thank me for. I just said what's true." He paused and put his hand on his screen. "I miss you, Morg."

"I miss you, too."

We stayed that way for a few seconds. Then I heard the door to the suite open.

"Got to go. The sorority sister-hoods are back. This should be interesting."

"Deus vobiscum, Morg."

"Thanks, Robert. I may need God's help."

I closed down my computer and got up from the table. I sighed. Someday maybe I'd have the guts to close with "Love you." The group came in talking loudly and laughing. Heather came over and put her arm around my waist.

"Hey, we missed you. Why didn't you come to lunch? We wondered if you and Mindy went off on your own." She looked around. "Where is she, anyway?"

I pulled away. "Mindy's in the brig. At least that's where she was headed last I knew."

She was visibly shocked. "What? Why?"

"For killing Darla Darling and Bix."

She held up her hands in front of her. "Wait, Mindy did kill Bix? But why would she kill that Darla woman? And what about her husband? I heard he was killed, too. Who killed him?" She seemed to finally notice my cheek then looked down at my arm, which also had a large bruise from Mindy's kick. Ice packs and make-up can only cover so much. "What happened to you?"

"Mindy and I had a bit of a fight. She was trying to stop me from turning her in."

Fireplug came up to us, her face set like an angry bulldog. "You turned her in? Bix was a bastard. If Mindy killed him, he deserved it. Why did you have to stick your nose into it?"

Heather stepped between us, facing Fireplug with her hands on her hips. "Because I asked her to. Back off before I make you."

Fireplug stepped back but her expression didn't change. "Mindy's your sister. Are you taking the side of this . . . this . . . this outsider over Mindy?"

"Morg is more of a sister, and a friend, than any of you will ever be. You're nothing but a bunch of Karens. Now get the hell out my suite." She looked over at the rest of the sorority group. "And if any of you feel the same as Sheri, go with her."

Fireplug turned heel and headed for the door. Texas, Fullback and Scarecrow hesitated, looking at each other, then followed.

Heather turned to Jennifer. "What about you? If you want to hang with them, go ahead."

Jennifer looked frightened. "Morg saved me from Dave and hell here on earth, maybe even saved my life. I know we'll never be as close as you two, but I'd like to be her friend." She looked at me. "If you'll have me."

Heather rushed over and hugged her. "I know she will. She does that with people she saves. I should know." She looked over at me. "Come on. Group hug."

To say that hugging was not my thing was like saying the Pope isn't Islamic. To say I'm not into group hugging is like saying he's not a member of Hezbollah. But Heather had stood up for me to the Gang of Four, so, I owed her. I went over and put my arms around my two friends. Or my sisters?

I noticed the time, 2:51, and drew back. "I've got to be somewhere at 3:00. I need to go."

Heather gave me a questioning look. "It's all over, isn't it? Mindy acted alone, didn't she? There wasn't another person involved, was there?"

"No, no, nothing like that. There were some people who helped me a lot and I'm supposed to meet with them. They don't know about what happened with Mindy."

"How about if we go too? I'd like to meet the people who helped you." Heather gave me a wistful smile. "I'm afraid I didn't do much. I was too concerned with fitting in again with the Sigmas."

"Sure." I thought about the sisters. "You'll enjoy them."

So we all headed to O'Malley's.

Chapter 61

When we arrived, Father Tim and the ladies were already there. Father Tim had a teapot and a cup in front of him and the ladies were holding two champagne cocktail glasses with a light golden drink

Lillian set hers down, stood and gently touched my cheek. "What happened, child?"

So much for my skill in the use of make- up. "I had a run in with our killer." I held up my hand. "No questions now. I'll explain it all in detail after I get a drink."

After introductions all around, Heather and Jennifer ordered chardonnay and I ordered a Jameson on the rocks. I hoped the ice rattling wouldn't be too loud. Once the drinks arrived, I gave a description of all that had occurred along with an explanation of how I came to my conclusions.

Father Tim had been leaning forward, intently listening the whole time. "So Mr. Maudlin and Miss Darling faked his death and they killed her husband before throwing his body overboard from the balcony of their suite. You must have had your doubts about the too-convenient broken watch from the first."

I nodded. "A bit too much like an Agatha Christie mystery. It set the supposed time of death at 3:17 a.m. When I found that the rain had been over before 3:00 a.m., yet the coat had been wet on top and the deck dry underneath, I knew it had been staged before the rigged time on the watch. Bix definitely had not committed suicide or fallen overboard. He had either been murdered or made it to look like he had been."

Dramatically, I paused and sipped my drink before continuing. I did enjoy melodrama of all of them raptly listening. "Darla must have slipped a key card to Bix here at O'Malley's the night before and he used it to enter her suite just after 3:00. I didn't know they'd poisoned Jerry and disposed of the body so that Bix could take his place until I went into their suite this morning. That's when I found only one bed had been used and the box for the mask. That box must have been in the gym bag I saw him carrying the night before. He had it sent to a P.O. Box registered to Frank Abagnale. That's the protagonist in *Catch Me If You Can*, and the real-life name of the guy it was about." I shrugged. "Sometimes it pays to be a movie buff."

He smiled at me. "Very impressive."

Judith cocked her head. "So that's why Boobsie had her thug keep me away from the Beast when Lillian and I were in their cabin."

I nodded. "I would imagine the mask wasn't fun to wear and so he wasn't wearing it then. If he kept turned away from you while in the wheelchair and wearing Jerry's clothes, you wouldn't be the wiser. I realized Jerry was dead and the switch had been made when I saw that only bed had been used with the K-Y gel in the nightstand. Jerry was pretty much paralyzed by his stroke and hardly in need of a sex lubricant."

"Hard-ly?" Judith suppressed a laugh. "Hard-less, you mean."

Heather and Jennifer giggled.

Father Tim cleared his throat and refilled his tea. "They used the poison to try to kill you. Why did you think Miss Darling used it on her husband before?"

"She went to a lot of trouble to get it before sailing. She didn't even know I existed then, so why bring it? To kill her husband." I paused. "Killing someone with your hands is not easy, emotionally. It can be traumatic for the killer, although obviously not as much as for the person killed. It's a lot easier to just drop some poison into food or drink than to, say, hold a pillow over someone's mouth until they die. He would have struggled even though they could easily have overpowered him. You could say poisoning was the coward's way."

"But why kill him at all?" Father time cocked his head. "While the Church and I are not in favor of divorce, 'tis far better than murder. While all sins are sin, that one is most heinous."

Heather leaned on the table, resting her chin on the palm of her hand. "I can answer that. Because of something called a pre-nup. It saved me a ton of money when my marriages bombed. I'll bet she'd get nothing if she got a divorce. She'd be broke."

I nodded. "He'd already been to the altar a few times before and it didn't last, so he knew the score. Plus she might not even survive if she split. He was one vindictive guy."

"Why not stay with him until he croaked and inherit his money?" Jennifer asked. "I mean he was pretty old and decrepit, wasn't he?"

"Maybe she wouldn't get much or even anything when he died. Or maybe she got impatient. When she married Jerry, he was an active, successful businessman who promised to produce a real movie for her to star in. Then came the stroke and she's stuck as a nurse for a shell of a man who can't produce any movie or really do anything anymore, especially in bed." I shrugged. "Hardly an exciting, satisfying life for her. And Bix was quite the charmer. Since Mindy cut him off and Jerry couldn't do it any more, those two probably hooked up again and came up with a plan to make both of them live happily ever after. Or at least for a year or two until they got tired of each other. With Bix apparently dead, no one would dun him for money again and they figured a way to get rid of Jerry in a way that she wouldn't be accused of his murder. Plus they would have lots of money. A win-win-win."

"Never underestimate the power of love." Judith winked. "Of money, that is."

Lillian was twirling her champagne glass, staring at it. "One thing you haven't explained is why so many people were going into their cabins after three in the morning." She looked at me. "Wasn't that odd?"

"I haven't asked all of them, but I assume that Darla called them like she did Mindy and Rex. She must have said something that got them out of their cabins. If any of them were seen where Bix faked his going overboard, they would become a suspect. Like I said, there were two puzzles with the pieces mixed together. One was what really happened and the other was a series of red herrings devised by Bix and Darla."

Jennifer was listening very intently. She hadn't even touched her wine while I had explained everything. "So Bix was going to try to pass as Jerry Steele through customs? If he had, then what? Keep up the charade? For how long?"

Father Tim held up a finger. "You know, there is an interesting similarity to a criminal who almost escaped from prison in South America, Brazil, if I remember correctly, disguising himself as his daughter with a high-quality mask of that sort. I saw pictures and it was amazing how well the mask changed his appearance. I would imagine it would be much easier for a man to use such a mask to pretend to be another man long enough to get thorough customs."

I nodded. "Don't forget, Jerry was in a wheelchair, covered with a shawl, gloves, a hat and sunglasses. Since Bix was portraying a stroke victim who could hardly speak, it probably would have worked. As to what their long-term intent was, I would imagine they would only have kept up the act long enough to drain Jerry's funds and escape to some country without extradition." I sipped my whiskey before continuing. "We'll never know."

At that point, we were interrupted by Olav coming into the bar. He saw us and came over.

"It was difficult to find you, Morg Mahoney. Here is the money for the man who threw his drink on you." He handed me five one-hundred dollar bills. "I have come from the captain with a message for you."

Uh-oh. He must not be happy that I continued my investigation when told to back off.

Olav continued. "Would you dine with the captain tonight? It is to show his appreciation for what you did for this ship."

Not what I'd expected. I looked around the table. "I would like to, but I was planning on celebrating with my friends. They helped me. Can they come too?"

Olav pulled out his walkie-talkie and had a conversation. I wished I understood Norwegian. When he finished, he flashed a big smile. "The captain would be honored for all of you to come to dinner at Rick's Steakhouse. There will be a special room reserved. Please be there at eight."

I gave him a quick salute. "Aye, aye, Chief Security Officer Larsen."

I turned to the group. "This meeting of the O'Malley's Pub Regulars is adjourned. We will reconvene at Rick's Steakhouse, eight o'clock sharp." I glanced over at Heather. "After I get some help from a make-up pro." I stood.

Lillian started to applaud. Then Judith joined in, quickly followed by Father Tim, Jennifer and Heather. They all stood, all applauding.

I felt myself redden. I'd never had a standing ovation before. Everyone in the place was staring. But it felt good.

Dinner with the captain was fantastic. He thanked me for solving the murders without involving the Coast Guard and gave me a bottle of very expensive Jameson Bow Street 18 year-old Irish whiskey. He must have felt guilty over how he'd treated me. Youssef wore his white dinner jacket again. The captain gave him a strange look, but said nothing when the two of us went into more Casablanca dialog.

After that, all of the Regulars returned to O'Malley's to listen to DJ until the wee hours of the morning.

Saturday

Chapter 62

After Heather and I stumbled into our suite, we had to pack and set our bags outside the door. Then we were up at six to get ready for docking and departure. The high of the night before dissipated in the drudgery of the morning. I barely spoke to Heather as I drank my morning coffee. Better to get my caffeine fix before I engaged my mouth.

After a knock at the door, Alasdair entered. "The captain has arranged for a limousine to provide transportation to wherever you wish in Southern California."

That, with the whiskey, meant he must have felt very guilty over how he'd treated me.

Alasdair handed me an envelope and continued. "Those are two tickets for anywhere we cruise for you and Heather." He gave a little grin. "In the same type of accommodations as you had on this cruise, of course." He turned toward the door. "If you will follow me, your limousine awaits."

I looked down at the envelope. The captain must have felt very, VERY guilty.

As we headed down the hallway on the gangway deck and Alasdair and Heather had turned a corner out ahead of me, Disco Ghost was coming toward me, holding a paper cup. When he saw me, he started backing up, without looking where he was going. He bumped into a large man that looked like a Hell's Angel, sporting a thick, black beard and ponytail. Disco's coffee went all over the man's grey T-shirt that said "Harleys Rule." The man looked down at his T-shirt, then grabbed Disco by his shirt front and landed a solid punch to his face. Disco went down like a bag of wet laundry. I almost felt sorry for him. But then I thought of our last encounter and didn't. I stifled my smile.

When we got to the gangway, Heather stopped and hugged me. "I'm sorry this cruise was such a disaster for you. You never even got ashore once."

I patted her back, thinking of four new friends I'd made, the O'Malley's Pub Regulars and Jennifer. Something of a record for me.

"You know, it really wasn't that bad. In fact, it was sort of fun and rewarding." I paused and brandished the envelope with the free cruises. "But I do hope no one gets murdered on our next one."